Not Until Christmas Morning

Morning

- A Hope Springs Novel -

Valerie M. Bodden

Not Until Christmas Morning © 2019 by Valerie M. Bodden.

Cover design: Ideal Book Covers

Valerie M. Bodden
Visit me at www.valeriembodden.com

Books in the Hope Springs Series

Not Until Christmas
Not Until Forever
Not Until This Moment
Not Until You
Not Until Us
Not Until Christmas Morning
Not Until This Day
Not Until Someday

Box Sets
Hope Springs Books 1–3 Box Set

Contents

A Gift for You . . .

Members of my Reader's Club get a FREE story, available exclusively to my subscribers. When you sign up, you'll also be the first to know about new releases, book deals, and giveaways.

Visit www.valeriembodden.com/gift to join!

"Though the mountains be shaken and the hills be removed, yet my unfailing love for you will not be shaken nor my covenant of peace be removed," says the Lord, who has compassion on you.

—ISAIAH 54:10

Chapter 1

*P*lease ring.

    Austin stared down his computer, perched on the scuffed card table in his cramped eat-in kitchen. These moments before his brother was supposed to call were the hardest. The moments when his mind went to all the things that could have happened to keep Chad from calling.

He folded himself into the rickety chair next to the table, sliding his crutches to the floor and pulling up the leg of his sweatpants. It'd been almost a year, but the jolt still went through him every time his eyes met the rounded end of his left leg. Even though he knew intellectually that his foot wasn't there anymore—even though he accepted it to some degree—it was still surreal every time he saw the empty space where it should be. He rolled the silicone liner over his residual limb, which ended about eight inches below his knee, then grabbed his prosthetic and slid his stump into it, standing to walk in place until the pin on the end of the liner locked with a series of clicks.

He lowered himself to the chair with a groan, tucking his legs under the table as his computer blasted the sharp alarm he'd set to indicate an incoming video call. As always, the sound set his nerves firing, ramping his heart rate to levels it hadn't achieved since the first days of Ranger training. But he wasn't about to lower the volume, in case he was ever asleep when his brother called. If he ever actually slept, that is.

The moment his brother's face filled the screen, wearing the same goofy grin as always, his heart rate slowed, and he could breathe normally again.

"Hey, man, it's good to see your ugly face." There was a delay between Chad's words and the movement of his mouth, but Austin didn't care. Seeing that his brother was still safe—still whole—was what mattered.

"Likewise." He kept his voice gruff, so his big brother wouldn't know how much he lived for these too infrequent calls. It was the only thing he lived for anymore, really. That and getting in shape to redeploy. No matter what the doctors said.

Only two percent of soldiers with injuries like yours return to the battlefield.

Well, Austin was going to be part of the two percent. There was no other option. No way was he going to leave his brother over there alone.

"How are things?" Austin asked the same question every time they talked.

And every time, Chad repeated the same bogus answer: "It's raining peaches." It had been one of their mother's favorite sayings when they were growing up, and after she'd died, Chad had taken it over as if he'd inherited it the same way he'd inherited her curly hair.

Usually, Austin let him get away with it. When he'd been stationed over there, he hadn't wanted to talk about what was happening with anyone back home either. There was just no way to make them understand.

But this was different. He did understand. He'd been there. He'd lost buddies there. Tanner and—

No. He couldn't go there right now.

Austin squinted at his brother, trying to see what he wasn't saying. "Stop churching it up and give me a straight answer. How many missions are you running? You look tired."

8

Chad's grin slipped, and he ran a hand over his unshaven cheeks. "You know I can't, Austin. I'm fine. We're all fine. God's got our back."

Austin shoved his chair out and pushed to his feet. Supposedly God had their back last year too. Right up until the moment everything blew to pieces. He'd feel a lot better when he got back over there. Then he could be the one who had everyone's back.

"Austin, don't be like that." Chad's voice followed Austin as he took three steps to cross his kitchen.

"I'm not being like anything," he called over his shoulder, loudly so the computer would pick it up. "I'm hungry."

He yanked the refrigerator door open. But aside from a bottle of mustard and a gallon of milk he was pretty sure was at least three weeks old, it was empty.

"Did you go grocery shopping? Got something in there for a change?" Chad's voice carried across the small room, a rough mix of reprimand and concern.

Austin slammed the fridge door shut with a growl, then stood with his head braced against it, the stainless steel cooling his overheated skin.

"Austin—" Chad's voice was gentler now, laced with big-brother authority. "You can't keep living like this, man. Something has to change."

"Yeah." Austin nodded with his head still against the fridge. "I have to get back there."

"No." Chad's voice was firm, and Austin jerked toward the computer screen. His brother's face was grim.

"What do you mean, no?" The snap of his words carried across the room, bouncing off the walls.

Chad had never been anything but supportive of Austin recovering and redeploying. So what was he saying now?

"Maybe you'll get back here, Austin, maybe you won't. But either way, you have to learn to live with it."

"I *am* living with it."

"Yeah? When's the last time you left your apartment or ate anything besides takeout or went on a date or even talked to another human being?"

Austin opened his mouth to respond, but Chad jumped in. "And I don't count."

"I leave my apartment three times a week for physical therapy. I have no interest in dating. I talked to my mailman this morning." He couldn't argue about the takeout, though. Still, three out of four wasn't bad.

"That's not a life, Austin."

He almost argued again. But the little voice in his head that said Chad was right got the better of him. "I know. But what else am I supposed to do?"

"Get out of town for a while. Go somewhere warm. Florida or Hawaii or something. You've got the money from selling Mom's house."

Austin lifted his lip. Go to Hawaii? That was his brother's answer? He had no desire to go to Hawaii.

"Chad, I'm not going—" But he cut off as his eyes fell on the single picture he kept on his refrigerator. A family of four: Mom, Dad, Chad at maybe four years old, and little baby Austin.

He snatched it out from under the magnet and strode to the table, his gait sure despite the uneven floor that often tripped him up. He held the picture in front of the computer's camera.

"Do you remember this?"

Chad squinted, and Austin waited for his delayed answer.

"Yeah. That was right before Dad was called up. I think it's the last picture we have of all four of us together."

Austin pushed aside the familiar stab of jealousy that Chad had four years with their father before Dad was killed in action. Austin had been too young then to remember the man at all.

"What was the name of the town again?"

"Hope Springs? Why?"

Hope Springs. That was right. His parents had grown up there, but after his father's death, Mom had found a job opportunity in Iowa. Every once in a while, she'd tell them a story about the town, though, and to Austin, it had always sounded like the perfect place.

"I'm going to go there." He said it with certainty, as if it were the most logical thing in the world. Even though some part of him knew it was the exact opposite.

"Go where?" Even with the poor video quality, Austin could see Chad's brow wrinkle.

"To Hope Springs." He dropped into the chair next to the card table. "To see where we were born. Where Mom and Dad grew up."

"Okay." Chad dragged the word out, and Austin could tell he was trying to avoid saying a whole lot of other things. "If that's what you want to do. But November in Wisconsin sounds even less pleasant than November in Iowa. I still think somewhere warm and—"

"No." Austin peered at the picture again. This was where he wanted to go. Where he needed to go, even if he didn't know why.

And if he left right now, he could be there before dark.

Chapter 2

Leah had no idea why she'd agreed to this.

Scratch that. She did know. Her sister-in-law could be persuasive, that was why.

She arranged her face into what she hoped was a polite smile as the waiter set a salad in front of her. Across the table, her date—ugh, she hated that word, date, but there was no other word for a man you didn't know sitting across the table from you and trying to make small talk—stabbed a forkful of spinach and brought it to his mouth.

Leah followed suit. At least the food would give her an excuse to stop searching for topics of conversation. So far, they'd tried to talk about his job as an accountant, her catering business, and the Packers. When even the subject of the team's winning streak hadn't been able to sustain a conversation of more than five minutes, Leah had known the date was doomed.

Well, that wasn't true exactly.

She'd known it was doomed from before she got here. Not because there was anything wrong with this guy in particular. She was sure Robert was a perfectly nice man. But she wasn't interested in dating him—or anyone else.

But it seemed that every time she told that to Jade, her sister-in-law simply took it as a challenge. One she seemed determined to win.

No more. After tonight, Leah was putting her foot down. No more setups.

Still, that didn't mean she wanted to be rude to this guy. He was probably just as uncomfortable as she was. As she understood it, he was in one of Jade's classes at the university, where she was studying for her education degree. He'd probably rather be anywhere than here as well.

"So, Jade said you have a daughter?" Leah set down her fork to take a long sip of water. If she'd had her way, she'd be at home in a bubble bath right now, after a long week of catering a corporate retreat. *Later*, she promised herself. Maybe she'd stop at the candle shop on her way home and get something fall-scented—apple cinnamon or pumpkin spice—to add an extra touch of relaxation to her soak.

"I do." Robert set down his fork too. "Savannah."

"That's a pretty name." Leah waited for him to elaborate about his daughter, but when he didn't, she poked at another forkful of salad.

"Thanks." Robert resumed eating as well.

"How old is she?"

"Six."

"Oh." Leah's mind tripped over other possible topics of conversation as she scooped up another bite. Had they talked about the weather yet?

"Did you hear if it was supposed to snow? It feels like it could." If she wasn't afraid he'd think she was rolling her eyes at him, she'd roll them at herself. But it was true. When she'd walked out of the conference center earlier, the air had nipped at her uncovered ears, and low clouds had formed a flat ceiling overhead. It was only early November, but that didn't mean it couldn't happen.

"I hope it doesn't." Robert slid his empty salad plate to the edge of the table. "I hate winter."

Leah almost dropped her fork. The guy hated winter? Her favorite season? Had Jade gotten no info on him before she'd set them up?

"A dusting of snow is just what we need." She kept her voice light. "It will put everyone in the Christmas mood."

Robert drew in a breath to speak, and Leah marveled that she'd finally stumbled on a topic of conversation that lasted more than two sentences. But her phone trilled from her purse on the chair next to her. She reached to grab it as people at the nearby tables swiveled to give her dirty looks. "Sorry, I thought I silenced this."

She slid her finger to dismiss the call, but when she noticed the number, she couldn't help the gasp. She'd assumed it would be months yet before she got this call.

"I'm sorry. I have to take this. I'll be right back." She swiped to answer as she hurried toward the restaurant's doors so she wouldn't disrupt the other diners.

"Hello?" Her greeting came out at the same moment the sharp November air hit her skin, sending prickles up and down her bare arms. She probably should have grabbed her coat, but she didn't care.

"Is this Leah Zelner?" The woman on the other end of the line sounded matter-of-fact and clinical, with no hint of the excitement Leah could feel building in her own belly.

"This is Leah." Her teeth chattered, but she couldn't tell whether it was from the cold or from the possibility that this was really happening.

"Ms. Zelner. This is Jen Peters, a caseworker with Child Welfare Services. I see you have completed your home study and that you received your foster and adoption licensing certificates a couple months ago."

"Yes." She said it louder than she intended, and she imagined the woman on the other end pulling the phone away from her ear.

"And are you still willing to take a placement of an older child?"

Willing? She was more than willing. This was what she was supposed to be doing right now. She just knew it.

But she forced herself to keep her voice calm. "I'm willing."

"I'm glad to hear that. We have a child we'd like to place with you. However—"

"Yes. I'll take him. Or her."

"Slow down." The caseworker cut in. "I appreciate your enthusiasm, but there are some things we need to go over before you agree."

Leah made herself take a breath. She could be professional about this, even if her heart had taken up a giddy two-step. "Of course. I'm sorry."

"First, you should know that Jackson has had some disciplinary issues and has been removed from his last three foster homes because of them."

"Okay." But Leah's heart had latched onto the name—her child's name. Jackson.

"The issues include truancy, fighting at school, fighting with foster siblings, and running away, among others. Do you understand that should you accept this placement, these issues are likely to still be present?"

Leah swallowed. She'd known when she started this process what she was signing up for. Older foster children often came with special challenges. But that was exactly why she wanted to take in an older child. Babies would always find a home, but older children were often forgotten.

But Leah could change that. She could make a difference for them. Change their life.

"I understand," she answered.

"I hope you do." Jen sighed into the phone. "But I'd like to fill you in a little more on his case history. Can you come to the office right now? We have about an hour before Jackson arrives."

An hour?

That was fast. Really fast.

Leah was good at waiting. She'd been prepared for the woman to say they had a child who would need a home in a month or even a week. But right now?

15

That was nowhere near enough time to get everything ready. Sure, the guest bed was all made up, the dresser was just waiting for a young person to stash their clothes in it, and she'd stocked a bookshelf with some of her childhood favorites. But she'd been picturing how she'd make the child's transition to her home a celebration. She'd prepare a special meal, get a cake from her friend Peyton, and gather all her friends and family to welcome the child. To let the child know that they were going to have more love than they knew what to do with.

"Ms. Zelner? I'm sorry to rush you, but if you can't take Jackson, I'll need to make other arrangements for him."

Leah wrapped her arms around herself. What was she thinking? Was she really going to give up her chance to make a difference in a kid's life because she didn't have time to get a cake?

"Yes, of course, I'm available right now." A thrill zipped up her spine. After months of going through the licensing process and then waiting for a child, she was suddenly going to be a mother. Or, a foster mother, more precisely. But that didn't matter. She'd love the child as her own.

She knew she would.

As she hung up, Leah pulled in a long breath of the sharp air, sending up a quick prayer for wisdom.

"I can do all things through Christ who strengthens me," she reminded herself.

Then she hurried back into the restaurant to grab her purse and jacket and offer a hasty explanation to Robert. She was pretty sure she left him with the impression that she was crazy, but she couldn't worry about that right now.

She sped out of the restaurant and jumped into her car, following the winding streets through downtown Hope Springs toward the Child Welfare office, tucked along a residential street near her church. She hadn't known the office was there until she'd started researching foster care after watching her brother go through the process of adopting his wife's baby. Something in Leah had shifted as she'd seen her younger brother become a dad. She may be content without a husband, but that didn't mean she didn't want a family. And if she could improve the life of a child who might otherwise be without hope in the process, all the better.

As she pulled up to a stop sign, she reached for her phone and dialed Jade. Her sister-in-law answered immediately.

"Why are you calling me while you're on a date?" Jade demanded.

"I'm not on a date, I'm—"

"Leah." Jade's exasperated voice interrupted. "Tell me you did not cancel on poor Robert."

"I didn't cancel. I went, but—"

"You ditched him? That's even worse. Hope, not so loud." In the background, Leah could hear her eight-month-old niece pounding on something—probably one of the toy pots and pans Leah had gotten her.

"I didn't ditch him. I mean, I did, but—"

"Seriously, Leah. Why do you—"

"Jade." Leah raised her voice, and Jade must have sensed the urgency in her tone because she stopped scolding.

"What?"

"Child Welfare called. They need me to come pick up a kid tonight. Right now."

"Oh my goodness. Wow." Jade took a breath. "That's great. Do you want us to come along? Dan is over at church, but I can go get him, and I can rally the others too if you want."

Leah took a second to consider how she wanted this to go. She'd been so sure that a big party was the way to welcome a kid home. But if things had been as rough for Jackson as the caseworker had implied, maybe it'd be better to keep it low-key. "You know what, I think I'll go alone. And then maybe I can introduce him—Jackson—to all of you tomorrow night at dinner."

"Jackson. That sounds exactly like the name I'd picture your kid having." Jade's voice held the smile Leah was sure she was wearing. "Do you want to move dinner here? It's no trouble. I can throw together some pizzas or something."

Leah had to swallow the lump of emotion at Jade's enthusiasm.

"That's okay. I think maybe it will be good to have everyone over to my house. Let Jackson get settled in before I drag him around to everyone else's places."

Jade squealed, then laughed as Hope joined in from the background. "Sorry. I'm just so excited for you. I know how much you've wanted this."

"I have." Leah squealed too as she hung up. *Thank you, Lord, for answered prayers. Please help me be the mother this child needs right now.*

She finished the prayer as she drove into the parking lot of the Child Welfare office. She should be nervous. She should be freaked out. She was about to take responsibility for a child, for goodness' sake.

But she wasn't.

She was absolutely confident this was what she was supposed to be doing. And she was ready for it.

Chapter 3

Two hours later, with Jackson hunched into the passenger seat next to her, Leah was less confident.

If she'd thought making conversation with Robert at dinner was difficult, talking to Jackson was impossible. Every time she asked a question—What do you like to do? What's your favorite food? Do you have any homework tonight?—she was answered with a nearly inaudible grunt.

After what she'd learned from the caseworker, she probably shouldn't be surprised. When he was only six, Jackson's mother had died of an opioid overdose—and he'd been the one to find her. The thought of it twisted Leah's insides into such tight knots that she wasn't sure they'd ever loosen. According to the caseworker, Jackson had been placed with nine different foster families in the past six years, and his last placement had lasted only three weeks. If he weren't in the car with her right now, she'd probably break down into tears over what the poor child had already faced, being passed around as if he were nothing more than a piece of clothing that didn't fit anymore.

But that ended now.

She was going to make things better for him, give him a forever home and a forever family.

"So—" She tried a new conversation. "You'll be able to keep going to Hope Springs Middle School, so that's good." Although she wasn't one hundred percent sure that was true. According to the caseworker, in the three weeks he'd been enrolled at the middle school, Jackson had received four detentions and one in-school suspension.

Another grunt from next to her.

"Anyway—" She kept talking as if he'd answered. "I was thinking, we'll have to figure out what you should call me. I feel like Ms. Zelner is too formal." It's what the caseworker had suggested so that she could establish authority, but Leah hated it.

Jackson turned toward her and opened his mouth. Leah held her breath. Was he actually going to say something?

"How about—" His lips twisted into a smirk as he suggested a curse word that nearly made her gasp out loud.

She blinked and worked to keep her face neutral, telling herself he was only trying to shock her. And he'd done a pretty good job of it.

His satisfied sneer told her she'd utterly failed at hiding her reaction.

She made herself count to ten, then, keeping her voice flat, said, "How about Leah for now? Maybe someday, you'll call me Mom. If you're comfortable."

Jackson stared out the windshield, his face a complete blank.

"Hey." Leah slowed to turn onto her street. "I don't know if the caseworker told you, but my hope is that this will work out and that I'll be able to adopt you eventually." She glanced toward Jackson.

The boy was still staring out the window, but his hands were fisted in his lap, and his jaw was clenched.

"If you want me to," she added.

Jackson's jaw twitched. "You'll get rid of me long before that."

Leah shook her head. It was going to take a long time to get through to this kid. "Of course I won't—"

But she broke off as she pulled into her driveway and her eyes fell on her neighbor's house. Miranda had left for a year-long mission trip a few weeks ago. So why were the lights on in her house? And why was a strange truck parked in the driveway?

She threw her own car into park and opened her door. "Stay here a minute," she ordered Jackson. "I'll be right back."

It didn't occur to her to be scared until she was standing on the porch, hand poised to knock. Then she realized that it could be an intruder in there. Or a squatter.

But she'd promised Miranda she would keep an eye on things.

She gave the door a sharp triple rap, then stood back, glancing over her shoulder to check on Jackson. But he was still sitting in the car's passenger seat, still staring straight ahead.

She turned back to the house. It wasn't a huge place. Surely whoever was in there should have opened the door by now.

She lifted her hand to knock again, but before she could, the clatter of a lock turning had her scrambling backward. She drew in a sharp breath as the door opened, praying she hadn't just made the dumbest mistake of her life.

Beads of sweat prickled Austin's forehead, and he cleared them with a hasty swipe.

It's just someone at the door.

Nothing to get all bent out of shape about. Certainly nothing to send his heart rate ratcheting to pre-mission levels.

Night had fallen since he'd arrived, and he searched the bank of light switches near the door, flipping one after another until he found one that turned on the porch light.

It illuminated a petite blond woman, arms crossed in front of her, mouth pulled into a frown.

"What are you doing here?" she demanded.

And here Austin had worried the people of Hope Springs would be too friendly for his taste.

"Excuse me?" His voice was hard and unyielding, and the woman took half a step back, her expression a cross between fear and indignation.

Her frown deepened, and she uncrossed her arms to gesture to the doorway he stood in. "This isn't your house. So what are you doing in it?" Her eyes flashed, blue-green swirls snapping at him.

"I'm renting it." Austin chopped each word short. He had no desire to continue this conversation. "I made arrangements with the owner this morning."

"You talked to the owner?" The woman's hands tightened into fists, and Austin smirked. Did she plan to physically remove him from the place?

"Yes." Austin kept his answers as clipped as hers.

"You talked to the owner?" The woman repeated. "In Croatia."

Austin shrugged. This morning he'd been talking to his brother in Afghanistan, so was it really so hard to believe he'd talked to someone in Croatia too? "I don't know where she was. I just know I talked to her."

The woman shook her head. "If Miranda had rented the house out, she would have told me."

Austin grabbed the door, closing it halfway. "I don't know what to tell you. I rented this house, and this is where I'm staying."

The woman's mouth opened wide, and Austin braced himself for whatever she was going to say next, but the sound of a car door closing drew her attention.

"Jackson!" Her shout was loud but uncertain, and Austin peered over her shoulder into the dark.

A car was parked in the driveway next door, and a smallish form trundled away from it. It was tough to tell in the dark, but Austin guessed the kid was about eleven or twelve.

The same age as Isaad.

He shoved the thought aside. Another person he couldn't think about. Isaad. Tanner. The list was too long, his capacity for forgetting too short.

"Jackson, come here." The woman's call was even less certain this time. Again, the kid ignored her, quickening his steps toward the sidewalk.

The woman threw one last look at Austin, then sprinted off his porch.

"Well, if that was all," Austin said wryly as he closed the door, but the woman was already halfway across his yard.

Chapter 4

Where on earth did Jackson think he was going?

Wherever it was, fortunately he didn't seem to be in a hurry, and Leah was able to catch up with him before he'd gotten halfway down the block.

She slowed her sprint to fall into step next to him. Her instinct was to grab his arm and pull him toward her house, but something told her if she did that, the boy would take off. Instead, she walked silently next to him for a few steps.

When he didn't acknowledge her presence, she took a deep breath and tried for a light tone. "Our house is actually the one we parked in the driveway of. So unless you're taking the long way to get inside . . ."

Jackson kept walking, giving no indication he'd heard her.

Apparently she'd have to try a different tactic. She worked to sound stern. "Mind telling me where you're going?"

Jackson didn't look toward her. "Got bored waiting for you to stop talking to your boyfriend. So I decided to go find something to eat."

Leah's back stiffened. "I don't even know that man. I was trying to figure out—" She broke off. This wasn't about her or the man who claimed to be renting her neighbor's house. Which she still had her doubts about. But that would have to wait.

One problem at a time.

"Let's go home, and I'll make us some dinner."

She set a tentative hand on Jackson's arm, wincing at his cold skin. The kid only had on a t-shirt, but when she'd asked at the Child Welfare office if he wanted to put on his coat, he'd shrugged and picked up a duffel bag that looked too light to contain a winter jacket. She made a note to herself to buy one tomorrow.

Jackson pulled out of her grasp but turned around and walked next to her as they retraced their steps to her driveway. She led him up the narrow cobblestone path to the house's small porch.

When she'd unlocked the door, she pushed it open and reached to flip on the lights, then stood aside and gestured for Jackson to enter.

She followed him inside, trying to gauge his reaction from his posture, since she couldn't see his face.

"I can see why you're fostering." Jackson strode through the living room and toward the back of the house. "Where's my room? Or am I sleeping on the floor?"

"I'll show you your room in a second. Why don't you come take your shoes off first?" Leah slid her feet out of her own shoes and tucked them into the front closet. "We keep shoes in here."

Jackson rolled his eyes as he turned back to her and dragged his feet toward the front door.

"What do you mean you can see why I'm fostering?" She kept her gaze on him, though he hadn't looked at her once since they'd met.

Jackson scraped his shoes off without untying them and kicked them into the closet, where they bounced off the wall before landing on top of Leah's favorite work shoes. She resisted the urge to straighten them.

"Obviously you need the money." Jackson gestured at her house, wrinkling his nose as if it were decrepit and falling apart. Which couldn't have been farther from the truth. Her house may not scream luxury, but it was cozy and welcoming.

"Actually, I have a successful catering company." She shrugged off her jacket and hung it in the front closet. "The money I get for

25

fostering is to buy things for you. Like a winter jacket, for starters. Is there anything else you need?"

Jackson turned away from her. "Where's my room?"

Leah swallowed the sigh that almost escaped. Maybe she should have taken Jade up on her offer to get everyone together. This alone time with Jackson wasn't going so well.

But she stepped past him with a smile. "It's this way. I didn't know if I'd be fostering a boy or a girl, so I tried to make it kind of neutral." She stopped at the end of the hallway. "I hope you like it." She stepped aside to reveal the cream colored walls and navy quilt she'd chosen. "There are some books and some art supplies over there. And you can unpack your stuff in the dresser and—"

But Jackson launched his duffel bag across the room, and it hit the far wall with a thud. Before she could react, he'd closed the door in her face. She scrunched her eyes shut, willing the emotion back. So this wasn't going how she'd imagined. That didn't mean she couldn't salvage the night.

"I'll go make us some dinner," she called through the closed door. "I hope you like chicken."

She waited a few seconds, half hoping there would be an answer from the other side of the door but knowing there wouldn't be.

As she shuffled to the kitchen, she pulled out her phone to check the time. It was almost seven o'clock, which meant she'd have to make one of her quicker chicken dishes so she could get Jackson to bed at a reasonable time.

What even was a reasonable time for a twelve-year-old to go to bed?

She was about to Google the question, but an email notification from her neighbor popped onto the screen. She should warn Miranda about the guy next door while she was thinking about it. Find out what her neighbor wanted her to do about it.

But the moment she opened the email, her mouth fell open. Apparently the guy had been telling the truth. Miranda was emailing to let her know she'd rented the house out and not to be alarmed if there was someone staying there.

A little late for that.

She scanned the rest of the email, grimacing at Miranda's PS: *He sounds cute. And he'll be right next door. Just saying.*

Leah clicked the phone off, setting it on the counter harder than she meant to in her exasperation. Would no one ever get it through their heads that she didn't need—or want—to be set up with anyone?

And anyway, the guy next door may have sounded cute from 3,000 miles away. But in person he was rude and stubborn and condescending and . . .

Leah forced herself to stop. It wasn't like she'd exactly been the picture of a warm welcome, yelling at him like that. She rubbed at her temples. At some point, she'd have to apologize.

But for now, she had bigger problems.

Like the preteen boy sulking in his bedroom waiting for some food. She pulled the chicken out of the refrigerator and got to work.

Half an hour later, she knocked on the door of Jackson's room to call him to dinner.

She'd thrown together a quick stir fry, and it smelled so enticing—if she did say so herself—that she was surprised he hadn't come wandering out on his own already.

"What?" Even through the door, the hostility was almost enough to knock Leah back, but she stood her ground.

"Dinner is ready." She infused an extra helping of enthusiasm into the statement as if that could make up for the boy's attitude.

"I'm not hungry."

Leah blew out a quick breath. Heaven help her, she was going to need an extra measure of patience tonight. "You were so hungry you were going in search of something to eat half an hour ago."

"I changed my mind." Jackson's tone crawled with defiance.

"If you're not hungry, you can watch me eat. We sit together at the table for meals in this family." She bit her lip. The truth was, she usually sat wherever she felt like sitting for meals—sometimes at the table but more often on the couch or, on nice summer nights, the deck. Still, it sounded like something a parent would say. And from now on, it's what they would do.

Five seconds went by. Then ten.

Finally, the shuffle of footsteps, faint but definitely there, reached her through the door. A moment later, Jackson emerged, looking as sullen as ever.

"It's a stupid rule," he muttered as he passed her.

She chose not to respond, instead following him to the kitchen and taking out two plates. "Wash your hands please."

Jackson gave her a look but went to the sink and ran his hands under the water. "There." Leah held a towel out to him, but he wiped his hands on his shirt.

She debated with herself for half a second, then put the towel down. Maybe some things weren't worth arguing over.

"Do you like stir fry? It's my favorite." She scooped a generous portion onto her plate, then held the pan toward Jackson.

"I told you I'm not hungry." His eyes darted toward the living room window.

Leah's eyes followed, just in time to see a pizza delivery car backing out of Miranda's driveway—or for now, she supposed, that guy's driveway. She hadn't even gotten his name, she realized with a flash of shame. She usually prided herself on her hospitality.

She set the pan of stir fry down and folded her hands in her lap. "We say grace before we eat."

Jackson looked at her as if she'd grown a pair of horns on top of her head. "What's that?"

"We thank God for our food." Leah faltered. Had Jackson never lived in a home where people prayed? "Fold your hands and close your eyes please."

Jackson folded his hands, but he stared at her—more defiance. She decided it was good enough.

Closing her own eyes, she offered a prayer. "Lord, we come to you with hearts overflowing with thankfulness for bringing Jackson and I together tonight. We may have just met, but we know that you have a plan in all things, including making us a family, and we ask that you would bless us as we get to know one another. Thank you for the food you have given us and the home. Most of all, thank you for your love. Amen."

As she finished the prayer, she looked at Jackson. But he was staring ahead, stony faced.

"Are you sure you don't want some stir fry?" She held the pan out to him again, but he knocked it away.

The pan tumbled out of her hand and hit the floor with a loud clang that reverberated through the house. Chicken and vegetables splattered across the kitchen floor.

Jackson sprang from his chair before Leah could fully register what had happened. "I told you I didn't want any."

Before Leah could answer, he'd taken off down the hallway. A second later, the slam of his bedroom door shook the house.

Leah closed her eyes, gripping the edge of the table. One extra measure of patience wasn't going to be enough tonight. She was going to need a whole truckload of it.

After cleaning the floor, she sat to finish her now-cold stir fry. Not that the temperature of the food mattered since she barely tasted it. She'd known bringing an older child into her home wouldn't be easy. She'd known all the potential difficulties. She'd thought she was prepared for them.

But it turned out that knowing something and experiencing it were two different things.

But that didn't matter. She'd promised to give Jackson a home and a family, and that was what she was going to do. Plate empty, she pushed back from the table with a new resolve. She wasn't going to give up on this kid after a few hours.

Scratch that. She wasn't going to give up on him, period.

After she'd washed her dishes, she pulled out a loaf of the homemade bread she purchased from Peyton's bakery every week, a jar of the strawberry jam she'd made this summer, and some peanut butter. Jackson may not be willing to eat her stir fry, but she hadn't seen a kid yet who could resist a PBJ. Especially when they were as hungry as she was sure Jackson was.

When the sandwich was made, she brought it to his room and knocked on the door. When there was no answer after a few seconds, she pushed it open.

Jackson was sprawled on the bed, staring at the ceiling. He didn't look over when the door opened, though she noticed his shoulders tense.

"Hey." She crossed the threshold with one foot, holding out the sandwich. "I know not everyone likes chicken stir fry. So I made you a PBJ. You can eat it in here if you want. Just for tonight."

Jackson didn't so much as twitch. She bit back her desire to stand here until he said something—anything—reminding herself that this was all new to him too.

"I'll put it on your dresser, in case you want it." She crossed the room and set the plate down, then stepped to within a few feet of his bed. "I know this is going to be an adjustment. But you should know that I'm on your side here."

Jackson blinked slowly up at the ceiling, not a single emotion registering on his face.

"I'll always be on your side," she added as she retreated from the room. "I'm sure you're tired. Why don't you eat your sandwich if you want it and then go to bed."

Ever since she'd begun the process of applying to be a foster parent, she'd envisioned the bedtime hug she'd give her child. But it would clearly be a bad idea to attempt that tonight. Jackson would probably sprint out of the house so fast she'd never see him again. Ignoring her disappointment, she pulled the door closed.

In the living room, she settled into the chair at the desk in the corner, shoving aside the latest payroll sheets and pulling out a blank piece of paper.

So today hadn't gone as well as it could have. Tomorrow was another day, right? As was the day after that. And the day after that. She had a lifetime of days with Jackson to show him he could trust her, that she wanted to be his family.

All she had to do was brainstorm some ideas how.

First up was introducing him to her friends tomorrow night.

She could take him to the petting zoo too. And maybe ice skating. They could tour the Old Lighthouse, though she'd have to check if it had closed for the season.

Her pen stilled. What else?

She spent the next two hours searching the internet for every event in Hope Springs and the surrounding area, until her list sprawled from the front of the page across half of the back. But it felt like something was missing. She rubbed her eyes, grainy from the long day and hours on the computer. Maybe she should just go to bed. Surely this had to be enough opportunities to bond with Jackson. But as she moved to put the list away, her hand brushed the day's mail—and a postcard announcing the annual Christmas decorating contest.

That was it. They'd decorate the house together and win the contest. She'd make this the best Christmas he'd ever had—the best Christmas any kid had ever had.

She made a note on her paper, then put it in the desk drawer.

Every muscle in her neck and shoulders protested as she stood and stretched. The day had taken its toll on her, and she needed some sleep.

On the way past Jackson's room, she nudged the door open softly. The boy was asleep—still clothed, still lying on top of the blankets. Leah padded to the linen closet and pulled out a spare blanket, then returned to Jackson's room and draped it over him. For a few minutes, she stood watching him. In sleep, there were no traces of the rebellion he'd shown earlier. He was just a sweet little boy who needed someone to love him.

And Leah would be that someone.

She blew him a silent kiss as she tiptoed out the door, continuing down the hall to her own bedroom.

She'd just nuzzled her way under the blankets, snug in her comfiest sweats, when a loud thud jarred her upright. She sat still, listening again. She had no idea what the sound had been or where it had come from, but her first instinct was to run and check on Jackson. Before she could swing her legs out of bed, though, the thud sounded again. This time it was louder—and clearly coming from outside.

She waited a few seconds, hoping whatever it was would go away, but the sound came again. And then again a few seconds later, taking up an oddly familiar rhythm.

She'd heard that sound plenty of times as a kid when her father had gone outside to chop wood. But it had always been during the day. Not at—she peered at her phone—nearly midnight.

It had to be the guy staying in Miranda's house. The elderly couple who lived on the other side of her had their lights out by eight o'clock every night.

Leah clenched her blankets in her hands as the thudding continued, seeming to grow louder with each thwack. She had to put a stop to this now—before the idiot woke Jackson.

What kind of person chopped wood at midnight?

Leah pounced out of bed and seized her robe, sliding her feet into her slippers.

Apparently, she was taking a midnight trip into the cold.

Chapter 5

The vibration of the ax making contact with the solid hunk of wood ran up Austin's arms. He savored the ache in his shoulders, the repetition of lifting the ax, swinging it in a downward arc, yanking it free, and starting again.

Another hour or so of this, and maybe he'd be exhausted enough to fall into a dreamless sleep. Though he doubted it.

It was why he rarely slept anymore. If he didn't sleep, he couldn't dream. And if he couldn't dream, he couldn't see that day again. Couldn't be dragged back into the horrifying images that he usually managed to keep at the edges of his consciousness when he was awake.

The doctor had prescribed sleeping pills for him and urged him to take them. But he had seen too many guys go that route. Become dependent on the pills. Turn to other pills to numb not only the physical pain but the emotional. That wasn't him.

A drop of sweat trickled into his eye, and he paused to blink it away, then lifted the ax again, bringing it down for one last whack. The log split with a satisfying crack.

He bent over the woodpile the owner had left unstacked and hefted another log onto the stump he was using as a chopping block.

He had the ax poised over his shoulder when a light sprang on in the backyard next door. His gaze jerked that direction in time to see a woman rushing outside. The same woman who had yelled at him earlier for being in the house he had rented and paid for.

With a barely suppressed groan, he dropped the ax. Why did he get the feeling she was going to yell again?

As she hurried toward him, her hair now pulled into a ponytail and a robe flapping around her sweats, his eyes caught on her feet. Hmm. He wouldn't have guessed she was a bunny slippers kind of woman.

Seemed more like a porcupine to him.

He leaned against the ax handle as he waited for her to reach him. Judging by her narrowed eyes and pinched mouth, she hadn't decided to make this a welcome visit either.

"What do you think you're doing?" she hiss-whispered the moment she was within five feet of him.

He gestured to the pile of split wood on the ground. That should be self-explanatory enough.

"It's nearly midnight." Her breath hung in the air between them. "I have a—" She caught herself, as if unsure how to continue, but when she spoke again, her whisper had sharpened. "I have a kid in there I'd like to get a good night's sleep. And this—" She gestured at the same pile of wood he'd pointed to, her lips twisting. "It's not exactly helping."

"Oh." Austin blinked at her. He hadn't considered the fact that normal people went to bed at normal times. That they slept through the night without worrying about being woken by nightmares. Or by a crazy neighbor chopping wood at midnight. "I'm sorry. I wasn't thinking."

The woman contemplated him, her face softening. "So you'll stop?"

He nodded. When had he become so inconsiderate? The guys had always razzed him about being Mr. Polite, but here he was, only thinking about himself. Then again, that was all he'd been thinking about for the past eleven months, wasn't it?

"Yeah." He leaned the ax against the stump. "I'll try to keep the midnight wood chopping to a minimum."

"Good."

He waited for her to turn back to her house, but she stood there studying him, her eyes raking over his face. In the dark, she probably couldn't see the jagged scar along his jawline, but still he shifted. He'd gotten plenty used to close scrutiny by doctors and nurses and therapists—but that didn't mean he liked it.

"Well, if that was all." He repeated the phrase from earlier, taking a step toward his own house.

The woman stepped closer, so that he could smell the tantalizing scent of apples and cinnamon that drifted from her. "Actually, I owe you an apology."

Now it was his turn to study her. Her cheeks were tinted pink, but he couldn't tell if it was from the cold of the night air or from embarrassment over admitting she needed to apologize.

"For what?" He couldn't resist asking. "Yelling at me now or yelling at me earlier?" The lightness in his tone sounded foreign, like he was speaking a language he'd once known but long since forgotten.

Her laugh sparkled on the crisp air. "Both. It's been a long day." She glanced over her shoulder toward her house. "It was my first day as a foster mom, and let's just say it could have gone better."

When she dragged her gaze away from the house, he caught the worry in her eyes. She looked as exhausted as he felt.

"But that's no excuse," she hurried to add. "I was rude, and I'm sorry."

"Apology accepted." Austin wasn't sure why it was important to him to see the tension in her face ease, but it was. "And you no longer believe I'm a squatter here?"

Her long ponytail flipped over her shoulder as she shook her head. "I got an email from my neighbor. Looks like you're on the up and up."

"That's a relief." He pretended to swipe a hand over his brow. "I was afraid you were going to call the FBI earlier."

"Honestly, I thought about it." There was that sparkly laugh again. "I'm Leah, by the way." She held out a hand, and Austin pulled off his glove to shake it. Her fingers were icy, and he felt an odd need to hold on longer to warm them.

"Austin."

He let go of her hand, and she slid it into the pocket of her robe. "So what brings you to Hope Springs?"

Austin stared over her shoulder. Beyond her house, everything was dark and quiet. Still. Peaceful.

"I was born here, but my mom moved us to Iowa when I was too little to remember. I guess I just wanted to see this piece of my history." He left out the part about how he was broken and had no idea where to go to be fixed. How for some reason, he thought this place might be it.

"That's so cool. What's your last name?"

"Hart."

She tipped her head toward the sky, apparently deep in thought. Austin followed her gaze until his eyes met the spread of stars far above. Hard to believe this was the same sky he'd slept under so many nights.

"I don't think I know any Harts," Leah finally said. "But I'll ask around to see if anyone remembers your family."

"You don't have to—"

"Nonsense." Leah's eyes twinkled almost as bright as the stars. "Figuring out how everyone in town is connected is sort of my hobby."

He was pretty sure the sound that came out of him was a laugh—but he couldn't be positive after so many months of not hearing it. "Strange hobby, but whatever you're into."

Leah's laugh was followed by a violent shiver.

"You'd better get inside before you freeze to death. Don't you know it's crazy to be outside at this time of night?"

Leah shook her head at him but turned toward her house. "Sleep well."

Austin sincerely doubted that would happen, but he appreciated the sentiment all the same. "You too."

He bent to stack the wood he'd chopped.

After a few seconds, her voice carried to him from the edge of her yard. "And Austin?"

He looked up in time to see her flash a grin. "Welcome to Hope Springs."

He gave a quick nod before returning to stacking the wood. It didn't make sense that his heart felt lighter after being here for only a few hours. But it did. Only a sliver, maybe. But a sliver was a start.

When he'd finished stacking the wood, he glanced toward Leah's house. The lights were now all off, and Leah was probably already asleep.

Austin tried to remember what it had felt like, once upon a time, to fall asleep instantly, to sleep through the entire night, to wake up feeling rested.

Maybe tonight he'd be able to do that.

He crossed the yard and returned to the house, letting its warmth thaw his raw face.

He puttered around for a while, but finally he couldn't put it off any longer. Between the drive, the cold, and the physical exertion, he had to admit he was exhausted.

He dropped to the side of the bed to pull off his prosthetic, then climbed under the blankets, sure he'd spend the next hour staring at the ceiling.

At least tonight he'd have something new to think about. This house. This town. The neighbor with the blue-green eyes.

But before he could decide what he thought of her, he was out.

38

Chapter 6

Today was a new day, Leah reminded herself as she set the plate of bacon and eggs in front of a glowering Jackson. He shoved it aside.

"Eat up." Leah infused her voice with all the enthusiasm she possessed in this world. "Big day at school today, and then afterward some of my friends and family are coming over for dinner so they can meet you."

If possible, Jackson's expression soured even more, but Leah pressed on. "I noticed you didn't have a backpack, so I dug one out of my closet. It's not in the greatest shape, but it should do for today. We'll get you a new one this weekend."

Jackson pushed away from the breakfast bar. But she wasn't sending him to school on an empty stomach.

"Eat at least half of that before we go."

"Or what?" Jackson shot a half-smirk, half-taunt at her. "What are you going to do to me?"

Leah's mouth opened and closed, and the breakfast she'd eaten before waking him rolled in her stomach. What would she *do* to him? Was he daring her to threaten him? Had he been threatened in the past?

"Or you're going to be hungry," she said simply, then turned to load the dishwasher. "What about lunch? Do you want me to make you something, or do you want to get lunch at school?"

Jackson didn't answer, so she responded as if he had. "How about a PBJ? I saw you ate the one I left in your room last night. Pretty good, right?" There hadn't been so much as a crumb left on his plate when she'd picked it up this morning.

"Whatever." But when she'd made the sandwich and passed it to him in a paper lunch sack, he took it.

Leah resisted cheering out loud at the minuscule sign of progress and led him to the car.

As she looked over her shoulder to back out of the driveway, she noticed a figure standing on the sidewalk. Although the hood of his sweatshirt hung low over his forehead, she immediately recognized Austin.

He waved to indicate he'd wait for her to back down the driveway, and as they passed, he flashed her a quick look. Not a smile, exactly—more an acknowledgment that he recognized her.

When she'd gone back inside last night, she'd lain in bed a while, her earlier exhaustion chased away by the cold night air. She'd tried to list in her head more things she and Jackson could do together. But she hadn't been able to focus as her thoughts kept drifting to the strange neighbor who felt the need to chop wood at midnight. She couldn't help wondering what his whole story was. The scar she'd noticed on his jaw earlier suggested there was a lot more to it than what he'd told her.

Not that it mattered. It wasn't like the guy owed her his whole life story. As long as he didn't chop wood at midnight anymore, that was all that mattered to her.

Not who he was. Or why he'd come. Or what had caused that haunted look in his charcoal gray eyes.

Leah pulled onto the street, watching Austin in the car's mirror. He took a few walking steps, bouncing a little as if warming up, then set out at a slow jog toward the outskirts of town. She made a mental note to tell him later that her brother was a runner too.

Jackson ignored all her attempts to start a conversation on the way to school, so she finally turned up the volume of the Christian radio station she always listened to.

When she reached the school, she pulled up to the curb where other parents were dropping off their children. "Have a good day."

Jackson didn't respond as he edged out of the car.

Groups of kids bubbled up the steps into the school, giggling and jostling each other. But none of them acknowledged Jackson. And he didn't acknowledge them.

An ache filled Leah's chest at the thought of how lonely the boy must be. According to the caseworker, this was the fourth school he'd attended in six years. No wonder he didn't talk to anyone.

The car behind her honked, and Leah forced her eyes off Jackson as she eased her vehicle toward the exit. After ten years of following the same routine every day, it felt strange to be starting her day by dropping a kid off at school. Strange but good.

The start of a new routine. One that would last for many years to come.

She didn't know what it would take to get it through to Jackson that he was here to stay, but she was going to figure it out. Even if it left her emotionally bruised and battered in the process.

The moment she reached the storefront that housed her commercial kitchen, she called the school to give them her contact information. The "oh" the secretary uttered when she said she was calling about Jackson was loaded with more meaning than any two-letter word should be able to carry. She chose to ignore it and simply relay the necessary information.

"Is there anything else you need from me?" she asked before hanging up.

"No, I'm sure we'll be seeing you soon." The secretary's voice hung with that same meaning she'd pushed into the word "oh."

Leah took a breath, commanding herself to ignore it. It wasn't going to help Jackson if she got into an argument with the school secretary. Besides, the caseworker had already warned her last night that Jackson was on thin ice with the school.

She only hoped his teachers would see his new circumstances as a chance for him to begin again.

She thanked the secretary and hung up the phone, throwing herself into preparations for the wedding she was catering tomorrow.

Wait, tomorrow. How could she cater a wedding tomorrow when she had Jackson to take care of?

Technically, at twelve, he was old enough to stay home alone, but was that wise? She supposed she could bring him with her—if nothing else, she could put him to work folding napkins.

By lunchtime, Leah was elbow-deep in prepping the pinot noir sauce she'd need for the filet mignon the bride had insisted on, when her phone rang. Normally, she'd let it go to voice mail if she got a call when she was in the middle of something like this, but she had a child to worry about now.

Please don't let it be about Jackson. She mouthed the prayer as she grabbed her phone off the counter. She didn't recognize the number, but it was local. Which she assumed was a bad sign.

"Hello?"

"Ms. Zelner? This is Hillary, the secretary from Hope Springs Middle School. We spoke this morning?"

Leah closed her eyes, still praying. "Yes? Did you need more information from me?"

"We're going to need you to come in and pick Jackson up. He's been suspended for the rest of the day."

Leah's chin dropped to her chest, but she forced herself to ask. "Why?"

"He was involved in a fight." Disdain dripped from the woman's voice. "Again."

Leah was already shoving ingredients back into the refrigerator. "I'll be right there."

When she pulled into the school parking lot fifteen minutes later, Leah slid into the closest spot. The sound of shrieking and laughter carried to her from the fenced yard behind the school. Most of the kids were apparently enjoying their lunch period.

But not Jackson.

Leah grimaced. This was not the first impression she wanted to make with the school.

She hurried toward the building and ran up the steps but stopped outside the doors to smooth her shirt, rubbing at the grease stain she'd gotten on the sleeve this morning.

Perfect.

Now they were going to think she was an incompetent mother *and* a slob.

She squared her shoulders and pushed through the front doors. It didn't matter what they thought of her. What mattered was that they give Jackson another chance.

The moment she said her name, the secretary pointed toward a door beyond the reception desk marked with the ominous word "Principal."

Mouth dry, Leah offered a grim thanks, then pushed the door open.

Jackson sat slumped in a straight-backed chair in front of the principal's desk, a bag of ice pressed to his cheek. Leah rushed to his side and dropped to her knee.

She hadn't been prepared to find him hurt. She silently lifted the ice bag off, wincing at the purple bruise that was starting to form on his cheekbone.

"Ms. Zelner. Thank you for coming so quickly."

Leah dutifully stood and shook the hand the older woman held out.

"I'm Mrs. Rice, the new principal here this year."

Leah simply nodded. She knew that Mr. Jessup—who had been principal when she was a student here—had retired last year, but she hadn't had an occasion to meet the new principal.

Until now.

"What happened?" Leah turned to Jackson, still slouched in the chair with the ice on his face. He stared at the floor. "Are you hurt?"

Mrs. Rice made a sound somewhere between a tsk and a snort. "It's the other boy you should be concerned about."

Leah's stomach lurched. "What happened?" she repeated.

"Jackson decided to—"

Leah raised her hand to stop the principal. "I'd like to hear it from Jackson, if you don't mind."

Mrs. Rice spluttered but gestured for Jackson to answer the question.

His mouth remained closed, his eyes focused on the floor.

From behind the desk, Mrs. Rice cleared her throat. "Nothing happened. Nothing ever does. He just decides he doesn't like the way a kid is looking at him that particular day and decides to beat the pulp out of them."

"Beat the pulp out of?" Leah reached for the back of the empty chair next to Jackson to steady herself. Was he that violent?

"Bryce now has a bloody nose and possibly a dislocated finger." Mrs. Rice gestured at Leah. "I understand you're his new foster mother."

Leah nodded, still clutching the chair back.

The principal rifled through a stack of papers on her desk, finally pulling out a puce sheet. "These are some resources we suggest for troubled students. I don't know how many of them his former foster parents have tried. But something has to be done. I'm afraid Mr. Young doesn't have many chances left."

Leah's shoulders tightened. What would happen then? Would Child Welfare take him away from her? Find her an unfit foster mother?

"Could I speak with you alone for a moment?" she managed to croak to Mrs. Rice.

The principal's lips flattened into a crooked line. "Jackson, go wait in the outer office."

Jackson didn't look at Leah as he slunk out of the chair and skulked to the door.

As soon as he'd closed it behind him, Leah drew in a deep breath. It felt like whatever she said now was going to set the course for the rest of Jackson's life.

No pressure.

She blew the breath out. "Mrs. Rice, I am so sorry that this happened, and I will talk with Jackson about it. It's not acceptable behavior, and I know that. I'm sure he does too."

Mrs. Rice raised an eyebrow. "Unfortunately, this is pretty regular behavior for him."

"Please try to understand." Leah stepped out from behind the chair to stand at the side of Mrs. Rice's desk so she could look the older woman in the eye. "Jackson has been through a lot in his life, and his circumstances—"

Mrs. Rice held both her hands up in front of her, as if erecting a barrier to the rest of Leah's explanation. "I know all about Jackson's circumstances. But I have a school to run."

"I know, and I can appreciate that," Leah jumped in. "But I hope you can also appreciate that Jackson is going through a period of transition, and he's struggling. I don't think we can even imagine what it's like to be moved from home to home like he has been." She touched a hand to her chest. "It breaks my heart."

Mrs. Rice's face softened. "Look, I appreciate what you're trying to do here. I really do. I hope you'll be able to make a difference for Jackson. And I'll do what I can to help. I'm just warning you that it might be a tough road. I hope you're prepared for that. Because if you're not, you might both be better off if you say so sooner rather than later."

Leah gripped Mrs. Rice's desk, every muscle in her body tensing. Did the principal really think Leah was just going to walk away from this boy? "Jackson is the way he is because he has been failed by every adult who has ever been part of his life." She spun on her heel and stalked to the door, her breaths coming in sharp gasps. "I refuse to be one of them."

Chapter 7

Three more reps, Austin pushed himself.

But the screaming pain from his knee stopped him after two more modified squats.

He cursed to himself. He could do this. He wanted to do it.

So why wouldn't his body cooperate?

He dropped to the couch, massaging what was supposed to be his "good" knee. The doctor had said it had some arthritis, but he'd assured Austin it shouldn't get much worse if Austin didn't work it too hard.

But not working it too hard wasn't an option. If he wanted to get off the temporary disability retired list and be fit for duty by the time of his next exam, he had to push himself as hard as he could.

The throbbing in his leg didn't abate, but Austin ignored it, reaching instead for his other leg to unfasten his prosthetic and pull off his liner. He massaged the end of his residual limb, feeling the spot where his tibia had been cut, refusing to wince as his fingers kneaded into the skin. The muscles of his lower leg had atrophied over the past eleven months, so that this leg was decidedly smaller than the other.

But just as strong, he told himself, bending to pick up the crutches he'd discarded on the floor this morning. He needed a shower. But as he settled them under his arms, a movement in his peripheral vision caught his attention. A flash of light against something metallic. He jerked his head toward the front window, breath catching in his chest. But it was only a car pulling into the driveway next door.

He meant to move away from the window then, but for some reason, he couldn't take his eyes off the car. Leah had gotten out and stood with her hand on her door, bending down to talk to someone inside. Must be her kid. The boy who'd taken off down the street last night.

Austin leaned his crutches against the couch and lowered himself onto the cushions. He didn't know why, but he felt compelled to watch them.

After a minute, the kid climbed out of the car, closing it with a force that made Leah jump. Her eyes followed him up the walkway to the front door. From here, Austin couldn't read her expression. But he was pretty sure it wasn't a happy one.

She closed her own car door so lightly that Austin doubted it had latched properly. Then she stepped toward the back door on the driver's side. But instead of opening it, she braced her elbows on it and dropped her head to her arms.

Austin recognized the move. How often had he done that over the past eleven months? Against his refrigerator, his apartment door, his bedroom wall?

It was a move of despair, of hopelessness.

Apparently, her second day as a foster mom wasn't going so well either.

As Austin watched her, he debated with himself. Something inside told him he should go out there, offer a kind word, maybe a listening ear. But another part of him—the smarter part—said that was absurd. Whatever was going on with his neighbor was none of his business—and he didn't want to make it his business. He had no desire to get close to her. And even less desire to get close to the kid. He wouldn't make that mistake again.

He rubbed at the scar on his jaw as he watched her slouched there, clearly in anguish. He tried to tell himself to look away, but he couldn't make himself obey.

After a few minutes, Leah lifted her head, swiped a quick hand over her cheeks and straightened her back. As she walked to the house, he could see the sheer force of will driving her there, and he was overcome by an irrational urge to cheer her on.

His phone dinged from beside him on the couch, and Austin glanced down at it, then looked away. It was an email notification. From the only person who emailed him anymore. The one person whose emails he couldn't bring himself to open.

Tanner's wife.

She'd been writing to him once a week every week since Tanner died. Which meant he had more than forty unread emails from her.

He had no idea what her messages said, and he couldn't risk looking. He was too much of a coward to answer the question she'd asked him the one time she'd visited him in the hospital.

How are you?

How was he? He was alive, that's how he was. When her husband was dead. And it was his fault. If he hadn't insisted on picking Isaad up. If he had been the one driving as he was supposed to be. If he had been watching the road instead of joking around with the kid.

But *ifs* didn't matter.

Austin had no idea how long he sat like that, staring at the phone screen even after it had gone blank. Finally, he put the phone away and lifted his head. The sun had dropped behind the trees across the street, leaving trails of deep pink and purple in the clouds. He glanced toward Leah's house, but she must have long since gone inside.

A set of headlights swept down the street, slowing as it approached, then turning into Leah's driveway. Before anyone had emerged from that car, another turned into her driveway. People spilled out of the cars, and their voices, indistinct but clearly joyful, carried across the yard and through Austin's closed windows. He counted four adults—and it looked like one of them was carrying a young child. As they made their way to the door, two more cars drove up, parking on the street in front of Leah's house. More people walked toward her door, more cheerful voices carried toward his house.

A grating kind of pain pressed at Austin's gut. He'd known camaraderie like that once. With Chad and Tanner and all the rest of the guys in his unit. If he were over there right now, if the past year had never happened, they'd probably all be sitting around, playing a game of poker and ribbing each other about whatever came to mind.

More *ifs* that didn't matter.

Austin grabbed his phone and hit the number for the pizza place—the only number he'd called since he got here. Then he pushed himself up from the couch, pretending not to notice as one more car pulled up to Leah's house.

He preferred to be alone, anyway.

Leah watched the timer on the oven tick off the seconds until the pan of meatballs was done.

Her friends were all in the living room, but she needed a few moments to herself. The day hadn't gotten any better after she'd picked Jackson up from school. She'd had no choice but to bring him to work with her, since she had to finish getting things ready for tomorrow's wedding. She'd tried to give him a job peeling carrots, but the moment she'd turned her back, he'd snuck off to a corner of the room, where he sat brooding the rest of the afternoon. She hadn't had time—or energy, frankly—to get him to do what she'd told him to do.

She'd hoped things might be better once he was surrounded by her friends and family tonight. But with each introduction, he'd grown more withdrawn, refusing to do anything but offer a limp handshake. He hadn't so much as said hello to anyone.

Last she saw, he was huddled in a chair, staring at the floor and refusing to answer even the simplest questions her friends asked.

She rolled her shoulders now, trying to ease the tension that had been building there all day. She was exhausted, frustrated, and much as she hated to admit it, embarrassed. When she'd told her friends she wanted to be a foster mother, they'd all been so supportive. They'd assured her she'd be a wonderful mother, that she'd make such a difference in a kid's life.

And now here she was, not even two days into fostering, and she was floundering big time.

Scratch that. She wasn't floundering. She was sinking. Fast.

"You need any help in here?" Her sister-in-law's voice nearly made Leah jump onto the countertop.

"Sorry. I didn't mean to startle you." Jade offered a sympathetic look. "Everything okay?"

Leah nodded. "Just thinking."

"About Jackson?"

Leah blew out a long breath. "Yeah. How'd you guess?"

"Give it time." Jade lifted a stack of plates out of the cupboard and set them on the counter.

"I don't know how to get through to him." Leah turned off the oven timer as it flipped to zero. "I know there has to be something I can do. I just haven't figured out what yet."

"You can pray about it," Jade prompted, and Leah marveled once again at the transformation in her sister-in-law. A year and a half ago, she would have scoffed if anyone suggested she pray—now she was the one offering that advice.

Still, it wasn't as if Leah hadn't thought of that. And she had prayed. Probably more than she ever had in her life. But it seemed like this was going to be one more prayer God answered with no.

She moved to the living room to let the others know dinner was ready. Her eyes went to Jackson, still slouched in his chair, not acknowledging the people who surrounded him. Beyond him, she caught the flash of lights out the window as a pizza delivery car pulled into the neighbor's driveway.

"Dinner time." She directed a pointed look at Jackson. "Why don't you lead the way, since you're our guest of honor tonight?"

But Jackson shook his head. "I'm not hungry."

That had to be a lie. He'd resisted eating the peanut butter and jelly she'd packed him for lunch until he thought she wasn't watching, then devoured it in about three bites. Was it just another act of defiance, his refusing to eat when she told him to? Or was there more to it than that?

Either way, he obviously needed food.

She tried to keep the frustration from creeping into her voice. "Jackson, you have to—"

But someone laid a gentle hand on her arm, and she glanced over to find Jade stepping past her into the living room, Hope on her hip. "Jackson, if you're not hungry, could you do me a favor and watch Hope while I get some food? I am absolutely starving, and she's at the age where she tries to knock everything off my plate."

"I'm not sure—" Leah jumped in. She appreciated what her sister-in-law was doing, but maybe putting the boy who'd been suspended for punching a kid in charge of a baby wasn't the best idea.

Jade shot her a look and set Hope on the floor by Jackson's feet, scattering a few toys around her. "She shouldn't be any trouble, but let me know if you need anything, okay?"

Jackson blinked at Jade, his expression shifting from opposition to something Leah hadn't seen on him before—a flicker of interest.

With a pat of Hope's head, Jade straightened and strode through the living room toward the kitchen, pulling Leah behind her.

"Do you think that's a good idea?" Leah kept her voice low so Jackson wouldn't hear her. "I told you about what happened at school."

"Trust me. Jackson's the one who better watch out. That little girl can soften even the hardest heart."

"What little girl?" Leah's brother Dan asked, dropping a kiss on his wife's cheek.

"Your daughter." Jade nudged him, and Leah was sure no father had ever lit up with a prouder grin.

The heaviness that had been dragging at Leah's heart since the car ride home with Jackson eased a little. Hope couldn't be more Dan's daughter if she had been his biological child. The same would be true of her and Jackson one day. It was like Jade had said, she had to give it time.

She joined the others in prayer, then dug into her own plate of meatballs, letting the sound of her friends' conversations soothe her frayed nerves. This was exactly what she needed—to be surrounded by all the people she loved best in the world.

"Leah, you have to come here." Jade's low, urgent tone carried to Leah from the opening to the living room as she was about to bite into one of the cupcakes Peyton had brought.

Appetite vanishing, Leah shoved her chair back and rushed to Jade's side. "What's wrong?"

But Jade didn't look horrified, she looked . . . awed.

Leah peered around Jade, and her breath caught. Was she seeing this right?

Jackson had slid out of the chair onto the floor, and Hope had crawled over to his side. Jackson was holding a rattle in one hand, shaking it gently as he held it out to her. But more amazing than all of that was his face—it was the first time Leah had seen him smile.

It made him seem both younger and older, vulnerable and responsible all at once.

"Wow," she breathed.

"I told you Hope could soften any heart," Jade whispered.

Chapter 8

The night air cut at Austin's lungs, but he drew in a deep breath, leaning his head against the back of the Adirondack chair he'd pulled off the deck and into the middle of the yard.

It was surreal, how like the Afghan night this was and yet how different. It had gotten this cold in the Afghan mountains, but the smells here were different. Less acrid smoke from the villagers' sawdust stoves, more pine trees and lake breeze.

It was nowhere near as dark here either. Although he'd turned off most of the lights in his house, warm patches of yellow light spilled from Leah's house next door onto his lawn.

The strangest part was that there was no danger here. He was sitting in the middle of a backyard, completely safe. While his brother faced who knew what on the other side of the world.

He flexed his left leg, wincing as needles stabbed through his nonexistent foot. The phantom pains weren't as bad as they'd been in the beginning, but they were still there, even when he wore his prosthetic. Still hampering his recovery.

He gritted his teeth and forced his mind off the pain. He was getting stronger. He knew he was.

He only hoped it was strong enough to prove he was fit to return to combat. He didn't have any desire to be stuck behind a desk somewhere. Or worse, retired from service entirely.

For the past fourteen years, the army had been his life.

Without it, he wasn't sure he knew who he was.

A clatter from next door pulled his eyes toward Leah's yard as she stepped out her back door, feet clad in boots this time instead of bunny slippers.

He meant to pretend he didn't see her, but instead his hand rose into a wave.

Leah did a double-take, then marched across her yard until she was standing in front of him. "What are you doing out here?"

Austin peered up at her. "Sitting."

Leah rolled her eyes. "I see that. I guess I should ask *why* you're sitting in the middle of your yard in hardly any clothes when it's like twenty degrees out here."

Austin snorted. Hardly any clothes? He was wearing his warmest fleece sweatshirt. The same one he'd worn so many nights in the mountains. And he'd never once gotten cold in it. "I'm good. What are you doing out here *in* clothes?"

Even in the dark, Austin could have sworn that Leah's cheeks flushed, and he chalked up a point for himself.

"I only wear my pajamas outside when I have to stop some lunatic neighbor from waking my kid. When I come out to get wood for my fireplace, I tend to dress more appropriately for the weather."

"How are things going?" Austin didn't know why he asked. He certainly hadn't planned to. And he didn't want to know the answer, not really. But when he pictured how defeated she'd looked earlier, he couldn't help it.

"A tiny bit better actually." Leah lifted her arms and drew her long hair into a ponytail, then let it fall. "I think we may have just had a breakthrough. He's in there playing with my baby niece. She has him wrapped around her finger already." The lightness in Leah's tone completely transformed her.

"So are you going to sit out here all night, or do you want to come meet some people?" Leah gestured toward her house.

If those were the two choices, he'd take sit out here all night. "No thanks, I—"

"You might as well say yes because I'm going to stand here and bug you until you do." Leah crossed her arms in front of her. "Plus, we have some food left. Meatballs. And cupcakes. I know all you've had for the past two days is takeout pizza."

So she was bossy *and* nosy. Good to know.

"I really should—"

"Come get some food? Yep." Leah held out a hand as if to help him up.

He contemplated it. He wanted to argue. Wanted to tell her to leave him alone, he was just fine on his own, thank you very much. But then he remembered the happy people he'd seen walking into her house earlier. The way they'd talked and laughed and joked together. The tightness in his chest that hadn't eased since then.

"Come on," Leah wheedled again. "I need some help carrying in firewood."

"Fine." He gave a resigned sigh. "But only to help with the firewood."

"Yay." She bounced on the balls of her feet.

He eyed her hand still stretched toward him but braced his hands against the arms of the chair to push himself upright.

An involuntary groan escaped him as he took a step.

Leah threw a concerned look over her shoulder. "You okay?"

"Yep." He tried to walk normally, ignoring the protest of his stiff leg muscles. "Just a little sore from my run this morning."

"Do you run a lot?"

It was an innocent enough question. She couldn't possibly know how fraught answering it would be for him.

"I used to," he answered finally. "I'm trying to get back into it."

She didn't seem to find anything strange about his answer. "My brother's a runner too. I bet he'd love to run with you."

Austin stared at her. Did she always go making plans for complete strangers?

They each loaded their arms with logs, then he followed Leah toward her back door.

"I guess we didn't think this through." Leah looked from her own full arms to his. With her elbow, she pounded on the door. "Hopefully someone will hear that. They're kind of loud in there."

But it was only a few seconds before someone opened the door.

"Thanks, Peyton." Leah smiled at the woman who held the door, then slid in past her. Austin followed Leah, trying to ignore the curious look the other woman gave him.

He kept his head down as he trailed Leah through the kitchen and dining room to the living room. People covered nearly every conceivable seating area, and Austin's eyes darted to the door. He forced himself to take a deep breath. As soon as he dropped this load of wood, he could get out of here. A couple of guys had sprung to their feet and were unloading the wood from Leah's arms. One started to grab logs off Austin's pile too.

"You should have told us you needed wood, Leah. We would have gotten it," one of the guys scolded.

"It's fine. I had a helper." As she passed the last piece of wood off, Leah gestured to Austin. "Everyone, this is Austin." She turned to him. "Ready for this?"

Before he could figure out what he was supposed to be ready for, she launched into rapid-fire introductions. "That's Sophie and Spencer over there, with their twins Rylan and Aubrey." She pointed to a couple seated on the floor, their legs extended to keep two crawling babies on the far side of the room. Both adults waved at him.

"And that's Peyton and Jared on the couch and Nate and Violet snuggled on that chair together. Ethan and Ariana on the love seat, and that's their little girl Joy eating a book." Everyone laughed as Ariana tugged the paper out of her daughter's mouth.

But Leah was still going. "Next to you is Tyler, and those are his twins running around. He's Spencer's brother." She leaned closer. "Twins run in their family."

"Someone could have told me that *before* I married into the family," Sophie called as she picked up one of her little ones to deliver a raspberry to her tummy.

"On the hearth here are Emma and Grace," Leah continued. "And over by the window is my brother Dan and his wife Jade."

Dan stepped around the others and held out a hand. Austin wiped his own hand subtly on his sweatpants before returning the gesture.

"And that's their daughter Hope on the floor next to Jackson. My—" She faltered, and Austin's eyes went to her. She took a quick breath, then said, "My foster son."

It was the first time Austin had seen the boy up close, and his heart jumped.

Dark hair. Bumpy nose.

Isaad?

But then he blinked, and the kid looked up, his expression surly.

Not Isaad.

His heart plummeted.

"So where'd you two meet?" The question came from the woman Leah had introduced as her sister-in-law.

Austin heard the undertone in her voice and nearly groaned. He never should have agreed to come inside. Not only was this place way too crowded for comfort. Not only was there a kid who looked disconcertingly like Isaad. But now he'd given Leah's friends—and probably Leah herself—the impression he was interested in her.

"We didn't meet," Leah jumped in defensively, a hand lifting to her hip as she shot her sister-in-law a look.

Okay, so maybe Leah, at least, hadn't gotten the wrong impression. That was a relief.

"So you brought a stranger over?" Dan sounded like he was only partially teasing.

"Wouldn't be the first time," the blonde woman on the couch chimed in. If he remembered correctly—which was unlikely—that one was Peyton. "Remember that time she brought home that hitchhiker and insisted on making him a warm meal before—"

"All right. All right." Leah held up her hands. "I promise Austin isn't a hitchhiker. He's renting Miranda's house for a while." She turned to him. "How long did you say?"

He shrugged. He had no idea. But if his physical went well, not long.

"His family was originally from Hope Springs. Hart. Sound familiar to anyone?"

They all shook their heads, but Dan stepped forward. "I can check through old church records. Chances are, if they lived in Hope Springs, they went to Hope Church."

Austin gave a noncommittal nod. Dan was probably right, since his mother had been a committed Christian and had raised him and his brother in the church. But whereas Chad remained a believer, Austin had long since come to his senses. Anyone who could still believe in God after the things they'd seen in battle was crazier than him.

"Come on." Leah tilted her head toward the dining room. "I promised you food. And food you'll get."

She smiled at him, and he tried to convince himself it didn't warm him. That was just the fire that one of the guys now had roaring in the fireplace.

Nothing else.

Chapter 9

"We still need those tartlets," Leah called across the wedding hall's kitchen to her assistant Sam.

"On it." Sam wiped her hands on the front of her already streaked apron and held up her mixing bowl.

Leah studied the schedule she'd laid out for the day. So far, there had been no major delays, and things were running smoothly. Which was something of a miracle, considering that her brain wasn't all here.

She was too busy worrying about her decision to leave Jackson home alone while she catered this wedding. She'd debated bringing him with her, but after the way he'd flourished with Hope last night, she hoped that perhaps giving him a little more responsibility and showing him some trust would improve things between them.

But that didn't mean she was certain about it. At all.

If only she could call to check on him, she'd feel better. But he didn't have a phone. She'd have to add that to the list of things she needed to get him, so they could stay in touch in situations like this.

Maybe she should call one of her friends and ask them to swing by the house. Or would that be too much like spying on him? Would he take that as a sign she didn't trust him?

She let out an exasperated breath and returned to her list. Why had no one warned her this parenting thing would be so hard? She was so used to feeling certain about everything, used to making snap decisions and not thinking twice about them. But now, she was questioning everything, second guessing herself at every turn. Was this what parenting was going to be like? For the rest of her life?

Okay, mushrooms. She needed to prepare the mushrooms. She pulled the carton out of the refrigerator.

Austin. The name popped into her head. She could call Austin and ask him to check on Jackson. It wouldn't be suspicious if the neighbor happened to stop by—maybe he needed to borrow some sugar or something.

She took out her phone and scrolled to his name. Good thing she'd made him give her his number last night, just as she'd done with all the rest of her neighbors when she'd moved into the neighborhood. Just as a way for everyone to watch out for one another.

Her finger hovered over the call button. Was this too weird?

Austin hadn't seemed entirely comfortable at her house last night. Of course, Jade's implication that the two of them had met and then intentionally sought each other out again hadn't helped.

But it seemed like there was more to it than that. He tried to hide it, but she hadn't missed the way his eyes had flitted to the door every few seconds, no matter what room he was in. And other than a quick glance, he'd entirely ignored Jackson.

Still, he didn't have to be Mr. Rogers to check on Jackson now.

She hit the button, cradling the phone against her shoulder and cleaning the mushrooms as she waited for him to answer.

When he did, he sounded winded.

"Did you just get back from a run?" She set the mushrooms down and leaned against the counter.

"No. Working out. What's up?"

Unbidden, an image of his broad shoulders sprang to mind. She banished it. "Could you do me a favor?"

"Maybe." Austin sounded hesitant. "Depends what it is."

Leah laughed. "That's fair. Can you look out your window and check something for me?"

"Sure. Check what?"

"Is my house still standing?"

The laugh that sped through the phone took Leah by surprise. She didn't know Austin well, but so far she hadn't gotten the impression he was the laughing type.

"It's still standing. Why? Are you expecting it to fall today?"

"I hope not." Leah had never been more fervent about anything. "Now for the favor."

"I thought that was the favor." Austin's bemusement crept through the phone.

"No. That was a question." Leah tucked her hair behind her ear and switched the phone to her other shoulder. "The favor is, can you go over to my house and check on Jackson?"

"Check on—"

"But don't let him know you're checking on him," Leah rushed on. "Tell him you need to borrow some sugar or something."

"I don't think—"

But now that Leah had hatched the plan, she was desperate to carry it through. It was the only way she'd have any peace of mind. "Then call me afterward and let me know how he's doing. Please."

"Leah, I think—"

"I'm sorry. I know this is weird. And I wouldn't ask if I wasn't desperate. But I need to know that he's okay there, or I won't be able to do my work here. And I don't want to ruin some poor couple's wedding dinner because I'm a basket case."

The moment Austin's sigh crackled through the speaker, she knew she had won. "Thank you so much, Austin. You're the best." She clicked the phone off before he could try to get out of it again.

"He's the best, huh?"

Leah jumped at Peyton's voice. She'd been so focused on her conversation with Austin, she hadn't seen her best friend come in and set her box of cake decorating supplies on the counter.

"He's going to check on Jackson. I've been so worried about leaving him home alone." Leah busied herself chopping the mushrooms. There was no reason she should feel embarrassed that she'd been on the phone with Austin.

But she knew the conclusion Peyton would jump to before her friend said it. "He seemed like a nice guy. Maybe you should—"

"No." Leah stilled her knife and lifted her head. "I'm not going to ask him on a date. I'm not going to ask anyone on a date. And for the record, none of you are going to ask anyone on a date for me either. Never mind the fact that I've told you not to a thousand times before."

Peyton's mouth opened, but Leah wasn't done. "Jackson is my priority right now. And he will be for a long time to come. So no more comments about asking Austin out. He's a nice guy, and I look forward to becoming friends with him. But that's as far as it goes."

Peyton raised her hands in front of her in a gesture of surrender. She started pulling supplies out of her box in silence, and Leah returned to her chopping.

But after a few minutes, Peyton slid her empty box off the counter and turned to Leah, watching her silently.

Leah blew a stray piece of hair out of her face. "What?" She'd rather pretend Peyton wasn't standing there just waiting to tell her something—something she probably didn't want to hear—but she knew Peyton would just bring it up another time—probably a time when it was even less convenient.

"It's just . . ." Peyton waved her piping bag at Leah. "You've put this guy into the friend zone before you've even gotten to know him. You're not giving him a chance."

Leah rolled her eyes. "Who says he wants a chance?" Austin had shown as little interest in her as she had in him.

"I'm not saying he necessarily does." Peyton opened a bag of powdered sugar and measured it into a bowl. "I'm just saying you're shutting him down before he can decide whether he does or not. It's the same thing you've done with every guy since Gavin."

Leah sucked in a breath. No one had mentioned Gavin in years, so why Peyton thought he had anything to do with anything now was beyond her.

"I got over Gavin years ago." Her voice was low, but there was a note of warning in it that she knew Peyton would recognize. And probably ignore.

"Maybe so." Peyton raised an eyebrow as if she didn't entirely believe Leah. "But that doesn't mean what happened hasn't affected you on some level. Affected the way you see men."

Leah pressed her lips together and pulled out a baking pan. Peyton knew the signal. The conversation was over.

"Come on, Leah." Apparently her friend didn't care about the signal today. "The guy dated you for two years. You thought you were going to get married. And then he decided he wanted to be friends."

Leah pushed past Peyton to grab a stick of butter out of the refrigerator.

"And then—" Peyton wasn't done yet. "He married someone else three months later. You can't tell me that didn't have an impact on you."

Leah dropped the cold butter into the pan harder than necessary. "Of course it had an impact on me. Then. Not now."

"So you're telling me that the reason you friend-zone every guy you meet has nothing to do with Gavin?"

"That's what I'm telling you." Why was it so difficult for Peyton to believe that the reason she was just friends with guys was because she was perfectly content as a single woman?

"Hey, Leah." Sam's call from the other side of the kitchen held a note of panic. "I don't think these Brie tartlets turned out."

Leah allowed herself a sigh of relief. She'd never thought she'd be grateful to hear that her star appetizer hadn't turned out. But anything was better than this conversation.

Chapter 10

Austin stared at the front door of Leah's house. How had she gotten him to agree to do this? And how stupid was he going to sound asking a twelve-year-old kid if he could borrow a cup of sugar?

Not that it mattered.

He was only here to do his good deed. He'd check on the kid. Ensure that both he and the house were in one piece. And then he'd get out of there, as fast as he could.

As he lifted his hand to knock, he steeled himself for the sight of the kid. *It's not Isaad.* He repeated it to himself as he waited for Jackson to come to the door. Maybe this way he wouldn't experience that painful jolt he'd felt every time he'd chanced a glance at the kid last night. The jolt that made him think just for a second that he'd gone back in time and Isaad was still alive.

He knocked again, but no one came to the door. He checked the time on his phone. Almost two o'clock. Even teenagers didn't sleep this late, did they?

He pounded on the door again, harder this time, the refrain *It's not Isaad* still playing in a loop in his head.

Another minute went by. Then another.

He debated. Technically, he'd kept his promise. He'd come over with the intention of asking for a cup of sugar. It wasn't his fault the kid had refused to answer the door.

But he'd also promised to let Leah know how it had gone. He could only imagine what would happen if he called and told her he hadn't seen or heard a sign of her foster son. He'd get yelled at again, for sure.

He tried the doorknob, but it was locked.

Great.

Was he going to have to break in?

Maybe before taking such drastic measures, he should try the back door. Pulling up his hood against the biting wind, he started around the house.

The moment he reached the backyard, he spotted Jackson, crouched under the large oak tree at the back of the lot, peering at something in the grass.

Despite his *It's not Isaad* mantra, the initial gut punch of the boy's dark hair drew Austin up short.

But as Jackson shifted, Austin got a glimpse of his face.

Not Isaad.

The boy glared at him, and Austin considered turning around. He could honestly report to Leah that Jackson was fine. But from the little he knew of her, that wouldn't be enough. He forced his feet forward.

Jackson reached into the grass, cupping his hands around something.

"What you got there?" Austin called out as he drew closer. The minute the words slipped from his mouth, he stopped. That was the first thing he'd ever said to Isaad too. The boy had been holding a rock, and Austin's first assumption had been that he was about to throw it at the American soldiers. But then the boy had pointed out the flecks of chlorite and serpentine in the stone, and Austin had realized he was a budding geologist. After that, Austin had made it a habit to search for interesting rocks to give the boy, who always knew exactly what they were.

He shook off the memory. This wasn't Isaad. It was Jackson. And whatever he was holding definitely wasn't a rock—it was moving.

Austin inched closer as Jackson regarded him, suspicion and mistrust fogging the boy's eyes. He turned his back to Austin, as if trying to protect his secret.

Austin shuffled closer, catching a glimpse of something squirming in Jackson's hands. "Is that a baby squirrel?"

Jackson eyed him again, then looked at his hands, giving a barely perceptible nod.

Stepping next to the boy, Austin bent to peer more closely. The squirrel fit entirely in Jackson's palm, a fine layer of fur covering most of its body. Its eyes were closed, as if it had curled up for a nap, and it's tail—nearly as long as its body—wrapped around its side.

Austin squinted upward, shielding his eyes as he searched the branches. Finally, he spotted a leafy nest near the top of the tree. "It must have fallen."

Too bad there was no way they could get it back up there. Strong as he was getting, there was no way Austin could climb this tree, and he was pretty sure Leah would skin him alive if he sent Jackson that high into the tree, especially considering the way the branches were whipping in today's wind.

"I'm going to keep it." It was the first time Austin had ever heard Jackson speak, and his voice was lower than Austin had expected.

"You should probably leave it. Its mom will come for it." Austin turned to leave. He'd done his job. Now he could go home, report to Leah that Jackson was alive and well, and maybe get in another workout before—

Before what?

Before he ordered another pizza and sat around all night with nothing to do?

It wasn't like his calendar was exactly full.

"The squirrel's mom isn't coming back." Jackson's voice jabbed at him, steelier than any twelve-year-old should ever sound.

Austin turned to the kid. "How do you know?"

Jackson studied the squirrel. "His body was cold when I picked him up. That means he's been there a while. If she hasn't come for him yet, she's not coming."

Austin scrubbed a hand across his short hair, letting it prickle against his fingers. *Go home*, he told himself. But he couldn't, not with that half-pleading, half-frightened look Jackson was giving him. Austin sighed. The kid was in foster care. Which meant he probably hadn't had the best experience with his own parents, right?

He was going to regret this. He knew he was. But he pulled out his phone and did a quick search for "how to take care of a baby squirrel." After a few minutes of reading, he looked up. Jackson was still cradling the squirrel, his left hand cupped over his right.

"It says to put a zipper bag filled with warm water in a box and cover it with a t-shirt and then put it at the base of the tree. That way the baby squirrel will stay warm, and the mom can come and get it."

Jackson shot him a challenging look.

Austin jumped in before he could argue. "You at least have to give her a chance to get her baby."

"What if she doesn't?" There was that hardness again.

"If she doesn't, then—" But Austin had no idea what they would do then. He couldn't go making promises to the neighbor's kid. But he wasn't about to be the one to tell him he couldn't keep the squirrel either. "Then we'll figure that out when we get to it. Deal?"

Jackson's nod was slow but emphatic. "Deal."

Satisfied, Austin held out his hand for a quick handshake. "I'll go get a box."

He sent Leah a text on his way back to his house to retrieve the shoe box he'd seen in the hall closet. *Everything fine here. Jackson playing outside.* No need to freak her out with the news that her foster son was hoping to adopt a squirrel. With any luck, the critter would be back in its nest with its mother within the hour, and he could get back to his own life—or lack thereof.

But three hours later, he was less optimistic. He and Jackson had been observing the box from inside all afternoon, and so far there hadn't been any sign of an adult squirrel. The temperature was dropping quickly—they'd already changed the bag of warm water half a dozen times to make sure the little squirrel didn't freeze—and now snow flurries were starting to fall. And it was getting dark. Austin didn't dare voice his fear that if the squirrel's mother didn't get it soon, it would become a meal for a hawk or a stray dog.

Jackson had been asking for half an hour already if they could bring the squirrel inside. Finally, Austin had to relent. He had no idea how it would traumatize the kid if the squirrel died—and he didn't have any interest in finding out.

As Jackson ran outside to collect the squirrel, Austin tried to figure out how he was going to explain this to Leah.

He couldn't quite decide if he dreaded the snap of fire in her eyes when she yelled at him—or if he looked forward to it.

"You're sure you don't mind finishing the cleanup without me?" Leah eyed Sam. Her assistant had only gotten married a few months ago and was probably eager to get home to her husband.

"For the twentieth time, I'm sure." Sam shoved Leah toward the door. "We're almost done. Go home to your son."

Leah couldn't help the grin. *Her son.* She hadn't gotten used to those words quite yet, but already she loved the ring of them. And Sam was right, she did feel a strong need to get home and check on Jackson. Austin's text earlier that Jackson was playing outside had given Leah enough peace of mind to get through the meal. But now that it was over, she wanted to get home and see for herself. Plus, if Jackson had ventured outside, maybe it meant he was over at least some of the sullenness that had followed him around like a chained puppy for the past two days.

As she drove home, careful not to press her foot to the accelerator too hard in her eagerness, her thoughts flitted to what Peyton had said earlier. About her friend-zoning guys because of what had happened with Gavin. It was absolute nonsense. Sure, she'd prayed Gavin would be her husband. And after things fell apart with him, she'd prayed that God would give her someone else to love.

But she'd stopped praying that prayer a long time ago.

It was clear that God's plans for her didn't include marriage. But just because she wasn't searching for a husband didn't mean she was deliberately sabotaging any relationship before it started.

And just because Austin was good looking and seemed fairly kind and even a little funny when he let himself be didn't mean she had to be interested in him as more than a friend.

Leah nodded to herself as she pulled into her driveway, vowing to put thoughts of Peyton and Austin and everything else that wasn't Jackson-related aside for the rest of the night.

But when she stepped through the door to her house, she realized that was going to be difficult, considering that Austin was sitting on the couch with Jackson. Her heart skipped at the picture of the two of them bent close together, peering into a small shoe box on the cushion between them. Anyone who didn't know them might assume they were father and son, despite Austin's light hair and Jackson's darker locks. They looked up as she closed the door behind her.

Both wore expressions of mixed guilt and hope.

"What's going on?" She concentrated on catching her breath after the surprise of seeing Austin in her house and seeing Jackson anywhere other than his room.

Austin gestured her over. "Jackson found this little guy on the ground, and he's taken care of him all afternoon."

"Little guy?" Leah took a cautious step closer. She wasn't sure she wanted to see anything that was described as little guy and fit into a shoe box. What if they had a spider in there?

Her eyes fell on a nearly naked creature, and she shrieked and jumped back. "Is that a rat?"

Two snickering laughs greeted her. "It's a baby squirrel." Jackson's voice held a note of *duh*.

"Oh." As long as it wasn't a rat, she could probably be brave enough to get a little closer. "What's a baby squirrel doing in my house?"

"It fell out of its nest, and we tried to find its mom, but she never came back for it."

Leah felt her mouth open. That was the longest string of words she'd ever heard Jackson utter.

"That was very kind of you." She kept her voice guarded. "We should call the humane society. If they don't take in squirrels, they'll know who does."

"Actually—" The rumble of Austin's voice cut her off as she was about to look up the phone number. "Jackson would like to keep it."

Leah froze. They wanted her to keep a squirrel? In her house? She glanced at Austin, who held her gaze, eyes pleading. Was it that Jackson wanted her to keep the squirrel, or that Austin did? But when she turned to Jackson the same pleading was reflected in his eyes.

She sighed. How was she supposed to say no to that? But her mind seized on something. A squirrel was a wild animal. "I'm sorry, Jackson. It's illegal to keep wild animals. Maybe we can get some fish or something." Fish were easy to take care of, weren't they?

But Austin and Jackson were both smirking at her. It was uncanny how much they looked alike when they did that.

"Actually, there are exceptions in Wisconsin, including . . ." Austin looked at her, and she could almost swear he was going to wink, but then he gestured to Jackson.

"Squirrels," the boy filled in. Austin grinned and held out a hand for a high-five, which Jackson returned with a matching grin.

Something twinged at Leah's middle, and she pushed it aside. She should be happy that Austin and Jackson had bonded today. Maybe it meant Jackson would open up to her too.

She reached behind her head and gathered her hair into a ponytail, thinking. Just because it was legal to keep a squirrel didn't mean she wanted one in her house.

"But we don't know the first thing about taking care of a squirrel. I'm sure they need special food and a cage and— What?"

They were both giving her that dorky grin again.

"I went to the pet store." Austin ran a hand over his cropped hair, as if self-conscious. "I got some food and a cage and some toys."

Jackson looked at Austin as if the man were his hero.

Leah stiffened. This had gone far enough. "You shouldn't have done that."

"It was no big deal. It was just a few things." Austin ducked his head as if she had thanked him.

"I mean, you shouldn't have done that without asking me first. I hope you can return it all. Because we're not keeping that squirrel. We'll call the humane society in the morning."

Both Austin and Jackson jerked their gazes to her. But this time, where Austin's was apologetic, Jackson's was insolent. He jumped to his feet, snatching up the box and stomping toward the hallway.

"I hate you." The ugly words were completely devoid of emotion, but Leah winced, turning away and blinking rapidly to clear the moisture that filled her eyes. She didn't need Jackson to know he'd hurt her.

She stared out the front window, where the flurries that had started falling earlier were now collecting in a thin layer on the grass.

"I'm sorry." Austin's voice was low. "I shouldn't have interfered."

She heard him push to his feet and cross the room but didn't turn her head.

A gust of cold air swept over her as he opened the front door.

"The way he took care of that squirrel, though. It was pretty amazing."

The door closed with a click, and Leah rubbed at her forehead.

Just when she thought parenting might be getting easier, her kid brought home a squirrel.

Chapter 11

Austin rubbed at his gritty eyes as he stared out his front window. When had the sun come up?

A nightmare had woken him well before dawn, and he'd been sitting here on the couch since then, but apparently he hadn't been paying attention to his surroundings.

He'd been too stuck in his own head, thinking about Chad and Tanner and Isaad. And Leah and Jackson.

Much as he tried, he couldn't get his mind off his new neighbors. Off the way spending time with Jackson had started to feel natural yesterday. Off the way he'd stopped thinking the boy was Isaad every time he saw him. Off the glint of tears in Leah's eyes when Jackson had said he hated her.

He never should have overstepped the way he had. He'd put Leah in an awkward position.

He should go over there and apologize. But she'd probably prefer if he left them alone. Pretended he'd never met them. Austin rubbed at his leg, but it didn't do anything to ease the tightness that constricted his chest.

He tried to shake himself out of it. He'd been on his own for months now. There was no reason to be disappointed that his budding friendship with his neighbors had ended. Hadn't he promised himself not to get close to anyone here anyway? He'd be leaving soon, and the fewer people he had to say goodbye to, the better.

Movement next door caught his eye, and he angled his head toward Leah's yard in time to see her stomping toward his house through the thin layer of snow that had settled on the grass. Apparently he'd been wrong about her preferring to leave it alone. She obviously hadn't yelled at him enough last night.

He got to his feet and pulled on his stocking cap, emerging onto the porch as Leah reached the bottom of the steps. The morning was sharp and clear, and the snow created a dazzling backdrop in the winter sun. For a second, Leah's hair seemed to glow, and he was almost tempted to reach out to see if it was real.

Fortunately, he had more sense than that.

"Good morning," he said cautiously.

"Good morning." She sounded equally uncertain as she climbed the porch steps to stand level with him.

"I'm sorry—" he said, at the same time she said, "I shouldn't have—"

They both broke off, then both started again. Austin forced himself to be quiet. Let her talk first, then he could apologize.

"I just wanted to say I was sorry about last night." She wrapped her arms around her down jacket, ducking her chin into the white fluffy scarf wound around her neck. "I was kind of blindsided by the whole squirrel thing. But I think you were right. I think I should let Jackson keep it."

Austin gaped at her. She wasn't yelling at him? She thought he was right?

"I just wanted you to know. And to apologize for yelling at you." She lifted her head so that her mouth was no longer covered by the scarf and offered him a slight smile. "Again."

Austin finally found his voice. "I'm sorry too. I shouldn't have overstepped like that. I was having fun with Jackson, but I didn't think long term." He tugged his hat lower over his ears against the sting of the morning chill. "What made you change your mind?"

77

She peered over her shoulder, toward her house. "Jackson's mother died when he was six. Drug overdose. He had no father, and he's been in foster care ever since. Nine families in six years."

Austin's stomach rolled. He'd seen kids in a lot of terrible situations in Afghanistan, but somehow he never thought of horrible things happening to kids in his own country.

Leah shrugged. "I started thinking about what it must be like for him, to find this baby squirrel that was abandoned. And the compassion he showed in wanting to take care of it. Maybe it's a sign that somewhere in there is a little boy who wants to be taken care of too." Leah tucked a stray piece of hair under her hat. "Anyway, it was pretty obvious he was happy with that creature." She hit him with a direct look. "And with you."

He lifted a hand, almost reaching for her arm, but then lowered it. "I shouldn't have shoved myself into a relationship with him like that." He'd seen the flash of envy in her eyes yesterday as she'd watched them together, and he couldn't blame her.

But Leah shook her head. "I'm glad you did. Right now, anyone who can get through to him is my hero. Speaking of which, maybe you should be the one to tell him he can keep the squirrel. You're the one who helped him take care of it, and he'd probably rather talk to you than to me anyway."

It would be fun to tell the boy, Austin had to admit that. But he wasn't going to take that joy from Leah too. "Nah. He should hear it from you. You're his mom."

Leah's brow creased. "I don't know if he'll ever consider me his mom." Her voice cracked, and this time he did touch her arm, only for a fraction of a second.

"Give it time. You care a lot. Anyone can see that. He'll figure it out eventually too."

"Yeah." She stuffed her hands in her coat pocket. "Aren't you freezing?" She gestured to his sweatshirt. "Why don't you ever wear a coat?"

"I'm good. You look cold, though. Do you want to warm up with some coffee? I've got a pot made." He didn't know where the invitation came from. For some reason, he had an urge to keep talking right now. Or maybe it was that he had an urge to keep talking to her.

"No thanks." Leah took a backward step down the porch stairs. "I need to wake Jackson up for church." She turned and bounced down the last two steps. At the bottom, she turned back, looking tentative. "You're welcome to come with us if you like. To church."

With the sun backlighting her like that, it wouldn't take much of a stretch to imagine she was an angel. But he'd long ago figured out angels weren't real. And neither was God.

He shook his head once, said, "No thanks," then turned to the house and stepped inside. On his way through the living room, he allowed himself a glance out the front window. Leah was almost back to her house already, and as he watched her walk through the snow, he let himself wonder, just for a second, what would have happened if he'd said yes to her offer.

Something tugged at his heart, but he ignored it.

"What do you want to do now?" Leah glanced at Jackson, who had sat stock still through the entire service, although at her prompting he'd at least stood at the appropriate times. With his blank expression, it was impossible to tell if he'd gotten anything from the service.

But her heart felt a million times lighter after worshiping her Savior. Dan's sermon about trust had been exactly what she'd needed to hear. A perfect reminder that God had never failed her—and he wasn't about to now.

Jackson shrugged. "I have to feed Ned."

Leah still didn't understand how the squirrel had gotten that name, but she wasn't going to fight it. At least Jackson was talking to her now. He'd offered a simple "thank you" when she'd told him he could keep the squirrel, but she'd seen the way his eyes brightened.

"What about after that? Is there anything fun you want to do? I'm not sure there's enough snow to sled yet, but we could go somewhere. I heard Rothman's Farm has opened their Christmas Wonderland. We could go feed some goats and stuff."

Jackson was silent so long Leah was sure he wasn't going to answer. Finally, though, he said, "Can Austin come?"

Leah forced herself to keep her expression neutral. Jackson wasn't trying to hurt her feelings, she was sure. "Don't you want to do something, just the two of us? Get to know each other better?"

But Jackson shook his head. "I want Austin to come."

Okay, maybe he *was* trying to hurt her. But she wasn't going to let him see how it affected her. "I guess we can ask him."

They rode the rest of the way home in silence, and the moment they entered the house, Jackson went to his room, presumably to feed Ned, whose cage they'd perched on Jackson's dresser. Leah set to work making him a peanut butter and jelly. She'd decided not to push him to eat with her—or to try other foods—for now. One step at a time.

She dropped the sandwich off in Jackson's room, then made one for herself and started to text Austin.

We're going to Rothman's Farm. Jackson wanted to know if you'd like to come.

She studied the words. She wanted to make sure it was abundantly clear that the invitation was from Jackson, not her. Finally satisfied that there was no way he could read more into it than was there, she sent it off. She tried to force herself to eat, but she couldn't help checking her phone every few seconds to see if he'd replied. She couldn't decide if she wanted him to say yes to make Jackson happy or to say no so that she and Jackson could spend the day alone together.

As she finished her sandwich, her phone dinged with his response.

Do you want me to come?

Ugh. Leah almost threw her phone across the room. How was she supposed to answer that question? And how did he even mean it?

If you want to. She eyed her response, then sent it off before she could change her mind.

This time she only had to wait a few seconds for his response. *Sure. Be over in a minute.*

Leah exhaled, relief and tension colliding in her belly. Much as she wanted to spend the day alone with Jackson, she had to admit that having Austin there as a buffer would almost certainly be helpful. Which was probably why her pulse quickened ever so slightly when she glanced out the window and saw him approaching.

"Jackson," she called down the hallway. "Austin's here. Time to go."

She opened the front door before Austin could knock, and he stepped inside, bringing with him the smell of the cold outdoors, but also something underneath that—something warmer and more masculine. She took a step back to widen the space between them.

"You're sure you don't mind if I come?" Austin spoke quietly, his face almost boyish with uncertainty.

"I told you—" Leah waved a hand as if it didn't matter to her one way or the other. "If you want to come, you should come. If you don't want to—"

"I don't want to get in your way."

She lifted a shoulder. "You—"

But before she could finish that sentence—which she had no idea how to end—Jackson traipsed into the room.

He went straight to Austin, who held out his hand for a fist-bump.

"I get to keep the squirrel." Jackson's voice was filled with more enthusiasm than Leah would have imagined he possessed.

"So I heard." Austin reached over to ruffle the boy's hair, and Leah pressed down a fresh pinch of jealousy. It was good for Jackson to have someone he could relate to, she reminded herself. Even if it wasn't her.

"Are we ready to go?" She took in Jackson's t-shirt and shorts. Clearly not.

She pointed toward his room. "There's snow on the ground. You need to wear something warm. Pants and a jacket."

Jackson nodded toward Austin. "How come *he* doesn't have to wear a jacket?"

Leah eyed Austin's sweatshirt in exasperation. Did no one around here know how to dress for the Wisconsin weather?

"I'm not his mom," she finally said. "Now go put on some warmer clothes."

"You're not my mom either," Jackson muttered, so low that Leah could almost convince herself she'd only imagined it—except for the searing pain cutting across her stomach. "And I don't have a jacket."

Leah dropped her head. That was true. Between his suspension on Friday and the wedding yesterday, she hadn't had time to get him one yet. Maybe this had been a bad idea. Maybe they should stay home after all.

"Go put on some pants like your mom told you to." Austin's voice was even. "I've got something you can wear for a jacket."

Leah braced for Jackson's outburst. But after watching Austin for a minute—who watched him in return, not blinking—Jackson spun and stomped down the hallway. Leah was pretty sure he muttered, "She's not my mom" once more before he ducked into his room.

She stared at the floor, trying to decide if she should thank Austin or ream him out for stepping in. Before she could make up her mind, he murmured, "I'll be right back" and disappeared out the front door.

She leaned against the wall and closed her eyes as she waited for both of them. *Please help us have a good day together, Lord. Help me have the patience to be a mother to Jackson.* She'd never had to pray for patience before—it generally came naturally to her—but she felt as if she'd used up her lifetime reserve of it, and now she was left without any right when she needed it most.

As she opened her eyes, they caught on Austin crossing the yard toward her house. He had a different kind of a walk—not swaggering exactly, but sort of stiff. She tried to decide if he had a limp or if it was her imagination.

Just as she'd decided it was her imagination, he looked up, and even through the window, his eyes seemed to snag on hers. She inhaled but found she suddenly couldn't exhale. After a second, he disappeared from the window as he reached the front steps, and she could at last breathe out again.

She sucked in a couple of quick extra breaths, working to get herself under control. That had been strange—and it wasn't something she wanted to repeat when he was standing right next to her, so she moved toward Jackson's room as she heard the front door open.

But Jackson had apparently been waiting for Austin, because he emerged from his room the moment the front door opened. At least he was wearing pants now.

"Here you go, dude." Austin held out a sweatshirt that matched his own, and Jackson shoved past Leah to grab it, immediately pulling it over his head. Great. In their matching shirts, the two looked even more like father and son.

"Now are we ready?" Leah grabbed her car keys and slipped past them to lead the way out the door. She and Austin reached for the door handle at the same time, their fingers brushing for an instant. She jerked hers back and let him hold the door open as she practically flew outside and down the steps, barely resisting the urge to stick her hand in the snow to cool the shock of warmth she'd felt at his touch.

Chapter 12

They'd been at the petting zoo for an hour already, and still Austin had no idea what had possessed him to accept Leah's invitation. Maybe it was the way she'd apologized earlier this morning. Or the earnest look she'd directed his way when she'd invited him to church.

Most likely, it was just that he'd enjoyed spending time with Jackson yesterday. One thing he knew: It had nothing to do with the warmth he felt every time he got anywhere near Leah. Sure, she was pretty, with that light hair and those enchanting green-blue eyes, and sure she was easy to talk to—when she wasn't yelling at him—and sure her smile was the most captivating he'd ever seen. But none of that meant he was interested in her as anything more than a neighbor. Or if he was, he shouldn't be.

Wouldn't be.

"Oh look." That captivating smile was back as she pointed past him. He followed the trajectory of her finger to a large sign that read "Christmas Wonderland."

His effort to suppress a groan failed, and Leah's eyes slid to his, the shock on her face almost comical.

"You don't like Christmas?"

Austin swallowed. That was a loaded question. He'd liked Christmas once upon a time. Looked forward to running downstairs with Chad to tear open the presents their mom had so lovingly picked out. There usually weren't a ton, but they were always just what Austin and his brother had wanted.

He'd had some good Christmases in the service too. Time spent with his brother and the other men in their unit. Usually, they managed to fashion some sort of Christmas tree or another. And they often received care packages with thoughtful gifts from people they didn't even know, which was always touching.

But last year had ruined Christmas for him. Losing your leg, your best friend, and the young Afghan boy you'd come to look at almost as a son would do that.

"I'll wait for you guys over here." He scraped the words out as he took a step toward a seating area made up of straw bales.

Leah tipped her head to the side, studying him. She opened her mouth as if to say something, then closed it and turned to Jackson, gesturing him toward the Christmas Wonderland.

But the boy shook his head. "I don't like Christmas either." He trailed Austin.

"What?" Desperation filled Leah's voice. "But I wanted to show you the Enchanted Forest and the First Christmas and—"

"I said I don't want to." Jackson folded his arms in front of him.

Leah's eyes met Austin's, pleading. The war in his chest was more heated than any battle he'd ever taken part in. Everything in him told him to avoid any reminders of Christmas. But then he looked at Jackson, defiant and clearly waiting for his lead. And Leah, broken and clearly needing his help.

He reached up with two hands to pull his knit cap lower over his ears. "Why don't we all go?"

Leah's relieved smile almost made the knot of anxiety crawling its way up his esophagus worthwhile.

But Jackson stood unmoving.

"I don't like Christmas," the boy repeated.

"This is going to be the best Christmas ever, you'll see." Leah took a tentative step toward her foster son. But Jackson shuffled away from her.

The renewed anguish in Leah's eyes was too much for Austin. "Come on." He clapped Jackson on the shoulder and led him toward the Christmas Wonderland. He wasn't sure if Leah's sigh as she fell into step behind them was one of relief or frustration, but he didn't turn around to find out.

As he steered them toward the sign, Austin scanned the area. It wasn't enclosed, so if he got in there and found he couldn't handle it, there were literally hundreds of escape routes. Some of them went through what looked to be employee-only areas, but that was no big deal. As long as he could always find a way out, he'd be fine.

He hoped.

As they passed under the sign, Austin dragged in a long breath. So far, so good.

They made their way through a trail that led past dozens of trees, each decorated in a different style, some formal, some more festive. One was even decorated in red, white, and blue and had soldier ornaments hanging from its branches.

Austin kept walking, until they reached a life-size stable with actors dressed in nativity garb. He veered in the other direction—he had no need to sit here and watch people swallow this neat and tidy little story about a cute baby who was supposed to be the Savior of the world. If he couldn't save Isaad and Tanner, how could he save Austin—or anyone else, for that matter?

But Leah's hand on his arm stopped him. "I'd like to watch this for a minute, if you don't mind." Her words were soft, as if she knew he wanted to protest.

He pressed his mouth closed but led the way to a section of bleachers that had been erected to the side of the stable.

"Do you know the Christmas story?" he heard Leah ask Jackson.

"Like about Santa? Yeah, everyone does." The boy's tone implied what he thought of Leah's question. If he kept this up, Austin was going to have to have a talk with him about speaking respectfully.

But Leah smiled at the kid and said gently, "I mean the true Christmas story. About Jesus."

When Jackson didn't answer, Leah gestured for Austin to find them a seat in the bleachers.

He scanned the mostly full benches. He could probably get to the top if he had to. But he'd rather not attempt it right now. Instead, he led the way to a section of the front row that had just enough room for the three of them. He sat, and Leah followed, leaving room between them for Jackson to squeeze in.

But the boy stepped to Austin's other side, gesturing that Austin should slide over so he could sit there. Austin glanced at Leah, the hurt in her eyes lancing his gut, but at her subtle nod, he slid closer to her.

The space was so tight that he had to angle his shoulder behind her to make enough room for Jackson, and their arms pressed against each other.

Leah's back stiffened, but she gave him a strained smile. Her warm cinnamony smell played with his senses, and he tried to take his focus off of her.

"This is stupid," Jackson muttered from his other side.

Austin felt the same way, but he owed it to Leah not to show it.

"Give it a chance," he whispered to the boy as music started to play over the speakers.

Jackson gave him a disagreeable look, but Austin's gaze went to Leah. She was watching as a man and a pregnant woman—presumably Mary and Joseph—walked toward the stable. The look on Leah's face—it was a look Austin would love to see there all the time. She looked at peace, filled with hope and joy. The look stirred something familiar.

87

He'd felt that way once, hadn't he?

He shoved the question aside.

Even if he had, he'd never feel that way again. And there was no point dwelling on it.

"I'm sorry about the Ferris wheel." Austin's apology sent a renewed stab to Leah's belly, but she shook her head as they stood together in her driveway after returning from Rothman's. It wasn't Austin's fault that after the nativity play, she'd suggested they go on the farm's small Ferris wheel—the first suggestion she'd had all day that excited Jackson. It also wasn't Austin's fault that it was a two-person ride. Or that Jackson had insisted on riding with Austin or not going on it at all.

Austin had tried his best to convince the boy to go with her, even resorting to bribery—he'd ride with the boy *after* Jackson took a turn with Leah—but nothing had worked.

She swallowed past the hurt that had been building for the past four days into a constant ache at the back of her throat and fought off the questions that had been swirling through her mind all afternoon. Why was Jackson resisting her affection? Why did he seem to adore Austin and loathe her? And worst of all, had becoming a foster mother been a terrible mistake?

"Thanks for coming," she finally managed to say. "It was good for Jackson."

Austin touched a hand to her elbow. "It will get better."

She let out a breath. "Yeah."

In church this morning, sitting next to Jackson, surrounded by her church family, she'd been sure that was true. But now she was less certain than ever.

The front door burst open, and Jackson stepped outside. He'd peeled off his socks and shoes, but he still wore the sweatshirt Austin had given him.

"Don't come out here barefoot," Leah called, though she was pretty sure her reprimand lacked conviction. She was too exhausted to summon any up right now.

To her surprise, Jackson pulled his feet back into the house, though he leaned his torso farther out the door. "You want to see Ned?"

Though she and Austin were standing right next to each other, Leah knew the question was directed to her neighbor.

"Oh, uh—" Austin hesitated, and Leah could feel his gaze slide to her.

She shrugged. "Might as well come in and see the squirrel you roped me into keeping."

"I'm not sure you could be roped into anything," Austin muttered. He gave her shoulder a gentle nudge, then stepped past her toward the house.

Leah followed, her feet dragging through what was left of the snow. When was the last time she'd been this exhausted?

Inside, she busied herself heating up leftovers from yesterday's wedding. She'd make a plate for herself and one to send home with Austin. And a PBJ for Jackson.

She was pulling the last of the food from the microwave when Austin emerged from Jackson's room.

"You have to admit Ned is cute." Austin stepped into the kitchen, flashing her a smile that she couldn't help but return. If she didn't know better, she'd say today hadn't been good for only Jackson. It'd been good for Austin too. He still wore that haunted look, but at least he'd started smiling more.

"Don't even start." But she couldn't keep a straight face. Aside from looking like a rat, the baby squirrel was fairly adorable. And the little sounds it made were precious.

"I guess I'm going to head out. Let you guys get some dinner."

But Leah wasn't going to have any of that. "You aren't leaving until I give you your plate, young man. No takeout pizza for you tonight."

Austin opened his mouth, and she was sure he was going to argue, but then he said, "I was hoping you'd say that. That food smells delicious."

She couldn't resist laughing. She passed him the plate that held Jackson's sandwich. "Would you take this to Jackson? You don't have to make sure he eats it or anything. He'll eat it later when no one is watching."

Austin's brow wrinkled. "Why?"

"That I haven't figured out. But for now I'm happy he's actually eating something."

Austin's gaze lingered on her another moment, then he took the sandwich and brought it to Jackson's room. He was back within a few seconds.

Leah examined the plate she'd made him. "I should cover this, so it doesn't get cold as you're carrying it home. Or—" She didn't know why she stopped. She had friends eat here all the time. It was no big deal if she invited him to do the same. He was becoming a friend, wasn't he?

Still, what if he took the invitation the wrong way?

Better to play it safe.

"Or I could put it in a container." She ducked into one of her lower cabinets, sticking her head farther into it than strictly necessary to fetch her favorite large container, mainly to hide the flush rising to her cheeks.

There's nothing to be embarrassed about, she scolded herself. *It's not like you wanted to invite him as anything more than a friend.*

By the time she'd nabbed the container and its matching cover, her face had cooled. She stood and fit the food into it, then snapped the cover on and passed it to him.

"Thank you." His dark eyes held hers. "I'll enjoy this."

She offered a silent nod, and he turned toward the door.

"Austin, wait." She bit her lip as he turned toward her, eyes searching.

"Why don't you—" But his mesmerizing gaze made her change her mind again. "Why don't you take one of these too?"

She opened the box of leftover cupcakes Peyton had left and passed one to him.

"Thanks." He turned toward the door again, hesitating a second this time.

But she held her tongue, and after a moment, he was gone.

Chapter 13

The resistance band pulled taut as Austin finished his last set of leg lifts. He swiped at his forehead, then picked up his dumbbells, glancing at the clock on the wall. Four thirty. That gave him just enough time to finish his workout and shower before Leah stopped by with dinner.

At least if she continued the pattern they'd fallen into over the last few days.

Austin tried to feel guilty for taking advantage of her kindness. But she truly seemed to enjoy giving him food—which probably explained her career as a caterer. And, maybe he shouldn't admit it, but he'd come to look forward to the few minutes they spent together each day as they exchanged dishes, his empty ones for her freshly filled ones.

Those were the few moments each day when he could let himself focus on something other than his rehabilitation and getting back to Afghanistan. When his thoughts didn't track to what had happened over there—what could still be happening to his brother.

When Leah was here, he could think about other things. Like her sparkling laugh. And her swirly eyes. And her easy kindness.

Austin shook his head at the dumbbells, resting motionless in his hands.

He was acting like a kid with a crush.

Which was the furthest thing from what he was.

He was simply a man who appreciated a friendly neighbor—and good food.

One of these days, he'd have to start cooking for himself again. But how could he? After what Tanner had said the last time he cooked?

If this is the last meal I ever eat, I'll die happy.

What was he supposed to do with the fact that it *had* been the last meal Tanner ever ate?

The blare of a video call nearly made him drop the still uncurled dumbbell on his toes. He set the weights down and dove toward his computer. Thursdays were Chad's day to call. If someone was calling on a Wednesday—Austin's throat closed.

No, not Chad. Please don't let anything have happened to Chad.

The moment he clicked to answer and Chad's face appeared on the screen, Austin crumpled onto the couch.

Chad was alive. He was in one piece.

"Why are you calling?"

"It's good to see you too, brother." Chad wagged his eyebrows.

But the scare of the call hadn't worn off, and Austin wasn't ready to joke.

"Seriously, Chad. What's wrong? Why are you calling early?"

"I'm hurt." Chad pressed a mock hand to his heart. "Can't a guy just want to talk to his little brother?"

Under the joking, Austin heard what his brother wasn't saying. He was going on an assignment and wanted to call in case—

Austin couldn't let himself go there. He worked hard to match his brother's joking tone. "A guy can. *You* can't."

A flash of relief crossed Chad's face. He knew Austin had caught on.

"So, how's Hope Springs?"

"Pretty quiet. Kind of peaceful, actually."

"Good. And have you met some actual people? Other than the mailman this time?"

"Yes." He didn't know why, but he wanted to leave it at that.

Chad's eyes narrowed. "Name two people."

"Leah, Jackson, Sophie, Spencer, Peyton, Jade, Dan." He paused, trying to remember the names of the others he had met at Leah's house.

"Whoa. Whoa. Whoa." Chad's eyes went wide. "Are you making up names now?"

Austin snorted. "No. But thanks for the vote of confidence."

"Where did you possibly meet that many people in under a week?"

Austin shrugged. "Just my natural charisma."

Now it was Chad's turn to snort. "No, seriously."

"My neighbor dragged me over to her house when she had some friends over."

"She?" Chad's eyebrows lifted toward his slightly receding hairline.

"Knock it off." But Austin couldn't deny the heat radiating from his face. Hopefully Chad's connection wasn't good enough to detect it from the other side of the world.

"Aw, does little Austin like a girl?"

"Seriously, Chad. Knock it off. It's not like that."

"Like what?" Chad blinked at him innocently. "Seriously, though, Austin. I hope you do like her."

"Why? For all you know, she's hideous."

Chad gave him a knowing look. "Is she?"

Austin groaned. He'd walked right into that one.

"No." The word came out begrudgingly. But Leah was the farthest thing from hideous. "She's actually kind of gorgeous."

"I knew it." Chad's chortle shot through the computer.

"Don't get too full of yourself." Austin had to find a way to change the subject. "Just because she's pretty doesn't mean I'm interested."

A knock at the door made him lift his head. On the other side of the front window, Leah was waving at him, wearing a bright smile.

"Ah, look at your face." Chad's amused voice yanked Austin's attention back to the computer screen. "It's her, isn't it? You are such a goner."

Austin rolled his eyes. "I'm not a goner. She has food, and I'm hungry."

"Wait, you two are having dinner together? And you say there's nothing going on?"

"We're not having dinner together." They kept their relationship strictly neighborly. "She noticed that I was getting takeout all the time and apparently made it her mission to give me good food. She's a caterer, so—"

"Are you going to keep the poor girl out in the cold all night, or are you going to answer the door?"

"I'll answer the door if you ever shut up for a minute."

"Actually, I'd love to stick around to see how this goes, but I have to fly."

"Oh." Much as Austin didn't want Chad hovering in the background of his conversation with Leah, he wasn't ready to say goodbye to his brother yet. Not if it might be the last time—

Stop thinking like that.

"Take care of yourself, bro." He swallowed down all the other things he should say but couldn't.

"You too. I'll call when I can. But don't be worried if it's not for a while. And in the meantime, I wouldn't mind a prayer or two."

Fat chance he wouldn't worry. Or that he'd pray. But Austin worked his face into a stoic expression and nodded.

"And Austin?" Chad leaned closer to the camera. "I'm happy for you. And your girlfriend. Now go let her in." The screen went blank, and Austin shook his head as a chuckle escaped. Chad always had to have the last word.

He must have still been chuckling when he opened the door because Leah took one look at him, then peered over his shoulder. "What's so funny?"

"Nothing." Austin tried to straighten his lips, but seeing her didn't do anything to erase the smile. "I was just talking to my brother."

"Oh, I'm sorry. I didn't realize you had company. I can go get more food. Give me five minutes." She turned toward the porch steps, and without thinking, Austin reached for her arm.

"It's just me. I was chatting with him online." He kept his hand on her arm as she spun back toward him—maybe for a second or two longer than was necessary.

Fine.

Maybe Chad was right.

Maybe he did like her.

But so what? It wasn't like he was going to do anything about it.

"Where does he live?" Leah passed him the container, and he had no choice but to lift his hand from her arm to take the food.

"Afghanistan right now." As he did every night, he lifted the cover just enough to smell the contents. "Oh, pork." He allowed himself another sniff. "My favorite." He snapped the lid closed so the food wouldn't cool while he talked to Leah. Because now that she was here, he didn't want her to go.

"That must be hard." Leah stepped closer and jabbed her hands into her coat pockets. "Having a brother over there. Do you talk often?"

"Once a week or so when we can."

Until last year, they'd been together every day. But he didn't want to talk about that right now. "How's Jackson?"

Leah's sigh sounded like it carried the weight of the world. Or of a mother.

"I've already been to the principal's office three times this week, and Jackson still won't talk to me, so . . . not great."

"I was sure letting him keep that squirrel was going to score you points."

Leah lifted her hands to her mouth and blew on them. "I'm not sure anything I do could score points with him. Unless I could become you."

There was no bitterness behind her words, but still regret swamped Austin. For whatever reason, Jackson had taken a liking to him. Maybe the boy sensed that Austin was as broken as he was.

"Anyway—" Leah took a step backward. "Enjoy the pork. There are some mashed potatoes and corn in there too." She took another backward step, then turned toward the stairs.

"Leah."

She stopped, but he had no idea what to say. He only knew he wasn't ready for her to leave yet.

But that was ridiculous. What was he going to do, ask her to stay and watch him eat the food she'd brought?

"This smells delicious. Thanks."

She nodded and skipped down the steps, leaving him to eat alone.

Again.

Chapter 14

This was getting ridiculous.

Thursday night, Leah eyed the food she was about to bring to Austin.

It wasn't that she minded bringing him dinner. In fact, she quite enjoyed it. Sharing food with others was one of her greatest joys, and since Jackson refused to eat anything beyond peanut butter and jelly, it was nice to have someone else appreciate her cooking.

And, fine, she enjoyed her conversations with Austin too.

But it would make a lot more sense to enjoy those conversations over dinner, rather than standing at his door dropping off food. Plus, if he happened to come to her house to eat, maybe Jackson would emerge from his room longer than the three seconds it took him to refill Ned's water.

So why didn't she just invite Austin over for dinner already? It wasn't like he would misconstrue her invitation, especially since he'd shown zero interest in her.

What was she afraid of? That her friends would find out and jump to conclusions?

So what if they did?

She was an adult. She didn't have to be ruled by what her friends thought.

Mind made up, she grabbed her coat and charged for the front door before she could chicken out.

The smile Austin met her with knocked a little of the confidence out of her. This *was* the right thing to do, wasn't it?

Not that she could turn back now.

"Hey, I didn't bring dinner tonight," she blurted, then gave herself an internal kick. That wasn't exactly an invitation.

"I see that." Austin's grin didn't dim. "You know you don't have to have food to knock on my door though, right?"

Her laugh sounded nervous even to her own ears. "What I meant was, instead of bringing food to you, I thought it might make more sense to bring you to the food. If you want to come over. I mean, Jackson has been asking about you, and I figured that way you could kill two birds with one stone—eat and see Jackson and—"

"Leah."

"Yeah?" She forced herself to stop and take a breath. Had she been babbling?

"I'd love to come over and say hi to Jackson."

"Oh." A flutter rippled through her belly, but Leah ignored it. "Okay. Good."

She took a step away from the door and waited for Austin to pull on his stocking cap and follow her out.

"You look a little bit like a cat burglar in that." She gestured to his black track pants, black sweatshirt, and black cap.

Austin's rich, full laugh warmed her. "I prefer ninja. Sounds tougher."

Leah eased into step beside him as they crossed the yard.

See, this wasn't weird at all.

When they got to her front door, Austin opened it and gestured her inside.

He followed, pulling his cap off and running a hand over his hair. "Smells delicious, as always."

"Ravioli tonight. And garlic bread."

Austin groaned and patted his flat torso. "I'm going to have to start running twice as far if you keep feeding me like this."

Leah highly doubted that. There was no way a guy built like Austin didn't have a six pack.

She strode toward the kitchen to banish the thought. "Everything will be ready in a minute. Do you want to say hi to Jackson first?"

She directed a cooling breath toward her face as he moved down the hall toward Jackson's room. What was her problem tonight?

It wasn't like she'd never had a friend who happened to be male over for dinner before.

As she got out plates and silverware, she gave herself a strict talking to.

It's no big deal. You're two friends having a meal. It's no different than having Peyton over for dinner.

Except Peyton didn't have broad shoulders and mysterious, slightly haunted eyes.

Leah huffed at herself.

Clearly, this talking to wasn't working.

"Everything okay?"

She jumped, nearly dropping the pan of noodles covered in her homemade marinara sauce.

"Yep." She only hoped she sounded less flustered than she felt. "Could you grab the water?" She nodded toward the pitcher on the counter.

Austin slid past her, his warm scent washing over her. She scooted to the table and set the pan down harder than she meant to.

"Nice oven mitts." Austin pointed at her hands, protected by a ratty set of red and white checked mitts.

"They were my dad's. He always wore them when he grilled out. I should probably toss them, but I can't make myself do it."

Austin nodded, and though he didn't say anything, she could read the understanding in his eyes.

They both took a seat, and she folded her hands to offer a silent prayer for her food.

Normally, she invited her guests to join in. But after the way Austin had shut down her invitation to church last Sunday and the way he'd watched the nativity play with barely disguised contempt, she decided it best to let it go.

Silently, they each dug into their food, and for a few minutes neither of them said anything.

Great. This was going to be just like her date with Robert.

Not that this was a date.

"Do you mind if I ask you something?" The question came out before she could think better of it.

Austin's eyes met hers, his smile slightly guarded. "Can't promise I'll answer. But you can always ask."

Leah nodded. At least he was honest. "Why didn't you want to watch the nativity play or go to church?" If nothing else, the question should solidify that this wasn't a date. Wasn't that the number one rule of dating: Don't talk about religion?

Austin wiped his mouth with his napkin and took a long drink of water.

She lowered her gaze to her plate, scooping another bite. He had said he might not answer. So she shouldn't be surprised. Or disappointed.

"I used to go to church." His voice was flat, but when Leah looked up, she saw the conflict brewing in his eyes.

"But you don't anymore?"

He shook his head and took another bite.

"Do you mind if I ask why? Did something happen at your church or—"

Another head shake. "Nothing like that. I just don't believe any of it anymore."

"Any of it?" Leah swallowed against the sick feeling that swirled in her stomach. It broke her heart every time she learned of someone who had once believed but had fallen away.

"Any of it." Austin sat completely rigid, and Leah could tell the conversation was over.

Fine. She'd let it go for now.

But if he thought that was the last he was going to hear from her on that topic, he was wrong. What kind of friend would she be if she sat back and watched him throw away his faith?

Their conversation turned to lighter topics, including Ned the squirrel, who had nearly doubled in size already. In spite of herself, Leah had to admit that the little critter was cute. And the way Jackson cared for the squirrel gave her hope that under the boy who got into fights at school, there was a sweet, caring young man.

They lapsed back into silence as they finished the meal, but Leah found she didn't mind.

After he'd scooped the last bite off his plate, Austin studied her. "My turn to ask you a question."

"And do I have to answer as thoroughly as you did?" She couldn't help the teasing note.

Austin returned her smile. "You can be as cryptic or as open as you want." At her nod, Austin continued, "What made you decide to become a foster mom?"

Leah pressed her hands to the table, thinking. There were so many reasons she'd wanted to be a foster mom—how did she begin to answer that question?

Austin apparently took her hesitation as a desire to be cryptic because he picked up his plate and moved to the sink. "You don't have to answer."

"No, it's not that. I'm just trying to figure out how to give you an answer that doesn't take all night."

Austin shrugged. "I don't have anything else to do."

"Okay." Leah lifted an eyebrow and led him to the living room. They settled on opposite ends of the couch but angled toward each other.

Leah lost track of time as she told Austin about how Dan had adopted Jade's baby after they were married. How right around that time she'd seen a news special about the great need for foster families. How there were twenty-five thousand kids over the age of eleven waiting to be adopted from foster care, and thousands of them would likely never find a permanent home. How her heart had broken for them and she'd known this was something she could fix. That she could make a better life for at least one kid. How it wasn't just something she *wanted* to do, it was something she felt *called* to do.

He didn't even roll his eyes when she told him how she'd prayed about it. How God had helped everything fall in place at just the right time so that she got this house right before she was due for the required home study.

"Plus, I've always wanted kids," she said now. "And time is kind of running out for me to have any biological children, so . . ."

Austin leaned forward, holding out a hand to stop her. "Hold on. You can't be more than thirty or so."

She laughed, not sure if she should be flattered or insulted that he'd gotten so close to her actual age. At least he'd been a couple years under instead of a couple years over with his guess.

"Thirty-two," she corrected.

"That's hardly running out of time to have kids. My friend Tanner—" But he broke off, clearing his throat. "People have kids into their forties these days."

"I know. But I have no plans to get married in the near—or distant—future. Which makes it a little harder." She smoothed her hands over her jeans. She had no idea why she'd told him all of this.

Or why he'd listened.

"Well, for the record, I think what you're doing is really great." With the haunted look buried farther in the background, Austin's eyes were warm, and she appreciated him saying it.

She only wished she could still be so sure it was true. "I hope so."

The couch shifted as Austin stood. "I should get home. You probably need to get Jackson to bed."

Leah lurched upright. "What time is it?" A quick look at her phone confirmed it was almost nine o'clock. Had they really been talking for two hours? She pushed to her feet and walked Austin to the door.

"Thanks for dinner." He reached for the door handle but didn't open it. His eyes searched her face, and he took half a step closer.

Panic flooded Leah's system, ringing in her ears and making spots pop in front of her eyes. Was he going to kiss her? Is that why he was looking at her like that?

She took two steps back, then spun and fled to the kitchen. "You should take some ravioli home," she called over her shoulder, barely able to get the words out between gasped breaths.

In the kitchen, she forced herself to count to ten and inhale through her nose as she found a container and scooped leftover pasta into it. She was overreacting. Austin hadn't wanted to kiss her. He'd simply been moving so he could get through the door.

But she made sure to stay just out of arm's reach from him as she passed him the food. His eyes lingered on hers a moment, his expression unreadable, then he said goodnight and was out the door.

As she locked it behind him, Leah drew in another deep breath, telling herself she didn't enjoy the subtle hint of him that still hung in the air.

Chapter 15

*K*eep going.

This was the farthest he'd run yet, and Austin could feel his muscles starting to give out. But he was only three blocks from home. He wasn't going to let himself quit before then. Even if his knees *were* screaming at him.

He lifted an arm to mop the sweat from his brow, trying to concentrate on his breaths. His stride was different with the prosthetic than it had been before—uneven now—and it always threw his breathing off.

He'd considered getting a running prosthetic, but he felt wrong doing that. Like it would be cheating. And he'd already cheated death. The least he could do was avoid making things easier on himself than they should be.

Inhale, two, three, four . . .

He lost count as his mind drifted to last night again. For the life of him, he couldn't figure out what had possessed him. Leah had invited him over for a nice, friendly dinner—emphasis on *friend*—and he'd ended up almost kissing her.

Good thing she had more sense than he did.

He couldn't remember the last time he'd kissed any woman, let alone one he'd known for only a week. Though it felt like he'd known her longer—like his days in Hope Springs were part of another life, one so far removed from his old life that he could escape it for a little while.

Maybe that was it. That was why he wasn't acting like himself.

In which case, he'd better get back to being himself if he wanted to be in shape for his physical.

No more distractions, he promised himself as he pulled up in front of his house. Even as he made the promise, though, he couldn't keep his eyes from traveling to Leah's house. Although it was still early afternoon, her car was in the driveway. Hopefully that didn't mean Jackson had been suspended again.

Maybe he should check in. Make sure everything was okay.

That was what neighbors did, right?

Or, it was the very definition of distraction.

Austin forced himself to walk up his driveway. Whatever it was, she could handle it on her own. And if she needed anything, she'd ask.

Unless he'd scared her away with that near kiss.

As he reached his porch, Leah's door opened, and she rushed outside. Seeing her did nothing to slow his heart rate.

But either she didn't notice him, or she'd chosen to ignore him. As she charged toward her car, disappointment hit Austin. She was leaving. He wouldn't be able to talk to her even if he wanted to.

But instead of getting into the car, she circled to the trunk and popped it open, loading bag after bag into her arms.

Don't get distracted.

But he couldn't just stand here and let her struggle with that heavy load alone.

Ignoring the voice of common sense blaring in his head, he crossed the yard, reaching her car as she turned to go inside.

"Oh, Austin." She jumped, looking ready to run.

Was it because he'd startled her? Or because he'd freaked her out last night?

"Sorry. It looked like you could use some help." He reached to take a few bags from her, then leaned into the trunk to lift out a red cake box tied with string. "This too?"

She nodded and closed the trunk. "Thanks. I had no idea this was going to take so long."

Austin followed her toward the house. "And what is this?"

Leah's sigh was exasperated. "I had the brilliant idea to throw Jackson a birthday party. So I had to go shopping to get stuff for it. But I had no idea what to get him for a gift, so it took forever. I ended up with this." She set her bags on the kitchen counter, then rummaged in one, pulling out a small box and passing it to him. "Do you think he'll like it?"

Austin opened the box, which held a sports watch. "I'm sure he'll love it."

Leah bustled around the kitchen to put groceries away. "I don't think he'll ever love anything I do, but as long as he doesn't hate it, that will be a start."

He held the watch out to her, and she scurried to take it, then began piling streamers and balloons on the counter before zipping across the kitchen to grab a punch bowl.

"Hey. Leah?"

"Yep?" She kept moving.

"Maybe you should slow down. You're moving faster than Ned the squirrel right now."

Leah threw him a frazzled smile. "Can't. I have way too much to do before I have to pick up Jackson and his friends. And—" Now she stopped and stared at him, her expression pure panic. "I have no idea what thirteen-year-old boys like to do."

Austin clapped his hands together and headed for the door. "I can help you with that."

"Wait. Where are you going?" Leah's voice trailed him.

Austin rushed to his own house, where he unhooked his video game console and gathered up his games and controllers.

He may not know how to act around Leah right now.

But boys and video games? *That* he did know.

Plus, maybe helping with Jackson's party would get things back to normal with Leah.

And neither of them would have to think about that almost-kiss anymore.

Leah could not stop thinking about how she'd been so sure Austin was going to kiss her last night.

All afternoon, as he'd set up the video game console and then helped her decorate, her eyes had tracked to him again and again. But not once had he shown anything other than friendly interest. Which could mean only one thing: She'd completely imagined his desire to kiss her.

What a relief.

So why did her eyes insist on going to him again now, as she stepped into the living room, balancing a tray of food?

"Oh! Smoked you!" Austin tossed his remote onto the couch and fist-bumped one of the boys she'd invited over.

She'd wanted Jackson to choose a few friends for the party, but when he'd refused, she'd asked one of his teachers who he got along with. After some hesitation, Mrs. Johnson had suggested Logan, Kayden, Tommy, and Braxton. Fortunately, all four had agreed to come.

And they all seemed to be having fun—even Jackson, whom Leah had heard cheering moments before. He'd even shown a smidge of interest in the watch she'd given him, though he'd set it aside without putting it on.

"You guys ready for some food?" She started toward the coffee table, but before she could take two steps, Austin was on his feet and lifting the tray of pigs in a blanket from her hands.

Jackson's friends lunged for the food the moment it hit the table.

"Aw, man." The boy who'd been playing the video game spoke around a mouthful of food. "Jackson, your dad is way too good at this game. It's not fair."

Austin froze, looking from her to Jackson. When Jackson shrugged, Austin turned back to her, the question clear in his eyes. Should he correct the boy and tell them he wasn't Jackson's father?

Leah gave a subtle head shake. So what if Jackson's friends thought Austin was his dad. It wouldn't hurt anything.

"Better come get some food, Jackson, before your friends eat it all." Leah tried not to sound too motherly so she wouldn't embarrass Jackson.

He didn't acknowledge that he'd heard her.

"This looks great." Austin leaned forward to grab one of the pigs-in-a-blanket.

"Jackson's mom, you make good food," Kayden said, helping himself to more.

Leah beamed at him. These boys were so polite. "Thank—"

But before she could finish the sentence, Jackson jumped in. "She's not my mom."

The rest of the boys fell silent, and aside from the sound of their chewing, the room went still. Leah worked to keep her smile in place even though it felt like her face had hardened into plastic. Her pulse roared in her ears, but fighting past it, she turned to Kayden. "You can call me Miss Zelner. Or Leah. Leah would be fine too." Her voice was too quiet, and she gave a single nod, then turned and walked out of the room.

But the kitchen wasn't far enough. She pushed through the door to the backyard, letting the Arctic blast of the cold front the forecasters

109

had been predicting for days buffet her. Her face froze instantly, except in the spots where hot tears tracked down her cheeks.

I'm trying here, Lord, I really am. Please help me. If ever she could use a *yes* in answer to a prayer, this was it.

But she was starting to doubt she would get it.

Austin passed his controller off to one of the other boys, throwing Jackson a dark look as he stood and followed Leah. If the boy noticed the look, he didn't acknowledge it.

He tried the kitchen first, but it was empty, although another batch of hot dogs boiled on the stove. Austin checked on them, then walked toward the hallway. But as he passed the back door, he caught sight of movement on the dark patio.

He opened the door slowly, so he wouldn't bump her. She shuffled out of the way but didn't look at him.

"He's never going to accept me, is he?" Her voice was broken, her face wet. "Every time I think things are getting better, he goes and reminds me that they're not. Not really."

"Sure they are." He nudged her shoulder with his. "He didn't say he hates you. Just that you're not his mom. Which, biologically, is true."

"He didn't correct them that you're not his dad," she muttered. "Maybe he'd be better off with you."

He held up a hand. Befriending the kid was one thing. But he most certainly wasn't looking to become a father. "I'm not in the market for a kid."

Leah turned to him, her normally light eyes shadowed in darkness. "Why not? You'd make a great dad."

Austin shrugged. "I don't think I could go it alone like you're doing. If I ever had a kid, I'd need a wife first. And there aren't exactly a lot of candidates seeking after that position."

Why had he said *that*? It wasn't like he was looking for candidates.

Leah gave him a sideways glance but didn't say anything further. After a few minutes, she wiped her tears and turned toward the house. "We'd better get back in there."

As Austin followed her inside, the shoe on his prosthetic snagged on the threshold. He pitched forward, shuffling his feet quickly to catch his balance.

But it was too late.

He careened into Leah, shoving her forward before landing on his knees behind her.

She spun toward him, eyes widening. "Are you all right?"

"I'm sorry. Did I hurt you?" He was still on his hands and knees, but he was pretty sure he hadn't injured anything.

"I'm fine." Leah reached to help him up. "What happened?"

He ignored her hand. "Just tripped," he muttered. Bracing his hands against the floor, he pulled his good leg out from under him. Leah moved her hand closer, as if he hadn't seen it the first time.

"I've got it." The words came out with more force than he intended. "Go check on the boys. I'll be right there."

He didn't look at her, but he could feel her eyes drilling into him. Finally, she left the room.

When she was gone, he slowly pushed up onto his right leg, pulling his left leg behind him and readjusting his track pants over the prosthetic. He didn't know why it was so important to him to keep his prosthetic hidden. He'd worn shorts all summer without giving it a second thought. Sure, he got looks sometimes, but it didn't matter. He hadn't cared who had known how broken he was.

But here things were different. No one here knew what had happened to him. They didn't see him as someone broken. As far as they knew, he was whole and intact. And knowing there were people who thought that gave him hope that maybe he could be again.

Someday.

The shadows on the ceiling shifted as the trees outside bent in the whistling wind. It was the only movement in the room, other than the rise and fall of Leah's chest as she tried to take relaxing breaths.

Austin had sent her to bed at midnight, promising to hang out with the boys until they dropped off to sleep and then go home. That had been three hours ago, and the sounds from the living room had long since died down, but still she couldn't sleep.

Every time she closed her eyes, all she heard was Jackson's sneered words, "She's not my mother." How many times would he say that? Would he insist on it for the rest of his life?

She'd meant it when she'd told Austin the boy would be better off with him. Or at least with both of them.

Her eyes opened wider in the dark. What had brought on that thought? She didn't want to raise a child with Austin.

She'd just been thinking about how much easier it was to deal with Jackson when Austin was around. How he always seemed to know what to say to get Jackson to do what he was supposed to do. How on occasion he could even make Jackson smile. And her—he could definitely make her smile too.

Stop it.

This wasn't about her or her feelings for Austin.

Not that she had any.

She punched her pillow into a new position and settled her head into it. Finally, her eyes drooped closed, and she let the heaviness of sleep start to carry her away.

But only moments later, her eyes sprang open as a yell of some sort echoed from the front of the house. She bolted upright and sprang out of bed. That wasn't the fun kind of yelling the boys had been doing as they'd played.

This was more like a terrified yell. A genuine cry of pain or fear.

Maybe one of the boys had gotten up to go to the bathroom and been startled. Or maybe they were having a nightmare. Hopefully no one was fighting.

She clicked on the screen of her phone as she approached the living room, so she'd have enough light to find her way without waking the boys—assuming they were still asleep after that commotion.

Boys were spread across every inch of the living room floor, and all of them appeared to be out cold.

Another yell sounded, this time making Leah jump. She swung her phone to the other side of the room. Austin was sprawled on her couch, eyes clenched tight, arm flailing, as if he were trying to reach someone. His yell was quieter this time but filled with more anguish than she'd ever heard from a person before.

She hurried through the maze of sleeping boys, careful not to step on anyone. Miraculously, not a single one of them stirred. There was a small opening between where one of the boys slept on the floor and the edge of the couch, and Leah wedged her feet into the space, then bent over and laid a gentle hand on Austin's arm. Under her hand, his biceps were rigid, and his shirt was damp with sweat.

"Austin." She shook him lightly as she whispered. "Austin, wake up." She'd barely been able to hear herself, and yet Austin woke with a start, eyes wild as he searched her face, hands coming to her shoulders.

"Shh. It's okay. You were having a dream." Instinctively, she stroked his hair.

"Sorry." He sat up so quickly she had to clutch at his shoulder to keep from falling over the boy on the floor.

"I should go." His whisper was hoarse.

"Yeah, of course." She let go of him and made her way through the sleeping boys. She didn't hear any footsteps behind her, but the moment she'd crossed into the dining room, he was there.

"I'll go out the back door, so I don't wake them." Austin was still whispering.

She wanted to ask him what the dream had been about. If it had anything to do with whatever gave him that haunted look.

But she simply passed him his coat and opened the door for him. "I'll bring your games back tomorrow."

He waved her off. "Let Jackson keep them." And then he was gone.

Leah stood outside the door, letting the night air poke needles into her skin as she watched him cross their yards and enter his own house.

He'd been through something traumatic at some point in his life. Of that much she was becoming more and more certain.

Maybe it was why he was able to make a connection with Jackson so easily. Maybe if she could help fix whatever it was that had hurt Austin, she could figure out how to fix Jackson too.

At any rate, it was worth a shot.

Because she wasn't sure how much longer she could survive with things as they were.

Chapter 16

He never should have gotten close to them.

Austin's feet dragged to a walk, though he couldn't have run more than a mile. But his limbs hung heavy with the need for sleep.

He hadn't even tried to go to bed when he'd gotten home from Leah's. After that nightmare, sleep would have been worse than the exhaustion that weighed on him now.

Because this time when the IED went off, it wasn't only Tanner and Isaad he couldn't save. Leah and Jackson were there too. He couldn't shake the image of their broken bodies lying on the sand. It had been enough to drive him from the house at first light. But even now, as the wind cut at his skin and the sky hung gray and bleak above him, he couldn't escape it.

He scrubbed his hands over his face, as if that could banish the image seared into his mind.

He knew it couldn't happen to them. There were no explosives alongside the roads here. They weren't in a war zone. They were in the middle of sleepy Hope Springs.

But that didn't do anything to loosen the vise that choked the air out of his lungs every time he thought of it.

Was this what it was going to be like for the rest of his life? Every time he got close to someone, he'd see them being blown to pieces? How was he supposed to live like that?

A sudden need to talk to Chad gripped him. But he couldn't. Chad was on a mission, facing who knew what kind of danger.

And there was nothing Austin could do to keep him safe.

His brother's request from the other day kept popping into his head: "I wouldn't mind a prayer or two."

Chad had never asked Austin to pray for him before. Had he done it now because he knew something he wasn't telling Austin? Was he worried he might not make it back this time?

Austin shoved the thought aside.

More likely, it had been one more of Chad's lame attempts to get him to turn back to God.

Well, his brother could forget that. Believing in God had never done anything good for him. And it wasn't going to now either.

But the words came almost automatically. *Please keep—*

No.

He wasn't going to fall for that again. Chad was a good soldier. And good soldiers had his back. He'd be fine.

Austin hadn't been paying attention to where he was walking, but now he pulled up short at a scenic overlook he'd never come across before. The ground dropped away at the side of the road to the lake below, where waves frothed against the beach.

He drew in a ragged breath and eyed the drop-off. It was steep but not so steep he couldn't get down it.

He lowered his right leg tentatively into the thin covering of snow. When it held, he brought his left leg down. The movement was familiar, comforting. If it weren't for the pounding of the waves below, he could almost close his eyes and be back in the Afghan mountains.

At the bottom of the hill, he stepped cautiously onto the sand, packed hard by the cold. The sharp scent of the water sliced into the tension he'd carried all morning.

"What am I supposed to do now, Chad?" He called out, as if the waves could carry the message to his brother. "And don't say pray."

The lake foamed at his feet, and the sky loosed a sheet of thick, wet snowflakes.

Austin shook his head. He refused to believe the timing was anything more than a coincidence.

Anyway, he didn't need an answer. He already knew what his brother would say. "Talk to someone."

And Austin would scoff, just like he did now. Because he was tired of talking about it. The shrink he'd been required to see while he was in the hospital had been big about talking.

You lost your leg. Do you want to talk about it? Your best friend died. Do you want to talk about it? You saw a kid die and blame yourself. Do you want to talk about it?

No, he did not want to talk about it. Not with his shrink. Not with anyone.

Austin tilted his head at the water, Leah's face refusing to leave his mind. She'd listen, he knew she would. But he couldn't possibly tell her the things he'd seen, what he'd lived through. She was too innocent for that. She shouldn't have to know about the horrors the world held.

She'd understand.

Austin sighed. He supposed she might. After all, she was raising a kid who'd discovered his mother dead. But that didn't mean he should bother her with this too. She had enough to shoulder already.

No. This was his burden to carry.

And he'd keep carrying it. Alone.

Leah blew on her hands and shook out her stiff fingers, then gripped the frigid metal of the ladder. She'd hoped the snow might let up, but if anything, it fell faster as the morning went on.

She knew some people thought it was crazy to decorate for Christmas before Thanksgiving. But she wasn't one of them.

If things hadn't been so busy lately, she'd already have the decorations up, and she was determined to get it done today. She'd tried to coax Jackson to help her after his friends left, but he'd only shot her a look of contempt and holed up in his room again. Even the lure of the Hawaiian grand prize hadn't been enough to prompt any interest.

But when they won, he'd see. He'd be glad she'd entered. Glad they got to spend the week in Hawaii together. Making mother-son memories.

She ignored the voice that said if he didn't enjoy spending time with her here, he wouldn't enjoy it in Hawaii either. It was Hawaii—how could anyone not be happy there?

Stepping carefully onto the second step from the top of the ladder, Leah reached to grip the gutter above her head. With her other hand, she attempted to fasten one of the clips she'd bought for hanging lights. But it slipped out of her numb fingers, clicking against the ladder before disappearing into the snow. She sighed and dug in her pocket for another.

This might be more than a one-day job.

"What are you doing?" The gruff voice startled her, and she dropped another clip. If she kept this up, she was going to have to make another trip to the hardware store before she got a single string of lights hung.

"You should really give some warning when you sneak up behind a person on a ladder." She turned toward Austin, reminding herself that the extra kick to her heart was only because he'd surprised her.

"It wouldn't be very sneaky then, would it?" He peered into the snow, then bent at the waist and dipped his fingers into it, fishing out the clips she'd dropped.

"How did you . . ." She shook her head as he passed it to her. "You must have eagle eyes. Did you get any sleep after you went home?"

Austin shrugged, hands in the pockets of his sweatshirt. "So what *are* you doing out here? Don't you know it's a snowstorm?"

"What does it look like I'm doing?"

Austin scrutinized her. "Trying to catch your death."

She blew on her fingers again. "Every year, Hope Springs has a house decorating contest for Christmas. The grand prize is a trip to Hawaii."

Austin watched her, face blank. Did he not see where she was going with this?

"And I thought if we won, it would be a good chance for Jackson and me to spend time together. Away from everything else."

"Have you won before?" Austin looked skeptical.

"Of course not. I've never entered before."

Austin spluttered, but she pushed on. "But I have a plan." She climbed down from the ladder and pulled out her phone, scrolling to the inspiration board she'd created. She wanted to transform her home into a gingerbread house.

Austin's eyebrows lifted toward his stocking cap. "That looks like a lot of work."

"I know." But she could do it. She hadn't created a successful business by shying away from hard work.

"At least put on some gloves." Austin pulled his hands out of his pockets, and before she realized where they were headed, he had them wrapped around hers. "You're going to get frostbite." He rubbed his warm hands back and forth over hers.

Leah scrambled for something to say. But the only thing she could focus on was his hands on hers. Why did they feel so good? So right.

Because they're warm and you're cold, she told herself. *That's the only reason.*

She tugged her hands back and tucked them into her own pockets. "Much better, thanks. I can't hold onto stuff with my gloves on."

Austin's hands went back into his pockets too, but he was still watching her.

More to escape his gaze than from any burning desire to climb the cold ladder, she reached for a rung.

But Austin held an open hand in front of her. "Pass me the clips."

She blinked at him. "I thought you didn't like Christmas." But she reached into her pocket and started depositing clips into his hand.

"I don't." Austin shoved the clips into his own pocket and took a step up the ladder, moving cautiously. "But I like—" He turned away from her, falling silent.

"But I like to help," he finally mumbled.

Leah watched his deft movements as he snapped the clips onto the gutter.

For a second, she'd been sure he was going to say, "But I like you."

But he hadn't.

Thank goodness.

Just because he'd helped hang the lights didn't mean he liked Christmas any more now than he had before today.

Though Austin had to admit that he *did* like spending the day with Leah—and if hanging Christmas lights was the price he had to pay to do it, he'd gladly pay again.

Nice job following through with that whole not getting distracted thing.

Austin ignored the snarky reprimand in his head as he hung the last string of lights around the last window. He tossed Leah the end of the cord, and she plugged it in with the other ones.

"We need Jackson out here for this." She ducked into the house to call for the boy. That kid had no idea how good he had it. Leah had spent the entire day out here—in the middle of a blizzard—to make this perfect for him.

"Austin's here," he heard Leah call.

Much as Austin had come to enjoy spending time with Jackson, it irked him that the only time the boy showed any interest in anything Leah said or did was when it involved him. He hadn't done anything to deserve the kid's respect or devotion. Not the way Leah had.

Austin heard Leah negotiating with Jackson to wear a jacket and boots. Fortunately, when the boy emerged a few minutes later, it looked like Leah had won.

"Ready for this?" Austin fist-bumped the boy. "I'll turn it on. You two go stand on the sidewalk, so you get the full effect."

When they were in position, he couldn't resist doing a countdown. "One hundred. Ninety-nine. Ninety-eight."

"Austin." Leah's laugh from across the yard warmed through him.

"Fine. If you can't be patient. Three. Two. One." He rushed through the countdown and flipped the switch.

"Wow." Leah's awed gasp drew his attention more than the lights. He walked down the driveway to join them, his eyes fixed on her face—the way her lips curved into a smile, the way her cheeks were pink and bright with cold, the way the lights from the house reflected in her eyes.

"It's perfect," she breathed as he came to stand next to her and take in the house.

Even as someone who didn't enjoy Christmas, he had to admit they'd done a good job bringing Leah's vision of a gingerbread house to life. The eaves were all outlined in white lights, while colored lights rimmed every window on the front of the house. Leah had wrapped some old wreaths in lights to make them look like candies. She'd made Austin try them in about a thousand different places before she'd decided to put them back in the first spot. Not that he'd minded. A line of lighted candy canes traced the footpath to the front porch, completing the effect.

Closer to the sidewalk, a spotlight shone on a hand-carved wooden nativity set. When Austin had pointed out that it didn't really fit with the theme of the rest of the decorations, Leah had simply given him a look and said that without Jesus, there was no point to Christmas. Unwilling to get into a debate about religion, Austin had simply nodded and dutifully placed the heavy figures where she pointed.

"What do you think, Jackson?" Leah's voice was tentative.

Jackson shrugged. "It's okay." But under the nonchalance, Austin could read it in his eyes—he was impressed.

Apparently Leah saw it too, because she clapped her hands. "How about some cocoa?"

Jackson gave a slight nod, and Leah turned to Austin, eyes questioning. "Join us?"

He should say no. He hadn't gotten in a workout at all today, aside from climbing back up the overlook, which had been more challenging than he'd anticipated.

Plus, what had happened to not getting close?

But the idea of spending the night by himself with his weights and his resistance band didn't hold much appeal.

"Sure."

Weak, soldier. Weak.

He moved closer to her. "But first, there's something I've been waiting to do all day."

Leah's eyes widened, and she took a step backward. Was she afraid he was going to try to kiss her again? Surely, she didn't think he was that foolish?

He bent to the snow and scooped a handful into a ball.

Leah's shriek said she'd figured out what he was about to do.

She took two running steps into a snowdrift, but she was too slow. His lob easily hit her shoulder, and she shrieked again as snow cascaded down her coat.

Before she could retaliate, he reloaded, this time firing the snowball at Jackson. The boy didn't quite shriek like Leah. But he did grunt and bend to make his own snowball. Both his and Leah's hit Austin at the same time, and snow trickled down his back. But he didn't care.

Seeing both of them smiling at the same time made it so worth it.

Chapter 17

"*R*eady?" The nervous buzz that had been percolating in her belly all day was ridiculous.

Austin had come over for dinner every day in the week since they'd decorated her house. And none of his actions had been anything more than friendly.

Just because they were eating at Peyton's tonight didn't make things any different.

She knew that.

She was sure Austin knew it.

She only hoped—prayed—that her friends knew it too.

"Let's go." Austin looked as nervous as she felt.

Was it too much, bringing him to her friends' house? But it was either that or let the poor guy starve tonight.

Besides, plenty of her friends had brought new people to their get-togethers.

She tried to ignore the fact that most of them were now married to the people they'd brought. That had absolutely nothing to do with her and Austin.

Austin led the way to his truck and moved to open the passenger door. Leah forced down a fresh surge of panic. A guy could open a car door as a friend—it didn't have to mean anything. Besides, Jackson had to get in this way too, so technically Austin had opened the door as much for the boy as for her.

Austin must have started the car earlier because it was already toasty inside.

That was thoughtful.

Leah pushed the thought aside. She had to stop reading into everything.

"How's your brother?" Leah had avoided asking much about his brother, but she'd added him to her daily prayers.

"Haven't heard from him." There was an undertone of worry to Austin's voice, though Leah could tell he was working hard to sound unconcerned.

"That's probably pretty normal, though, right? I mean, I'm sure communication there is spotty and—" She cut herself off. And what? She didn't know the first thing about what it was like over there. But she felt an overpowering need to offer him some reassurance. "I've been praying for him."

Austin grunted. Apparently that conversation was over.

"Jackson, do you have homework this weekend?"

A grunt from the backseat. If only these two weren't so talkative.

Still, things had been going so much better this past week that she couldn't complain. That snowball fight with Austin last weekend seemed to have loosened Jackson up a bit. And with Austin coming over every night for dinner, Jackson had started eating at the table with them. He still only ate PBJ, but at this point, she'd take the small win. Plus, she'd only been called to Mrs. Rice's office once this week, and that was because he'd skipped science. But at least he hadn't punched anyone else.

As for Austin, he seemed to laugh more readily every day. And the look that had haunted his eyes—the one that made it seem like he wasn't entirely present—had receded farther and farther into the background, so that sometimes she didn't see it at all.

Now if they could just get through this dinner without her friends making things awkward between them.

Two hours later, Leah had to wonder what she'd been so worried about. Her friends had been on their best behavior—though Jade and Peyton did keep shooting her significant looks.

But Austin had gotten involved in a game of darts with the guys the minute they'd stepped through the door and had barely talked to her once since then. As they ate now, he sat in the living room, joining in an animated conversation with Jared and Ethan about their work as volunteer firefighters, while she sat in the kitchen with Sophie and Spencer and Ethan and Ariana and their little ones. A pang went through her middle every time Sophie wiped at her twins' faces or Ariana made a silly face at Joy.

Adopting an older child had been the right decision. She still believed that. But she couldn't deny that every once in a while she wondered what it would be like to have a baby too. Maybe next time she could adopt a little one.

If she survived this time.

She turned toward the living room to check on Jackson. She'd packed him a PBJ, but she knew he wouldn't eat it with everyone around. Maybe later, when everyone was involved in a game of charades or something, he'd find a quiet spot in the kitchen to eat it. She was learning not to push it. And for now, he seemed content playing on the floor with Hope.

One more sign that a little sibling would be good for him. Someday.

Her gaze left Jackson and traveled to the spot where Austin sat on the couch, right at home with her friends. His eyes caught hers, and he grinned. Her eyes jumped to the other side of the room, but it was too late.

She could already feel her face warming. Hopefully no one else noticed.

She stood, gathering her plate, along with those of her friends, and carried them into the kitchen, where Peyton was stacking a tray with Christmas cookies.

Her friend smiled. "It's a little early, but—"

"You know I don't mind." Leah chose a bell-shaped one and took a bite, closing her eyes as memories of Christmases with her family washed over her. "Perfect."

Peyton checked over her shoulder, as if to make sure they were alone. "Speaking of perfect, I'm glad you brought Austin."

Leah snorted. "Subtle, Pey."

But Peyton poked her shoulder. "I'm serious. He seems much more comfortable than the first time we met him. His eyes don't keep going to the door. Though they *do* keep going to a certain someone."

"Whatever." Thankfully, there was no way Peyton could see the warmth pooling in her middle.

"Don't be like that, Leah. It's obvious you two are good together."

"We haven't been together all night."

"My point exactly." Peyton shot her a triumphant smile. "You guys are working so hard not to be together that it's obvious you *are* together. Or you want to be."

"You're delusional. Go serve those cookies before you say something even more nonsensical." She shoved Peyton toward the living room. "Austin and I are friends. But that's all we're ever going to be. Capisce?"

"I think you're wrong—"

Leah held up a warning finger. "Capisce?"

Peyton gave a half nod, then shook her head vigorously and escaped the room.

"You are the most exasperating friend ever, did you know that?" Leah called after her.

The only answer she got was Peyton's gleeful laugh.

127

That had been more fun than Austin had anticipated. He'd already known Leah's friends were nice from the first time he'd met them, but he hadn't been sure how he'd do with being in such a large crowd again. But now that he knew them, it turned out they didn't feel so much like a crowd—more like a good-sized family.

He'd also been more than a little concerned that Leah's friends would detect his interest in her. But he'd done a pretty good job of keeping that hidden, if he did say so himself.

Actually, he'd done such a good job that it felt a little ridiculous now as he pulled into Leah's driveway to drop her and Jackson off.

He hopped out of the car to walk them to the door. Jackson disappeared inside after giving him a fist-bump, but Leah turned to him.

"I hope you had fun." She could barely suppress her yawn.

"I did." *Do not tuck her hair behind her ear.* "Sorry if I was ignoring you. I didn't want your friends to . . ." He toed at the step with his prosthetic. How did he say this?

Leah looked at her own shoes. "It's fine. It's not like we're a couple."

"Right." He yanked his hat tighter over his ears and turned toward the steps.

"Wait. Austin."

His pulse slid upward. Was this the part where she said she wanted to be more than friends?

"There's this thing tomorrow at Jackson's school. Some kind of father-son event. I offered to take him, but you can imagine how well that went over." She met his eyes, and he could read the uncertainty there. "And he could really use a male role model. So I wondered if maybe you might be willing to go with him."

Austin swallowed against a sudden scratchiness at the back of his throat. She had so many male friends. And a brother. But she considered him a role model for Jackson?

"You know what, never mind. I shouldn't have asked. It was silly." Leah reached for the door, but Austin threw out a hand to stop her. Her fingers were warm under his, and he had to make himself pull his hand away.

"It's not silly." He cleared his throat and met her eyes. "I'd love to go."

"Thanks." Leah's whisper slipped right through to his heart. He couldn't take his eyes off hers. It would be so easy to bend down and kiss her right now.

But this was about more than the two of them. It was about Jackson. And he wasn't going to exploit her gratitude over this to get a kiss.

Assuming she'd even kiss him—and not run away again.

Which was highly unlikely.

He forced himself to reach past her and open the door. "Goodnight."

She stepped inside, and he pulled the door closed behind her, staring at it a few seconds longer.

Taking Jackson to a father-son event was a no-brainer. Figuring out what to do with these feelings for Leah?

That was a whole new level of complicated.

Chapter 18

Austin pulled into the driveway of the sports complex Leah had given him the address to, glancing over at Jackson. The boy hadn't said much on the way over, but Austin understood. He hadn't had a father either. He couldn't count how many times he'd watched his friends hanging out with their fathers, wishing that just once he could be like them. But his mom had never thought to ask another male role model to take him to these kinds of events.

It felt surreal to be going as a father figure now. But in a good way.

He tried not to worry about the fact that the event must be some kind of sporting activity. He'd always been athletic, and as long as they stuck to the basics, like basketball, he'd be fine.

He let Jackson lead the way to the front doors, then made him pause for a photo. "Your mom made me promise to take lots of pictures. Say 'fun.'"

Defiance sparked across Jackson's face. "She's not my mom."

"She is." Austin injected authority into his voice, the same way he had on the rare occasions he'd had to deal with insubordination among his men. "And she cares about you very much. I don't know if you realize this, but that's not the easiest thing to find in this world. You should be thankful for her."

He snapped the picture and texted it to Leah, hoping it was dark enough that she wouldn't notice Jackson's petulant expression.

"I don't need anyone to care about me."

Austin stopped in front of the boy, laying a hand on his shoulder. "That might be what you tell yourself. But we all need someone to care about us."

"Whatever." Jackson shrugged out of his grip. "You're not my dad."

The words shouldn't have cut at Austin the way they did. He knew he wasn't Jackson's dad and that he never would be. But that didn't lessen the sting.

"No, I'm not." He kept his voice even. "But I am your friend. And as your friend, I'm telling you—"

Jackson pushed through one of the building's glass doors, letting it swing shut behind him. Austin grabbed it just in time and followed him, trying to summon up some of that incredible patience Leah always showed.

Inside, a wall of noise hit Austin as boys and dads grouped in the lobby, dads laughing together, boys shouting and chasing.

Jackson had already tucked himself away at the far end of the bank of doors, and Austin followed him. He should probably encourage Jackson to greet the other boys, but the truth was, this spot as far from the crowd as possible suited him perfectly as well.

"Hey." A guy with reddish hair and a green sweater approached. "Is this your dad, Jackson?"

Jackson gave the man a disgusted look. "No."

"Oh." The guy looked taken aback.

"I'm a friend of the family." Austin shook the hand the man offered. "And you are?"

"Mr. Wickel. Jackson's science teacher."

Austin resisted the urge to increase the pressure on the guy's hand. If he was Jackson's science teacher, shouldn't he know the boy didn't have a father?

"We're going to get started in a few minutes. Looks like you don't have any gear, so you can head down the corridor to the right to rent some. We'll see you in there." Mr. Wickel held out a fist to Jackson for a fist-bump, but Jackson sneered at it.

Austin didn't blame him. "That guy is an imbecile," he muttered as Mr. Wickel moved off.

The comment earned him Jackson's first smile of the night. But Leah probably wouldn't approve.

"Don't tell your mom I said that."

This time he was almost sure he heard a laugh.

"Come on." Austin clapped a hand on Jackson's shoulder. "What kind of equipment do we need to rent?"

They followed the line of kids and dads down the hall. A couple of boys said hi to Jackson, but most ignored him.

"I wonder what we're . . ." Austin lost his words as the crowd ahead of them thinned enough for him to see what they were waiting to rent.

Hockey gear.

His heart dropped. He knew the military had a hockey team for amputees. Those guys were whizzes on the ice—the single-leg amputees on skates and the double-limb amputees on sleds—but Austin had never been a hockey player, and he'd had no inclination to learn during his recovery. He didn't figure there'd be much call for hockey players once he got back to Afghanistan.

He pulled at the collar of his t-shirt. Now what did he do? Should he try, for Jackson's sake? But maybe here, in front of a hundred kids and their dads, wasn't the place to reveal his prosthetic to Jackson. At the thought of all those eyes on him—all the questions he'd be asked—he almost bolted.

But he made himself stand his ground to talk to Jackson. Leaning close to the boy, he spoke in an undertone. "I can't play hockey."

Jackson rolled his eyes. "You stand on skates and hit a puck with a stick. It's not that tough."

The line shuffled forward, and a guy behind Austin cleared his throat, gesturing for Austin to move up. Instead, Austin reached for

Jackson's arm and tugged him out of line, motioning for the next group to go ahead of them.

"We can stay if you want. I'll watch you. But I can't skate."

Disappointment flashed in Jackson's eyes, but he blinked, and it was gone. "Whatever. I didn't want to come anyway."

Austin nudged him toward the line. "Go on. I'll rent you some equipment. I bet you've got killer skills. I want to watch you."

But Jackson twisted out of his grip and marched toward the lobby.

Austin followed, the weight of the prosthetic he usually didn't notice dragging at him.

"Hey." He pulled up next to Jackson. "How about we do something else? Just the two of us." He racked his memory for what he'd liked to do at Jackson's age. "How about bowling?"

Jackson directed a withering look at him.

"Or we could hang out here. Shoot some hoops. I'm sure they have an open court."

But Jackson angled for the door. "I want to go home."

Austin followed him outside, his exasperated sigh fogging the air in front of him. He hit the key fob to unlock the truck and watched Jackson climb in. As he followed, Austin tried to figure out if there was a way to salvage the night.

But he came up empty.

Queasiness rolled through him at the knowledge that he was failing Jackson.

And what was Leah going to think?

She'd asked him for this one simple favor, and he couldn't even do that. The worst part was, he couldn't begin to explain why.

The ride home was silent, but when they pulled into Leah's driveway, Jackson spoke, not looking at Austin. "Don't worry. I'll tell Leah I had a good time. We all know that's the only reason you went anyway."

Austin's head whipped toward the boy. "Do you really believe that?"

Jackson shrugged.

"I like your mom. She's nice. And we get along well. But I went tonight because I like *you*. I wanted to spend time with *you*."

"Whatever." Jackson's eyes rolled back farther than Austin would have thought possible.

Before Austin could say anything else, Jackson jumped out of the truck and slammed the door. Austin watched him shuffle toward the house, debating whether he should follow or take the coward's way out and go home.

He really wished he didn't already know the right answer to that one.

Steeling himself, he followed Jackson's tracks to the front door. But Leah beat him there, stepping outside as he reached the bottom of the porch steps.

"What happened? Why are you back already? Did Jackson refuse to participate?" Little puffs of steam clouded in front of her as she spoke, and she wrapped her arms around her elbows.

Austin swallowed. Apparently, Jackson hadn't said anything. It'd be so easy to let Leah believe her assumption was correct. But he couldn't do that to her. Or to Jackson.

"It was me." He dug his hands into his pockets.

Leah's lips tipped into a frown. "What was you?"

"I'm the one who wouldn't participate. It was hockey, and I don't skate."

Leah's mouth worked, no words coming out, but her eyes snapped. Finally, she seemed to find her voice. "And you couldn't try? For him?"

"I'm sorry." In his pockets, his hands clenched. "I couldn't."

"Why?" There was fire in her voice. "Why couldn't you try? He wouldn't have cared if you were bad at it. All he cared about was being there with you. And you blew that."

"I blew that?" Austin puffed out a hot breath. "I blew that?"

This woman was incredible. He'd taken her son to a father-son event, as a favor to her, and now she was telling him he'd blown it when he hadn't been able to skate because he didn't have a leg?

"So what if you weren't the best? You could have tried anyway. There's no reason—"

But he'd had enough. He reached down and gripped the left leg of his track pants. "You want to know *why* I couldn't skate?"

His breaths were ragged and sharp, and he almost did it.

He almost pulled up his pants leg and revealed his prosthetic.

But he stopped himself.

This wasn't the way to tell her. Not in anger.

Her hand went to her hip, and she raised an eyebrow, her expression saying "I'm waiting" as clearly as words would have.

Austin breathed in and out. His grip on his pants leg loosened.

"I just couldn't. I'm sorry." He turned and stalked to his truck. He could feel her eyes on him as he backed out and parked next door.

But he didn't look over at her.

Leah leaned into the porch railing as Austin disappeared into the house next door.

A long sigh scraped against her trachea in the cold.

At least that was over. The feelings she'd had for Austin lately had been growing dangerously close to attraction, and she'd started to think it might be mutual. But if the guy couldn't spend one evening with her son, that had to end right now.

She and Jackson were a package deal.

Anyway, this made things easier. Austin had been occupying way too many of her thoughts lately. Thoughts that would better be spent on figuring out what to get Jackson for Christmas or finalizing plans for the annual community Thanksgiving meal she always managed.

She moved toward the door, its colorful lights winking at her. Lights she'd held as Austin hung them. They'd felt so much like a team that day.

Just went to show that feelings couldn't always be trusted.

What mattered now was providing Jackson with stability and with adults he could trust. She'd thought that might be Austin. But apparently she'd been wrong.

As she returned inside, she pulled in a breath. She'd close the door on whatever feelings she'd been starting to develop for him.

Now.

With a hard shove, she latched the front door.

She only hoped the door of her heart was closed as tightly.

Chapter 19

He'd wanted fewer distractions.

And now he had fewer distractions.

Austin curled the weight, an involuntary grunt exploding from his lips. He'd already punished his muscles harder than he should this morning. And it was only nine o'clock.

But his physical was just over a week away. And he had nothing else to do anyway.

He dropped the weight and reached for his water bottle, his eyes going to the window, the same way they had a million times in the past two days. And just like it did every time, that same ache rose in his middle.

Maybe he shouldn't, but he missed them. Two days of not seeing them, not talking to them, was too long.

He'd considered going over to apologize for everything that had happened the other night—he'd even gotten as far as opening his front door yesterday. But what was he going to say? Sorry I couldn't skate, but I don't have a leg?

That's a start.

But he pushed the thought away. It was better this way. It wasn't like he was going to be here forever. Next week, he'd have his physical, and then he'd be on his way back to Afghanistan.

That didn't exactly leave time for a relationship—with Leah or her kid.

He forced his eyes off their house and moved toward the bathroom. He should shower and get on with his busy day of doing nothing.

His eyes flicked to his laptop, open on the coffee table. Still no word from Chad.

He tried to ignore the dread that nearly strangled him every time he thought about his brother.

It had only been two weeks since they'd last talked—and Chad had warned that it might be a while before he could call again.

There was nothing to worry about.

Austin sat on the small stool he'd placed next to the shower and hiked up the leg of his track pants. He'd learned it was easier to take his prosthetic off first, then the pants.

He was about to push the button to release the pin that held the prosthetic in place when there was a loud bang on the front door.

He considered ignoring it. It was probably a solicitor.

Or it could be Leah.

He pulled the leg of his pants back down and stood, telling his heart to knock off its silly thumping as he strode to the front door.

Eagerness shot through him as he opened it.

But it wasn't Leah.

It was Jackson, shivering in only a t-shirt.

"Hey, dude." Austin reached for the boy's arm, dragging him into the house. "Get inside before you freeze to death."

Jackson's eyes darted around the room.

"I'm glad you came over." Austin gestured for Jackson to sit, but the boy didn't move. "I wanted to apologize—"

"Leah's not getting up." Jackson's voice was scratchy, and he blinked as if holding back tears.

"What?" Austin tried to switch gears, even as his heart heaved. "What do you mean, she's not getting up?"

"She's always up by now, but I pounded on her bedroom door, and she didn't answer." Jackson shook harder.

"Okay. It's okay." Austin locked a reassuring hand on the boy's shoulder. "Maybe she decided to sleep in, and she's wearing ear plugs or something." Though he had to admit that didn't sound like Leah.

"What if she's dead?"

Austin's mouth opened. Leah was a young, healthy woman. Why would Jackson jump to that conclusion?

And then he remembered—Leah had told him that Jackson had found his mother dead of a drug overdose. She'd probably been young and healthy as well.

"She's not dead." He grabbed his coat and threw it around Jackson's shoulders, then pulled his stocking cap onto his head and steered the boy to the door. "Come on. I'll check on her."

At first, Jackson's feet didn't budge, but after a few nudges, Austin got him moving.

They sped across the yard as fast as they could through the six inches of fresh snow.

"She's in her room." Inside, Jackson pointed down the hallway but seemed unwilling to step beyond the front door. He stood there, Austin's coat still draped over him, face pale, shaking.

Austin patted his shoulder, then strode down the hallway to Leah's closed bedroom door at the end.

He gave a gentle knock. "Leah?"

When there was no answer after a few seconds, he knocked and called again, a little louder this time. He glanced over his shoulder, but he couldn't see Jackson from here. He stuffed down his own mounting concern and raised his hand to knock again, but the door opened.

He allowed himself a tiny sigh of relief.

Until his eyes fell on her.

Her cheeks were flushed, sweat beaded on her forehead, and dark circles bruised her eyes, which she seemed barely able to open, although they widened when they fell on him, and a hand went self-consciously to her hair.

"What are you doing here?" She wrapped her arms around her middle as a shiver wracked her frame, despite the fleece pajamas she wore.

"Jackson came over. He said you weren't getting up." Austin reached for her elbow to lead her back toward the bed.

"I'm fine." Leah tried to escape his grasp but stumbled. His arm went around her to steady her, and he tried to ignore the warmth in his chest as she leaned into him.

"Yeah, you seem fine." He touched his free hand to her forehead, wincing at the heat that radiated from it. "You're burning up. Let's get you back to bed."

But Leah tried to pull away again. "I can't. I have to get everything ready for the community dinner tomorrow. I have twenty turkeys to cook and mashed potatoes and stuffing and—"

"There must be someone else who can do that." They'd reached her bed, and he lowered her gently onto the white comforter.

"I cook the meal every year. I like to do it. I want to help people."

Austin bent to lift her legs and swing them into the bed. "I know you like to help people." He made his voice gentle. "But this year, you're going to have to let people help you. Who should I call to make the meal?"

She closed her eyes and lifted a hand to cover them. "My assistant is the only one I'd trust. But she's out of town for Thanksgiving. Maybe if I rest for a little bit, I can go over later. It'll be tight but . . ." Her words had gotten slower, and she looked half asleep.

"That's right. You rest." Austin tucked the blankets around her, then strode to the bathroom and wet a rag with cool water. After ringing it out, he folded it into a neat rectangle, then placed it on her forehead. She half-sighed, half-moaned but didn't open her eyes.

Austin let himself watch her for a few seconds, until he was sure she was sleeping. Then he headed for the living room to recruit Jackson. They had a lot of work to do.

It looked like they were making Thanksgiving dinner.

For the entire town.

"I knew there'd be a list." Jade waved the piece of paper triumphantly in front of Austin as she emerged from the office at the back of Leah's commercial kitchen downtown. "I'm always teasing Leah about all the lists she makes, but this time I have to admit that it's helpful."

Austin did too. He wasn't sure they'd be able to pull this off otherwise. Even with the list, it was going to be a challenge.

"I still can't believe Leah asked us all to help make the community Thanksgiving dinner. The last time we offered, she practically laughed in our faces." Jade's husband Dan came up behind her and read the list over her shoulder. "She must be really sick."

Austin nodded. No need to mention that technically it hadn't been Leah who had texted to ask her friends to help with the meal. It had been Jackson's idea to "borrow" Leah's phone and contact her friends to see if anyone would be able to help with the cooking. Austin had agreed, making it clear to the boy that the only reason it was acceptable was because they were doing it to help Leah.

He'd been apprehensive at first, but he had to admit now that it had been a good idea. In addition to Dan and Jade, Peyton and Jared, Ethan and Ariana, Grace, and Emma had made it.

Austin glanced toward the building's small lobby, where Jackson was keeping Hope and Ethan and Ariana's little girl, Joy, entertained.

"So, where do we start, chef?" Dan teased.

Austin scanned the list Jade passed him. He'd thought Leah had been exaggerating when she'd said she had to make twenty turkeys, but judging from this, she hadn't been.

He swallowed. "How many people does this need to serve?"

"A couple hundred. Mostly homeless people or people who have nowhere else to go for Thanksgiving." Jade was studying the list. "I can handle the mashed potatoes. Pretty hard to mess that up, right?"

Austin made a mark on the paper. "And I can take care of the turkeys." He divvied up the rest of the tasks among the others.

As they broke off to do their jobs, Austin rummaged in the industrial-size refrigerator for the herbs he'd need for the turkeys. He snapped off a piece of sage, the smell a punch straight to the gut.

He'd promised himself he'd never cook again, and everything in him rebelled at the idea, from his trembling hands to his churning stomach. But what else could he do?

You could turn around and leave. You don't owe these people anything.

But that wasn't true. Leah could have written him off that first night they'd met, when she'd found him chopping wood at midnight. Instead, she'd gone out of her way to make him feel at home here. And her friends had all been more than welcoming too.

Austin threw the sage back in the bag. Today was not the day to get caught up in those old memories. Today was a day to make new ones. If not for his own sake, then for Leah's.

With a quick breath, he grabbed the rest of the ingredients from the fridge.

For the rest of the day, the kitchen bustled with activity as everyone worked on their tasks. As Austin understood it, they'd make all the food today, then transport it to the church, where they'd let it warm tomorrow during the Thanksgiving service so that no one had to miss worship to prepare the meal.

"It smells good in here." Jackson stopped in front of Austin, carrying baby Hope. "Way better than she smells."

From next to Austin, Jade laughed and took her daughter. "Unless you want to change her?" She wiggled her eyebrows at Jackson, who gave her the kind of revolted look only a thirteen-year-old boy could pull off. "I'll take that as a no." Jade carried the still smiling baby off.

"So it smells good, huh? You want a bite?" Austin leaned closer and whispered. "I won't tell anyone."

But Jackson's mouth dropped into his more typical scowl. "I don't want it. It just smells good."

Austin studied the boy. There was a reason he wouldn't eat more than peanut butter and jelly, he was sure of it. But if Leah wasn't going to push it, neither was he.

"All better." Jade passed a fresh-smelling Hope back to Jackson. The baby immediately gripped his ear, and Jackson's scowl transformed into a smile as he tickled the little girl into letting go. Too bad Leah wasn't here to see that smile. On both kids.

Actually, it was too bad Leah couldn't be here, period. Surrounded by her friends, the dull longing he'd felt after not seeing her for two days had grown into a need to be near her. And it didn't help that they kept mentioning her name.

As Jackson took Hope back, Jade leaned her hip on the counter and regarded Austin. Peyton came and stood next to her. Austin eyed the two women. They were ganging up on him about something, he could feel it.

"It was nice that you did this for Leah." Peyton gave him a wry look that said he'd been busted.

He tried to play it off. "Oh, I didn't do— She was the one who—"

But both women were shaking their heads and laughing at him.

"Nice try," Jade said. "But Leah could be dead, and she still wouldn't give this up. You must really care about her."

"I didn't— I don't—" He turned his full attention to the turkey he'd been carving. "I was just trying to help," he finally mumbled.

Jade's grin gentled. "I know. And we all appreciate it." She gestured around the room, where everyone was now cleaning up. "And so will Leah."

He lifted the turkey pieces into the large roaster they'd use to warm it tomorrow. He tried to ignore the fact that the women's eyes were still on him.

"Can I tell you something about Leah?" Peyton asked.

Austin shrugged, as if he couldn't care less what she had to say about Leah. He doubted they bought it.

"If you like her, you're going to have to make it painfully obvious."

His eyes swung to Peyton, then to Jade. Both looked completely serious.

"And be persistent," Jade added. She grabbed a rag and wiped up the juices that had dripped from the turkey.

Austin opened his mouth to argue, but clearly there was no point. These two had already made up their minds.

And it wasn't like they were wrong.

Not that it mattered after the way he'd left things with Leah the other night.

Peyton set a hand on his arm. "I can tell she likes you too. Or, she would if she let herself. But you're going to have to fight if you want to get out of the friend zone. She's been hurt in the past. So she tends not to give men much of a chance, beyond friendship."

Austin's shoulders tensed. He hated the idea of anything hurting Leah. "Oh, I—"

But he had no idea how to finish the thought. Did she even consider him a friend anymore? And if she did, did he want her to think of him as something more?

No.

But the weak voice wasn't enough to convince even himself.

Chapter 20

With a gasp, Leah sprang upright, her eyes flashing open. What was she doing in bed? How long had she been sleeping?

A faint trace of light leaked in through the curtains above her bed, and she reached to open them. The sun was low in the sky, faint lines of pink and orange oozing from its center into the clouds.

Could it really be sunset already?

But no, that couldn't be right. The sun set on the other side of the house.

It *rose* on this side.

She jumped to her feet but had to pause as a remnant of yesterday's headache pounded at her temples. She waited for the dizziness to pass, then sprinted for the bedroom door. Somehow, she'd slept through an entire day and night.

The day and night she was supposed to spend preparing the community Thanksgiving dinner.

She had to call Dan. Maybe he could get the word out that the event was canceled before people started showing up.

A sick feeling not at all related to her illness swirled in her stomach. She shouldn't have insisted that she had to be the one to prepare the meal. She should have listened to Austin yesterday when he'd suggested that she call someone else to make it. It would have been better than letting an entire community down.

Austin.

She stopped as her thoughts caught up with the spinning in her head.

Austin had been here yesterday. He'd tucked her into bed. She could still feel the soothing coolness of his hand on her forehead. The rag he'd placed there.

She'd woken once in the middle of the day yesterday to find a glass of water that she'd gulped down. She could only assume he'd left it. And the note.

He'd left a note.

Saying that he would take care of everything.

She rushed back to the nightstand, grabbed the note, then burst into the hallway. She'd run over to his house, find out what still needed to be done, and then get to work. Maybe the meal could be salvaged.

Jackson's bedroom door was open, but he wasn't in there.

She padded to the kitchen, already calling for him. "Jackson, do you know if . . ."

But she lost track of what she was going to say as her eyes fell on Austin standing at her kitchen island.

"Good morning." Austin raised a coffee cup toward her, his eyes finding hers and sending a tingle from her toes up her spine. "How are you feeling?"

"Much better." But her voice was scratchy and dry, and the words came out sounding more frog than human. She probably looked more like a frog right now too.

Austin grabbed a glass from the cupboard as if he'd lived here his whole life, filled it from the refrigerator, and passed it to her.

She took a long drink, letting the water soothe her throat, still struggling to recover from the shock of finding Austin in her house first thing in the morning. "Where's Jackson?" At least she sounded more like herself now.

"In the living room. I hope you don't mind, but I said he could watch TV."

"I got your note." She lifted it. "I'm going to go change and then I'll run over there and finish things up. What needs to be done yet?"

She braced for his answer. Hopefully she'd be able to accomplish at least some of it in the few hours before hungry people started to arrive.

"Nothing."

"What do you mean, nothing?" Even she usually left a few last things for the morning. "What about the turkeys?"

"Roasted, carved, and ready to warm."

"And the stuffing?"

"Stuffed."

"Potatoes?"

"Mashed. I think you can see where I'm going with this. Your friends all pitched in. Jackson too. He kept the little ones occupied all day. You would have been proud." He stepped around the counter and passed her a cup of coffee, his eyes seeking out hers. "I'm sorry about the other night."

But Leah couldn't worry about the other night right now. Or about how it felt to have his eyes on her. Or about how much she'd missed seeing him for the past few days. Those kinds of thoughts would only confuse her.

"Do you want some breakfast?" Austin cleared his throat and escaped to the other side of the counter. "You must be starving after not eating at all yesterday." He picked up her cast iron pan and started wiping it out with a paper towel. Somehow the guy who didn't cook knew not to submerge a cast iron pan. And had cooked a turkey dinner for the whole community.

"No thanks." Leah watched him a moment longer. She had so many questions. But now wasn't the time. "I should go check on Jackson."

"He didn't sleep very well last night. He got up every hour to go to the bathroom, but I think it was just so he could check if you were still—" Austin looked toward the living room and lowered his voice. "Still alive. He seemed pretty freaked out."

Leah pressed a hand to her chest. She highly doubted that Jackson cared what happened to her. But if her illness had triggered memories of what had happened with his mom, she was terribly sorry for that.

Something else Austin had said snagged at her. How did he know Jackson had been up? "Did you stay all night?"

A trace of pink rose in Austin's cheeks. "I didn't want to leave Jackson. And I didn't know if you might need anything . . ." He swallowed and directed his eyes to the now gleaming pan in his hands.

"Oh." Hopefully he'd figure the flush of her cheeks was still from her fever. "I'll go check on Jackson."

She gulped in a clearing breath as she made her way to the living room. Just because the man had taken care of her, taken care of her son, taken care of the meal she was supposed to prepare, didn't mean anything. Aside from the fact that he was a good friend. A *really* good friend.

Jackson looked up as she entered the living room. He looked smaller than usual, curled into a tight ball in his chair, and his eyes were heavy. He didn't say anything when she greeted him, but she could almost believe a flash of relief sparked in his eyes. Was it possible that Austin had been right? Had Jackson actually been worried about her?

"Happy Thanksgiving." She dared to slide a few steps closer, and Jackson went so far as to nod. "I'm going to go shower and get ready, and we'll leave for church right after that. Then we'll go serve the meal everyone made yesterday. Austin said you were a big help."

This time the corner of Jackson's lip lifted into what Leah could almost convince herself was a smile.

"Thank you for that." She wanted to say more. To tell him how much it meant to her. But maybe this was where she should leave it for now. Baby steps.

She padded back toward the kitchen to let Austin know it was okay if he went home now. She had things under control.

But at the sight of him wiping her counter, she paused, taking a moment to watch him. He looked up, and she snapped her head toward the refrigerator as if it were the most interesting thing in the world.

But she could feel her face heating again. There was no way he hadn't noticed her staring.

"I'm going to get ready for church," she mumbled, taking a step down the hallway. But halfway to her room, she turned back. "Would you like to come with us?"

She held her breath as she brought her eyes to his. He stopped wiping the counter and stared at her.

She should have known better than to ask. He'd already declined multiple invitations to church.

But he offered a slow nod. "I think I might."

She could feel the grin lifting her lips, and she didn't try to restrain it. Chalk one up to God for an answered prayer.

Chapter 21

Austin's shoulders tightened as he drove into the church parking lot. He'd insisted they take his truck, since a fairly heavy snow had started to fall about half an hour before they'd left. Already, a slick half-inch of snow covered the roads.

"Should I drop you off at the door and then find a place to park?" Austin glanced at Leah out of the corner of his eye. In her black leggings and an oversize pink knit sweater that hung almost to her knees, she looked cozy enough to snuggle.

He knew he should chase the thought from his mind, but he couldn't. He'd spent all night considering what Jade and Peyton had said. About how he must really care about her. About how he'd have to fight if he wanted to get out of the friend zone.

And somewhere around two in the morning, as he'd laid a hand on her forehead and been swamped by relief to find it at last cool and fever-free, he'd realized—he did want to get out of that zone. He wanted to tell her how much he cared for her. But he hadn't figured out exactly how to do that yet.

"That's okay." Leah's smile strengthened his pulse. "Let's all walk in together."

Austin nodded, pulling into one of the few remaining parking spots. He jumped out of the truck, then sped around to the other side to help Leah down from her seat. The feel of her warm hand in his made something in his throat jump. It didn't make any sense, how he felt about her. He'd only known her for three weeks. And yet, in that time she'd become a constant in his life.

She hit him with another smile as she walked around the truck with him. "I'm glad you came."

He nodded, but his muscles tensed as they joined the river of people flowing toward the building. He hadn't considered how many people might be here this morning. Sweat pricked the back of his neck even as snow landed on his face.

He never should have said yes to this. But he hadn't wanted to see the disappointment that flitted on Leah's face every time he declined her invitations to church. Plus, his mom had always taken them to church on Thanksgiving, and he'd felt a sudden, unexpected nostalgia for that family feeling this morning as he'd stood in Leah's kitchen.

As they stepped through the doors, Dan greeted him with a handshake and a pat on the shoulder. Austin's eyes darted around the large lobby, crowded with groups of people talking and greeting one another. Beyond them, the sanctuary was even more packed. His jaw tensed as he checked over his shoulder for the door. As long as he could see it—as long as he knew there was a way out—he'd be fine.

He was pretty sure.

"Where do you—" Leah cut off as her eyes searched his face. "What's wrong?"

He shook his head, clearing his throat and trying to put on a halfway normal expression. "Nothing. What were you going to say?"

Concern hovered in Leah's eyes, and she moved closer to his side. "I was going to ask where you want to sit."

He did a quick survey of the sanctuary. "How about there?" He pointed to a small section of open seats near the back. It might be a tight squeeze, but it was better than being in the middle of the crowd.

Leah gave him an odd look but led the way. He silently thanked her for not pointing out that there were at least two nearly empty rows near the front of the church.

After squeezing past three people's legs, they settled into the empty spots, Jackson on one side of him and Leah on the other. As Leah folded her hands and closed her eyes and Jackson picked at a hangnail, Austin concentrated on taking a few calming breaths.

He wasn't in danger here. There was no reason for him to count the number of steps from here to the exit.

Fourteen.

Solely to distract himself, he picked up a Bible from the rack hanging on the back of the seat in front of him. He paged through it, not paying attention to the words. It wasn't like they meant anything.

Next to him, Leah shifted, her arm brushing against his, and he couldn't resist turning toward her. Her smile was as ready as ever.

He almost leaned over and told her how beautiful she looked, but at that moment, her brother's voice came over the church's sound system.

Leah turned toward the front of the church, and Austin followed suit.

As he went through the familiar motions of the service, he worked to steel his heart against what he was hearing. Just because he was here didn't mean he was going to fall for all this mumbo jumbo again.

Every once in a while, he allowed himself a glance at Leah, who appeared to be loving every moment of the service.

Austin almost envied her. His life would certainly be simpler if he hadn't had to learn the hard way that God was no more than a fairy tale or a nice idea.

At the front of the church, Dan stood at a small podium.

He took a moment to look around the crowded sanctuary. "So, how's your Thanksgiving going so far? Do you have a lot to be thankful for? Food? A home? Family?" Dan bobbed his head up and down a few times, as did many of his listeners.

Austin stopped himself from rolling his eyes. Could this be any more cliché?

"Yeah, me too." Dan braced his hands on the podium and leaned forward. "Now, I know it's Thanksgiving and all, but let's be real here for a second. Are there some things you're *un*thankful for? Things you're maybe angry with God for?"

Austin stilled. Were preachers allowed to say things like that in church?

"Maybe you lost your job this year," Dan continued. "Or maybe you've had some health issues. Maybe someone close to you died."

Tension zapped through Austin's body, and he winced as a phantom pain sliced his missing foot.

"So what are we supposed to do with those things? Say, 'Thanks God, but no thanks? I'll thank you for everything else, but I can't really be grateful for *that*?'"

Dan paused, as if thinking, then picked up his Bible. "Actually, listen to what God calls us to do. In First Thessalonians, Paul says we are to 'Rejoice always, pray continually, give thanks in all circumstances, for this is God's will for you in Christ Jesus.'"

Dan closed his Bible and shook his head. "Unbelievable, isn't it? You're telling me God expects me to give thanks in *everything*—even the bad things? Not only that, but he wants me to *rejoice* in them? What is he, crazy?" Dan held up a hand. "I know, I know. You're thinking I shouldn't be standing up here calling God crazy. But you know you're thinking it too. You're thinking, if God wants me to thank him for those things, he can think again."

Dan stepped out from behind the podium to pace in front of the church. "But that's exactly what God is saying we need to do. He says, 'Give thanks for *everything*.' Even the bad things."

Dan ran a hand through his hair. "But why? Why would God want us to thank him for the bad things that happen to us?" He stopped pacing and scanned the congregation.

Austin wanted to make himself look away, but he couldn't. He had to know—why would anyone give thanks for all the bad that had been heaped on them? Why should he give thanks for losing his leg and his friends?

"It's because—" Dan spread his arms wide. "It's because those things are blessings too."

Austin let out a harsh breath and shook his head. Unbelievable. It was one thing to say he should be thankful that he'd lost so much. But to say it was a blessing? That was taking things too far.

Leah glanced over at him, but he couldn't face the concern in her eyes. He needed to pull it together, think about something else until Dan was done talking.

But he couldn't shut out Dan's voice. "I'm not saying we're always going to see these things as blessings. Maybe we'd be better off calling them blessings in disguise. And sometimes the disguise is really good. So good that we might never see how they could be blessings while we're on this side of heaven. But God sees. God knows. He knows how even these hard things, these things that make us so angry, are working for our good. In Romans 8:28, Paul writes, 'And we know that in all things God works for the good of those who love him, who have been called according to his purpose.'" Dan looked up, and Austin could have sworn that his eyes traveled straight to the back of the church. "It's pretty easy to see that, to believe it, when things are going well for us, isn't it? When we have the dream job and money in the bank and a healthy family. When we're coasting."

Austin tried to remember the last time he'd felt like he was coasting. Maybe before Mom died? Maybe longer ago than that?

Dan started pacing again. "But what about when things go wrong? What about when we hurt? What about when the people we love hurt? Is that all for our good? Because if it is, maybe I don't want all things to work for my good, right? I'll take okay, I'll take medium instead of good, if it means I don't have to have all these heartaches, right?"

Austin's jaw clenched until his teeth ached, and he was suddenly too aware of the press of bodies around him.

Only fourteen steps to the exit. It was no big deal. He wasn't trapped. He wasn't in danger.

And yet.

He couldn't sit here another second.

He half rose, and Leah leaned closer, whispering, "Are you all right?"

But he could only shake his head and try to remain inconspicuous as he climbed over first Jackson and then the three people at the end of the row.

Eight more steps.

He pushed through the doors into the lobby, sucking in a deep breath as they closed behind him. Away from the press of bodies, Austin's pulse slowed, and the squeezing in his chest loosened. But the lobby must have had speakers because Dan's voice had followed him out of the sanctuary.

"But God doesn't want okay for you," Dan was saying. "He doesn't want medium. He wants *good* for you. Eternal good. And sometimes the way he brings about that good is through blessings in disguise."

Austin eyed the exterior doors. Maybe he should wait outside. He took a few steps toward them, but something in Dan's voice made him slow and then stop. He dragged himself to the far side of the room, where a comfortable looking couch sat in front of a large stone fireplace.

"I'm going to ask you to do something now. Something that it's going to feel really weird to do on Thanksgiving. But humor me." Even from out here, Austin could hear the congregation's gentle chuckle before Dan's voice picked up again. "I want you to close your eyes." He waited a second. "Go ahead. If everyone does it, no one will look foolish." Another twitter from the crowd.

"Good. Now—" Dan continued. "I want you to make a list in your mind of all the things you're *not* thankful for this year. The things you're mad at God about. And I want you to confess those things to

God. Tell him, 'God, I'm mad about this.' Don't worry, he's a big God. He can take it. I'll give you a minute for that."

Austin stared at the rough stone of the fireplace. He wasn't going to close his eyes, but that didn't stop him from making a list. He was angry about his leg. And Tanner. And Isaad. He was angry that Jackson had found his mother dead and had grown up without a family. He was angry that he'd grown up without a father. He was angry that he was too broken to ever be fixed.

"Got your list?" Dan's voice came over the speaker again, and Austin let out a shaky breath.

It wasn't rational. He knew that. How could he be mad at God when he didn't believe in God anymore?

But that didn't change the fact that he was.

"Now—" Dan lowered his voice, but Austin could still hear him too well. "Here's the tough part. I want you to surrender all of those things to God. Ask him to change your heart and to give you peace with each one of those things. Ask him to help you see them as blessings in disguise."

No.

Thankfully, there was no one else in the lobby to see how hard he was shaking his head, to see him get up and pace in front of the fireplace.

No.

This was where he drew the line.

He could maybe admit that he was mad at a God he claimed not to believe in. But he wasn't about to ask that same God to give him peace with those things. He didn't want peace with them.

He wanted to be angry.

He had a *right* to be angry

He worked on tuning out the rest of the service.

It didn't matter what Dan said.

It wasn't like Austin believed any of this anyway.

Chapter 22

$\mathcal{L}$eah's eyes tracked to Austin.

Again.

Instead of working on the serving line with her, he'd chosen to stay in the kitchen, filling glasses of milk and juice. She'd tried to talk to him after church, to make sure he was okay, but all he'd say was that he'd needed some air.

But there was more to it than that, she could tell. That haunted look, the one that had started to fade over the past couple weeks, had overtaken his expression again.

She forced herself to dollop mashed potatoes onto the next plate. With one hand, she gripped the edge of the table to hold herself upright. She'd never tell anyone, but her head had started to pound again, and the whole room seemed to be swaying.

As she scooped another batch of potatoes, a warm hand covered hers. "Why don't you take a break?" Austin's voice was low and close to her ear, and a warm shiver went down her back. "I'll take over for you."

She shook her head. She hadn't been able to help prepare the meal. The least she could do was serve it.

But Austin had already stripped the spoon out of her hand.

He dropped a serving of mashed potatoes onto a plate. "I promise we'll come find you if we need anything. Why don't you go lay on that comfy couch in the lobby?" He rested the potato spoon in the bowl and stepped back from the serving line. In one deft movement, he pulled his blue sweater over his head, revealing a plaid button-down underneath. He held the sweater out to her. "Use this for a pillow. Or a blanket."

Leah took it, trying not to notice that it was still warm from the heat of his body. Or that it carried his pleasant scent.

She should argue, but the prospect of lying on a couch right now was too tempting. Reluctantly, she took off her apron and slipped out of the kitchen and through the quiet hallways to the lobby. Being sick for Thanksgiving hadn't been part of the plan. But at least she had people she could rely on to take care of things.

People like Austin.

It was her last thought before she nestled her head into Austin's sweater, closed her eyes, and was out.

She was pretty sure it was only ten minutes later that someone was shaking her.

"Leah."

The voice whispering her name was familiar, comforting, and her lips slid into a smile.

"Leah." The voice was more insistent this time, and she cracked her eyes open to find Austin's face inches from hers.

"Hey." His mouth curved into a teasing smile. "Going to sleep all day?"

She blinked, trying to focus. "Sorry. What do you need?"

"Nothing. Just you."

Her eyes snapped open all the way, and he seemed to realize what he'd said. "I mean— To take home— To come with me so I can drive you home."

Leah was pretty sure her face must be as red as his, but she pushed herself into a sitting position. The moment she did, the headache that had eased while she slept returned with renewed vigor. She closed her eyes and rubbed at her temples.

"Here. Let me." Even without opening her eyes, she could feel Austin step closer. His hands gently nudged hers out of the way, then his fingers were pressing gently into her temples, moving in slow circles.

Leah's shoulders tensed, but the motion eased her headache, and after a second, she relaxed into it. Austin's hands slid further back on her scalp, into her hair, still moving in those slow circles.

"That's much better," Leah murmured.

"Good." Austin's voice was low, but he kept massaging.

Leah should tell him to stop. Her headache was almost gone now. But having his hands in her hair felt too good.

"Dan sent me up to see what was taking so . . ." That was Peyton's voice. Leah would recognize it anywhere. Along with the laughing, I-told-you-so note to it as she trailed off.

Austin's fingers jerked out of her hair, and he took three quick steps backward before bumping into a chair.

Leah could only pray Peyton wouldn't say anything stupid that would make her friendship with Austin awkward.

As Peyton reached them, her eyes flicked from one to the other, and she could barely suppress her smile. But apparently God had heard Leah's prayer because Peyton simply said, "Dan wanted you to know your mom can't make it to dinner because of the storm. And he said to tell you not to feel obligated to come if you're not feeling up to it."

Leah had never missed Thanksgiving dinner with her family. But right now the idea of doing anything but going home and snuggling into bed was more than she could handle.

"I do have a headache." Leah rubbed at her head again to show Peyton that was why Austin's hands had been in her hair. And for no other reason. "Is it really that snowy out?"

"There's a good eight inches out there already." Austin glanced toward the church doors, where the afternoon was quickly darkening into dusk.

"Maybe I better skip it this year." She turned to Austin. "Unless you wanted to go? I'm sure I'll be fine."

Austin shook his head. "I think we should get you home."

Leah pretended not to notice the pointed look Peyton directed her way.

"I'll send Jackson up." And with that, Peyton was gone again, though Leah was almost sure she saw her friend shoot Austin a wink as she sauntered down the hallway.

An awkward silence descended on them. Leah started to rub at her temples again, then dropped her hands into her lap. The last thing she needed was for him to think she wanted another scalp massage.

"I'll go pull the truck up," Austin finally said. "That way you won't have to walk through the snow."

"That's all right. I'll be—" But Austin was already on his way out the door.

A minute later, his truck pulled up outside, just as Jackson entered the lobby.

"Hey, dude." Leah tried to gauge Jackson's mood. "How did you like helping with the meal?"

Jackson shrugged, but his eyes looked brighter than usual.

The moment they stepped through the front doors, Leah gasped. She knew Austin had said they'd gotten eight inches of snow already. And she'd seen eight inches of snow plenty of times in her life. But the world had been completely transformed between the time she'd gone into church this morning and now.

The parking lot had been recently plowed, but a thick layer of snow covered the few remaining cars. Snowflakes filled the sky as well, sparkling in the streetlights that had just turned on. One landed on her lashes, and she blinked it away, smiling. Winter had always been her favorite season, and she was fine with it coming early. It made everything feel more Christmassy.

Austin already had the passenger door open for her, and she climbed into the truck. They rode in silence for a while, but finally she couldn't stand it any longer. "So, are you going to tell me where you learned to cook like that? People were raving about how good the turkey was." More than they usually raved about her turkey. She'd have to get him to spill the recipe.

"Picked it up here and there." He turned down the street that led to her house.

"Well, I feel like a sucker, making you dinner all these nights." Leah kept her voice light, so he'd know she was joking. She enjoyed making food for people, whether or not they knew how to cook for themselves. "Why were you always getting takeout if you could cook like that?"

Austin's shrug was easy, but the line of his jaw tightened.

Apparently, cooking was a touchy subject.

She closed her eyes and snuggled into the warmth of the truck. But too soon, she felt the vehicle slow and turn, and then the engine shut down.

"We're home," Austin whispered. A second later, he was opening her door and reaching to help her down. Against her better judgment, she set her palm into his. She was too tired to trust she could step down herself without landing on her face. A zip of recognition flew up her skin at the touch, but she pretended not to notice it.

As soon as she was down, Austin let go of her hand, but instead of moving ahead of her through the snow, he wrapped an arm around her shoulders and tucked her into his side. She should protest. But she was too sleepy. And his warmth felt too nice.

At the door, Austin let go of her, and the night air crawled down her neck. She shivered.

"I know you're tired." Austin opened the door for her. "But could we talk for a minute?"

Everything in Leah told her to say no.

Austin had hurt Jackson with his refusal to participate in the father-son event the other day.

But he'd also gotten Jackson involved in helping out with the community dinner.

And he'd pretty much saved the whole meal from disaster.

The least she could do was take a minute to listen to him.

Chapter 23

*A*ustin sat on Leah's couch, cracking his knuckles as he waited for her to make the tea she'd insisted they needed.

Now that he'd decided to do this, he just wanted to get it over with.

Not that he was sure doing this was the best idea. But he owed her an explanation for what had happened with Jackson the other night. And if he was going to ask her to consider a more-than-friends relationship with him, she needed to know the truth.

But the longer she took, the less certain he was that he should do it. Not the part about telling her about his leg. That he was going to do one way or the other. But what he wanted to do after that—asking her on a date—that he was a lot less sure of.

"Here we go." Leah's voice sounded strained as she carried two mugs into the living room, and he rose to take them from her, setting them on the coffee table and gesturing for her to sit.

She looked tired.

Maybe he should wait until a better time.

No.

No more excuses.

"So what did you want to talk about?" Leah's fingers fidgeted with a strand of her hair. Was she nervous? Did she sense what he wanted to ask her? Did she want him to?

Austin pushed the questions aside. First, he had to get past telling her about his leg.

He exhaled. Here went everything. "I wanted to apologize for the other night. I feel like I owe you—"

Leah waved a hand for him to stop, and he obeyed. "You don't owe me anything. I get that it was probably weird for you to take your neighbor's kid to a father-son thing. I shouldn't have put that on you." She blew on her tea and took a sip, not lifting her eyes to him.

"That's just it." Austin slid closer to her on the couch, so that their knees nearly touched. "It wasn't weird at all. I was looking forward to it. I like spending time with Jackson." He didn't add that he liked spending time with her too. That would come soon enough, assuming this part went well.

Leah let her eyes meet his for a second, and he had to look away before he kissed her right here and now.

"What was it then? Did I give you the impression I expected more?" Her cheeks grew fiery, and he almost reached a hand to cool them. "You know," she mumbled, "between us?"

Austin nearly laughed out loud. She had most definitely not sent that signal.

"It was hockey," he said simply.

Her forehead creased. She was clearly waiting for more, but he couldn't get the rest out.

"And you didn't want to make a fool of yourself because you don't skate?"

Austin shook his head. "I don't mind making a fool of myself now and then." His voice was hoarse, and he bent to grip the cuff of his pants. "I couldn't skate because of *this*." With a quick inhale, he pulled the hem up to his knee, exposing his entire prosthetic, from the black carbon fiber shell at the top to the titanium rod that disappeared into the semi-lifelike foot shell inside his shoe.

Leah's hands jumped to cover her mouth, but he heard her gasp through them. Her eyes filled with tears, and his stomach sank.

He didn't know what he'd hoped.

That she'd take one look at it, say, "That's nice," and move on with her night?

"I'm sorry." He spoke past the knives at the back of his throat. "I didn't mean to upset you."

But before he could comprehend what was happening, her arms went around his back. They were warm and soft, and he found himself sinking into them, his arms coming up to circle her. He inhaled her cinnamony scent, and his heart eased for the first time in a year.

"I'm sorry." She pulled away after a minute, and Austin had to fight the urge to gather her back to him. "I didn't mean to—"

He tried to convey that he hadn't minded—far from it—with his smile, and she seemed to accept that.

"I had no idea. I mean you run and you climbed my ladder and . . ." She cut herself off. "But I shouldn't have assumed you were blowing Jackson off about the skating. I'm sure when you tell him, he'll understand."

Austin's stomach flipped. Telling Leah was one thing. But telling Jackson, who'd already seen so many awful things in his short life? That he couldn't do, not yet.

Leah must have read it in his expression. "You don't have to tell him yet. But I think you should. Soon."

He nodded. He wasn't making any promises. But he'd try.

"Do you mind if I ask how it happened?" Leah's voice was tentative.

He longed to say that he didn't mind. That he'd be happy to tell her everything. But he couldn't talk about it. Not with her. Not with anyone. His last therapist had called it avoidance. He called it survival.

Still, he owed her something at least. "I was in Afghanistan." Saying it felt like peeling off his own skin.

He looked at the ceiling, trying to come up with something else he could tell her without collapsing the careful walls he'd built up around that day.

Next to him, he could hear the quiet in and out of her breathing. Its softness calmed him.

Without meaning to, he found himself talking.

He tipped his head back to rest on the couch cushion and closed his eyes. "It was last Christmas."

"Oh." Her voice said that she finally understood why he didn't like Christmas.

He could feel the muscles in his jaw working, but it took a minute to get the words out. "We were on a routine patrol, my buddy Tanner and I. I was supposed to be driving, but he wanted to. Said it would remind him of being home for Christmas and driving his wife and kids to visit family." Already he had to stop and clear his throat. "He was driving, and we saw this kid we'd befriended playing along the side of the road."

He opened one eye a crack and tipped his head toward her. She watched him, her expression a mixture of compassion and tension. "He was about Jackson's age. Isaad." He rubbed a hand over the rough scar on his jaw. That kid had been something special. "I told Tanner to pull over and pick Isaad up and we'd give him a ride, kind of as a Christmas present."

His hands fisted and he pressed them into his eyelids. "We weren't supposed to do that, and Tanner was a rule follower. But he was also a good guy." He licked his lips. "He stopped, and Isaad got in. I was joking with him about giving him a lump of coal, and he was laughing." Even now he couldn't help smiling at the memory of the sound. "He had the best laugh, and I was watching him. I wasn't scanning the road in front of us, the way I was supposed to be." His voice cracked, and he sucked in several deep breaths.

A soft hand fell into his, and he squeezed it, unable to look at her. But now that he'd started talking, he couldn't stop. Even though he knew he should. Leah shouldn't have to carry this burden too.

"It all happened so fast. One minute Isaad was laughing, the next everything was chaos. It felt like the world had blown apart." He exhaled. "Which I guess it had."

Leah slid closer, pressing her other hand into his arm.

"It was an IED." He opened his eyes and stared at the ceiling. "I mean, I had seen what they could do. I'd picked up bodies that had—" He cleared his throat again. She didn't need that image in her head. "But I never knew what it was like to go through it. The funny thing is, some guys don't remember it at all afterward. But I can't forget." He gripped the back of his neck.

He remembered what it felt like to fly through the air, his body completely out of his control. He remembered hitting the ground and having no idea where he was or what had happened to Tanner and Isaad. He remembered sitting up and seeing his leg completely mangled and knowing right in that moment that there was no way he'd be able to keep it.

"I prayed," he whispered. "Before I looked for them. I prayed so hard that Isaad and Tanner had survived too." But when he'd opened his eyes, the first thing he'd seen was Isaad, staring up at the sky with empty eyes. He'd clawed his way to the boy's side, even though he knew it was too late. Then he'd crawled across the sand and rocks, pain screaming through his shattered leg, to find Tanner. Only he'd blacked out before he got to him. He didn't find out Tanner was gone until he woke in the helicopter.

He pressed his lips together and closed his eyes again, but moisture rained down on his cheeks, and his breath was ragged. "Neither of them made it."

"I'm so sorry." Leah's whispered words washed over him, and he dared to look at her. Tears glistened on her cheeks too, and he reached to wipe them away.

The feel of her soft skin under his fingertips reminded him of the reason he hadn't wanted to tell her any of this in the first place.

He sat abruptly, pulling his hand away and scrubbing at his own cheeks. "I'm sorry. I didn't mean to burden you with all of that." He shifted to stand—he should go—but she grabbed his arm and held him in place.

"Thank you for telling me." Her voice was a balm, and he leaned closer to her.

Her eyes went to his jaw. "Is this from then too?" Her fingers lifted to touch the jagged scar that ran from his jaw up to his hairline, and he flinched involuntarily.

She lifted her hand. "Sorry, does it hurt?"

He shook his head. "No. It's just kind of hideous."

Her eyes locked onto his. "It's not hideous. It's beautiful. A reminder of what God brought you through."

"Yeah. Right." He wasn't exactly sure it was God who had brought him through. More like sheer dumb luck. Otherwise, why hadn't Tanner and Isaad made it too? They certainly deserved to survive more than he did.

"It is," Leah insisted. "And God knows what it's like to be scarred. Jesus had scars too. For us."

Austin swallowed. It sounded like something Tanner would say. But he wasn't in the mood for a conversation about Jesus.

Even so, he couldn't make himself leave her side.

"I should get home," he whispered. "Let you get some rest."

She nodded, but neither of them moved.

Austin searched her eyes. There was something there that hadn't been there before.

He bent his head a fraction closer. She didn't move. He dared another fraction. And then another.

One more fraction, and their lips would meet. Austin inhaled and closed his eyes. He could already feel—

"Ned needs more food." Jackson's voice sent Leah rocketing to the far end of the couch.

Austin exhaled a long breath, watching the squirrel scurry from one of Jackson's shoulders to the other.

The critter would be a lot cuter if he hadn't just cost Austin the kiss he'd been dreaming of for days.

"I'll put it on my list." Leah's voice was stilted, and Jackson gave each of them a weird look before retreating to his room.

Leah jumped to her feet, and Austin pushed himself off the couch more slowly, heading for the door. Ever since that first time he'd almost kissed her, she'd stopped seeing him out when he left. But this time he could feel her right behind him.

He turned to say goodnight, but before he could say anything, she lifted a hand to his scar again.

He closed his eyes as her fingers traced it.

She was making it nearly impossible to fight the urge to kiss her.

"Austin." Her whisper drew him closer. He only had a second to grasp what was happening before her lips met his.

His gasp was buried in their kiss as his arms went around her back. Her lips were just what he'd imagined—warm and soft, with the slightest hint of cinnamon.

When she pulled away, a smile tickled her lips, but worry lines furrowed her brow.

"I'm—"

He lifted a hand and smoothed a palm over her cheek. "Don't you dare apologize for that."

Her giggle was slightly giddy, and the sound went right through him. He could not make himself stop grinning.

"I was planning to decorate the tree tomorrow." Her smile was just as persistent as his. "If you wanted to come over and join us."

Decorating a Christmas tree was the last thing he wanted to do.

But if it meant spending time with Leah . . .

"I'll be there."

Chapter 24

Joy hummed through Leah, and she did a twirl in her bedroom as she got dressed the next morning.

She should be absolutely freaked out. She should be trying to figure out a way to stuff Austin back into the friend zone he'd so deftly escaped.

But she didn't want to. Not even a little bit.

She brushed a finger over her lips, swiping on a thin layer of gloss.

Hoping to attract Austin to your lips again?

Leah giggled to herself. She couldn't deny that she'd very much enjoyed kissing him. She could still taste the faint peppermint of his lips on hers. Another giggle sneaked out, and she covered her mouth. Jackson was going to think she was crazy, laughing to herself in here.

Her eyes fell on the bouquet of silk flowers she'd caught at Dan and Jade's wedding. Though, to be fair, she hadn't so much caught it as Jade had chucked it right at her head.

Obviously, Leah didn't put any stock in that old superstition. She'd only kept the bouquet as a fun memento of the wedding.

But as she considered the flowers now, she flashed back to all the times she'd prayed for a husband in the past. When God hadn't seen fit to answer that prayer with a yes, she'd switched to praying for contentment with her single status. And God had more than given her that.

She was beyond content on her own.

Or, at least, she had been.

But now? Now everything was a mess. A big, confusing, delicious, kissing mess.

Should she start praying for a husband again?

With a sigh, she sank onto the bed. Look at her. She was being foolish. One kiss and here she was, picturing herself walking down the aisle.

Help me to know your will in this, Lord. She ducked her chin as she sank into the familiar intimacy of prayer. *Guide Austin and I in our relationship, whether that's as friends or as . . . more.*

The thought sent a thrill through her, but she ignored it. She had to wait on God's will.

A knock echoed through the house, and Leah jumped, pressing a hand to her middle as an unexpected case of the flutters hit her. How was she going to greet him? Would he try to kiss her? Did she want him to kiss her?

She couldn't decide if it was fortunate or unfortunate that she'd never find out, since Jackson was already on his way to answer the door, Ned balanced on his outstretched arm.

"Don't let him get outside," Leah called down the hallway. The squirrel had grown a lot, but after it had been hand-raised, Leah didn't want to contemplate what would happen if it got outside.

"Duh," Jackson shot over his shoulder as he pulled the door open, then snatched the squirrel's tail just in time to keep it from jumping.

Leah's eyes went from the squirrel to the doorway. Maybe it was the morning light, or maybe it was his soft smile, but Austin looked different today. Happy.

"Good morning." His voice reached for her, and she stepped closer.

"Morning." She couldn't make herself speak louder than a whisper.

"How did you sleep?" Austin's eyes held a gentle light.

Jackson thrust the squirrel at Austin before she could answer. "Ned wants to say hi."

Austin turned to the boy as the squirrel scampered up his arm. "He's gotten big. You must be taking good care of him."

Leah let out a slow breath. She had to get her feelings in check. She could be in the same room with Austin without needing to kiss him the entire time.

Or even one time.

Anyway, they had a Christmas tree to decorate.

Two hours later, as she placed the last ornament on a branch, Leah had to wonder. Maybe she'd been wrong. Maybe she and Austin were best off as friends.

Jackson had ducked out of decorating almost immediately, leaving her to work side-by-side with Austin. Alone.

And yet Austin hadn't made a single attempt to kiss her again. Or to hold her hand. Or to touch her in any way.

If anything, he seemed to be doing everything he could to keep his distance.

They'd talked. Laughed. The same way they had dozens of times before.

As friends.

Which was . . . fine.

Like she'd said, she'd wait for God's will on this one. And if his will was for them to remain nothing more than friends, she could live with that.

Scratch that. She could more than live with it. She preferred it.

"There." She stepped back from the tree. "Perfect."

"Mmm hmm." But Austin's eyes were on her, and she felt suddenly self-conscious.

"How about some hot cocoa?"

Austin nodded, but he seemed to be deep in thought. As she retreated to the kitchen and got out the mugs, she worked to convince herself that she was content. That they could pretend last night had never happened and move on with their friendship intact.

By the time the cocoa was ready, she had a plan. She knew exactly what she was going to say.

She wouldn't apologize for the kiss, exactly, since he'd asked her not to. But she'd make it clear it wouldn't happen again.

Confident that it was the right decision, she picked up the mugs and carried them to the living room. But the moment Austin's eyes landed on her, she nearly lost her resolve.

He strode across the room, took the mugs from her, and set them on the table, then caught both of her hands in his.

"Austin, wait." She had to get this out. "I think we need to talk about last night."

He shook his head. "I told you not to apologize for that."

"I'm not." She had to look away, or she wouldn't go through with this. "I'm just saying I didn't mean for it to happen. And it won't happen again."

She tugged her hands out of his and moved toward the Christmas tree, her eyes falling on the heart ornament her dad had given her two years ago—his last Christmas on earth. He'd reminded her that there were many kinds of love in this world and that they were all wonderful. But the one love she always needed—the one love that would always be there for her—was the love of God. His agape, never-ending love.

"Why not?" Austin's voice was soft, and she appreciated that he didn't move closer.

She shrugged. "It's not a good idea."

"Why not?" he repeated, and Leah blinked back the sting behind her eyelids. She wanted so badly to say, never mind, they should absolutely kiss again.

173

But what happened when Austin realized that kissing had been a mistake? When he came to his senses and realized he only wanted to be friends with her after all—and maybe not even that?

She didn't have only herself to think about. There was Jackson to consider too. If she and Austin dated and then broke up, what would that do to the boy?

She heard Austin come up behind her, but he didn't touch her. "Peyton and Jade warned me that you've been hurt before." His voice was so gentle.

She swallowed but nodded. There was no point in denying it.

"You know I would never hurt you, right?"

But Leah couldn't answer. It was what Gavin had said too. And she believed he'd meant it. No one ever *wanted* to hurt someone. It was just what happened.

"Look, I'm not asking you to kiss me again."

Leah couldn't help but laugh at that. She glanced over her shoulder at him. He looked completely earnest and slightly vulnerable—and entirely adorable.

"All I'm asking—" He reached for her, and she let him wrap his hand around hers. "Is if we can do something together sometime. Go somewhere."

"I was going to take Jackson—"

"Without Jackson." His voice was firm, and he spun her to face him. "Peyton said I had to be absolutely clear about this, so— I want to go as more than friends, Leah. I want to take you on a date."

Coming from him, the word had a pleasant undertone that made her feel warm and kind of melty inside.

She bit her lip, and his eyes tracked to that spot.

Did he suddenly want another kiss as much as she did?

"Okay." Her whisper came out sounding uncertain, and she cleared her throat and tried again. "Okay."

"Yeah?" The smile that spread across his face was so wide it brought out a dimple she'd never noticed before. "Are you sure?"

She swatted at him with a laugh. "Are you trying to unconvince me now?"

"No, absolutely not. In fact, just in case you need a little more convincing . . ." He bent his head closer, moving slowly, as if giving her time to change her mind.

But she lifted her face to his, closing her eyes. She had no desire to move away.

The instant his lips fell on hers, she knew.

They'd gone way past the line of friendship.

And she couldn't be happier.

Chapter 25

*A*ustin couldn't believe he'd managed to wait an entire week for this day.

Although he'd continued to have dinner with Leah and Jackson every night—and although he and Leah had exchanged more than one goodnight kiss—he'd been half waiting all week for her to cancel their date.

He finished ironing his blue and white dress shirt, then pulled it on. As he buttoned it, his mind hooked on his physical earlier today. He'd already analyzed it from every angle three dozen times. But no matter how he looked at it, the exam felt . . . anticlimactic. And disconcerting.

The doctor had asked a few questions, performed a regular physical exam on him, and then dismissed him. When Austin had asked whether the doctor could tell him if he qualified for reinstatement to active duty, all the bushy-eyebrowed man had said was, "You'll get a letter in the mail in the near future." He hadn't been able to give Austin a date or a time frame.

Which meant Austin was left with more waiting. More worrying about Chad, whom he still hadn't heard from.

He fastened the final button and shook off the thought. There was nothing he could do for Chad right now. All he could do was trust that his brother was safe.

Chad's words from the last time they'd spoken rang in his head yet again. *I wouldn't mind a prayer or two.*

Austin sighed and lifted his chin toward the ceiling. He'd gone to church with Leah and Jackson again on Sunday—and this time he'd managed to stay in his seat for the whole service. He even had to admit that some of the things Dan said—like about how this world was a bleak place full of man's corruption—made sense. No one had to tell Austin that twice. He was living proof. What he wasn't sure of yet was what Dan had said after that: That despite the evil in this world, people could know peace because Jesus promised he had overcome the world. That one day, those who believe in him would be called from this world of pain and sorrow to be with him forever in heaven.

"If there really is a heaven," he muttered now to his ceiling. *Please keep Chad safe.* It was the fullest extent of a prayer he could offer, but if God *was* real, it would have to be enough.

He pulled on his jacket and stocking cap, picking up the flowers he'd bought this afternoon.

A shot of adrenaline coursed through him as he opened the door and the night air hit him. A fresh layer of snow blanketed the grass. That would make tonight even more perfect.

With Peyton's help, he'd found a place so perfectly Leah, she could have created it herself.

At her door, he considered letting himself in, as he'd started doing lately. But this wasn't just dinner with a friend. It was a date with someone he hoped was becoming much more than that.

He rang the doorbell, examining the lights they'd hung together as he waited. But the door remained closed.

She wasn't going to stand him up, was she? Her car was in the driveway, and the lights inside were on. If she was trying to pretend she wasn't home, she was doing a pretty poor job of it.

He was reconsidering letting himself in when the door opened.

Austin gasped as his eyes fell on Jackson. The boy's nose was swollen to twice its normal size, and ugly black and purple bruises extended from the bridge of his nose down the sides and under his eyes.

"What happened?"

"She says she'll be ready in five minutes." Jackson turned and shuffled into the house.

"Seriously, dude. Did you get in another fight? I thought you were done with that." Austin followed the boy to the kitchen and laid a hand on his shoulder.

But Jackson shrugged him off. "What's it to you?"

"It's a lot to me, actually." Austin blocked the boy's exit from the room, and Jackson's eyes darted past him. "I care about you. And your mom."

"Whatever." Jackson grabbed a plate stacked with a PBJ off the counter and shoved around Austin.

Austin watched the boy march toward his room, debating whether to follow. But he decided to let it go for now. Instead, he moved to the cabinets and found a vase for the flowers, placing them in the middle of the counter. Then he went to the sink and started putting away the clean dishes. After so many meals here, this kitchen was more familiar to him than the one in his own rental house.

His back was to the kitchen entryway, but still he knew the moment Leah was there. He set down the plates he'd been stacking and crossed the room to wrap her in his arms.

"The flowers are beautiful. Thank you." She sighed and leaned into him, and he pressed his lips to the top of her head.

"I saw Jackson. I understand if you need to cancel tonight. We can stay here and watch a movie or something."

Leah leaned back far enough that he could see her eyes. She looked tired, but that familiar light still shone in them. "There's nothing else I can do at this point. I've talked and talked and talked. And I'm not sure if I'm getting through to him at all. I think I need a little space from him right now, to be honest."

Austin smiled at her. "In that case, grab your coat. And a hat. And gloves. Maybe a scarf. Oh, and make sure to wear boots."

She gave him a startled look. "Where are we going? Sledding?"

He grinned as he waited for her to bundle up. "Not exactly."

He wouldn't ruin this surprise for anything.

Not even for the adorable pout she was giving him right now.

Chapter 26

She'd tried pouting. She'd tried cajoling. She'd even tried kissing. But Austin wasn't budging. The man could keep a secret.

A ripple of anticipation winged through Leah as Austin squeezed her hand and looked over with a smile. "Almost there."

After the way her day had gone, this was exactly what she needed.

Just when she'd thought she was making progress with Jackson—or, to be more specific, that she and Austin were making progress with him—he went and punched a kid again. For no apparent reason, according to Mrs. Rice. She'd have to take the principal's word for it, since Jackson hadn't said a thing to her since she'd left work early to bring him home from school.

She didn't understand why every step forward with him brought forty steps back.

"Here we are." Excitement crept into Austin's voice as he pulled into a narrow gravel driveway. Leah worked to force out thoughts of Jackson. Tonight was about her and Austin.

"Where is here?" She peered out the window. There was a small handmade sign near the entrance, but in the dark, it was impossible to read what it said. As far as she could tell, they were in the middle of nowhere.

"You'll see." Austin's grin lit up the inside of the truck, and she couldn't help but return it.

He drove toward a large barn and parked the car behind it.

"Are we milking cows?"

Austin's chuckle warmed her. He jumped out of the truck and jogged around to open her door for her, holding out a hand to help her down.

"Come on." He tugged her toward the far side of the barn. A jingling reached her ears before they got there, followed by the soft nickering of a horse.

"Is this— Are there—" Leah's mouth fell open. He couldn't possibly have known. She swiped a gloved finger under her eyes.

"I'm sorry." Austin's face fell. "I should have asked if you liked— I wanted it to be a surprise, but we can leave if you don't want—"

She tightened her grip on his hand. "It's not that. I love sleigh rides. When I was a little girl, my dad started taking me on one every year, just me and him. Last year was the first year I hadn't been on one in probably twenty-five years. I really missed it, and . . ." She swiveled to take in the trees, the velvet of the night sky, and the man standing next to her. "And it's perfect. Thank you."

He let go of her hand and wrapped his arm around her shoulders instead, hugging her close to his warmth. "I'm glad you like it."

She could only nod, breathing in that warm scent that always said Austin to her.

A sleigh pulled by two beautiful black horses—one with a white patch over its eye—stopped alongside them, and the woman driving it invited them to step up.

Austin's hand moved to the small of her back as he helped her into the sleigh, then followed her up and slid onto the seat next to her. He unzipped his jacket to reveal a red plaid blanket, and she laughed as he tucked it around them.

"What other surprises do you have in store?"

But he only smiled and held her closer as the horses set off, their bells jingling merrily.

She relaxed in Austin's arms as the sleigh slid into a wooded area. With the tree branches glittering above them, the snow shushing beneath them, and a few snowflakes dancing around them, it was like a scene from a painting.

A very romantic painting.

When Austin had asked her on a date, she'd pictured dinner at the Hidden Cafe. Not a moonlit sleigh ride. Thank goodness Austin had a more romantic imagination than she did.

She sighed, completely content, and he leaned over and pressed a kiss onto the top of her head. "You like it?"

She nodded, her head rocking against the firm muscles of his arm.

Too soon, the sleigh slowed, and Austin helped her down. She tried not to show her disappointment that the ride was over already.

But as her feet hit the ground, she realized they weren't in the same place they'd started. "Wait. Where are we? Where's the barn?"

Austin steered her toward a trail lined with small lanterns. "Let's take a hike. There's a surprise at the end."

"Another surprise?" Leah let herself be led along, her gloved hand tucked into his. In spite of the cold, she'd be happy to stay out here all night.

But after a few minutes, they came to a bend in the trail.

Austin pulled her to a stop. "Close your eyes."

"What?" She spun in a circle, but there was nothing to see here aside from more trees. "Why?"

"Trust me."

She nodded and closed her eyes. She did trust him.

He wrapped a hand around her elbow, leading her forward. They walked like that for maybe fifty yards—it was hard to judge with her eyes closed—before Austin told her to open them.

"What was that all— Oh." She pressed her hands to her cheeks.

She'd never seen anything like this.

In front of them was a small village of glass-enclosed gazebos, each lit by strings of Christmas lights, each with smoke puffing out of a chimney on top, each with a single couple inside, seated at a candlelit table.

"We're in that one." Austin pointed to the left, toward an empty gazebo with white fairy lights strung across the ceiling and a flame dancing in the fireplace.

"What is this place?" Leah gazed around in wonder. It was like they'd been transported to some sort of winter wonderland. "How'd you find it?"

"I have my sources." He pulled her toward the gazebo and opened the door for her. A heady mix of wood smoke and savory herbs—thyme and rosemary, if she had to guess—drew her inside. The small space was warmer than she'd expected, and she pulled off her hat and gloves, running a finger through her locks to combat the hat head she was undoubtedly sporting.

As if reading the self-consciousness in the action, Austin stepped closer and caught her hands in his. "You look beautiful." He ducked his head and lowered his lips to hers.

She let herself be drawn into the kiss, but he pulled away much too soon.

"Sorry." He took a step back. "I promised myself I wouldn't do that until the end of the date." His eyes danced in the firelight, and Leah couldn't resist closing the space between them.

"Maybe we should call this the end of the date then."

His eyes widened, and she offered a smile. Where had those words come from? She wasn't the flirty type. Couldn't remember a time in her life she'd ever flirted, actually.

But right now, she was feeling playful, and the room made everything slightly magical, slightly unreal—or better than real.

"I guess we could do that." Austin's throaty response drew her closer, and before she could overthink it, she rose onto her toes and brought her arms around his neck, drawing him in until their lips met in a long, slow kiss.

Before Austin, she'd never known a kiss could make her feel like this. That it could make her feel precious and safe and beautiful and cared for and—

She refused to let herself think the last word that hovered at the edge of her thoughts. It was much too soon for that.

When they at last pulled apart, Austin ran a hand over her cheek. "Looks like you're full of your own surprises."

"I guess I am." She led the way to the table at the center of the gazebo, where candles flickered on either side of a covered platter.

She pulled off the lid.

"Oh my goodness. Seared scallops. My favorite. How did you know?"

He gave her a mysterious grin. "I told you—"

"It was Peyton." Leah laughed. She should have known. "Peyton helped you set this up, didn't she?"

Austin's expression turned sheepish, and he lifted his hands in surrender. "Sorry, I—"

But she shook her head. "Don't apologize. I think it's sweet that you went out of your way to make this special." She stepped around the table to kiss him again.

When she pulled back, she could not stop smiling. Goodness, she liked kissing this man.

Austin smiled too and reached for her plate to serve her a generous helping.

Leah took it from him with a grateful sigh and sat at the cozy table as he filled his own plate.

When he was seated, she folded her hands and bowed her head to offer a silent prayer.

"You can pray out loud if you'd like." Austin's voice was low and guarded, and she looked up to find him watching her.

"Do you want me to?" She wasn't going to force it. If praying with her made him uncomfortable, she wouldn't do it. Though she'd pray for a time when he might want to join her.

But he nodded. "I think so."

She gave him a gentle smile, then took a deep breath, sending up a quick silent prayer before she began. *Guide my words, Lord.* "Heavenly Father, thank you for this beautiful night you have given us together. Thank you for Austin, who is a thoughtful and giving man who has sacrificed so much for people who will never know what he's done for them." She swallowed back the emotion at the thought. If there were a way for her to tell the whole country what Austin had given up for them, she would. But she knew that wasn't what he was looking for. "Thank you for everything he has done for me and for Jackson. We ask, Lord, that you would touch Jackson's heart and help him to know not only how much we care about him, but how much you do. How you love him more than anyone on this earth ever could. Thank you that you love us so much that you sent your son to die for our sins. Even after Jackson has only been with me for such a short time, I can't imagine giving him up to save someone else. And yet you did that, Lord. You gave up your perfect son to save us, though we were anything but deserving. Help the knowledge of that guide everything we think, say, and do every day. Amen."

She kept her eyes closed for a moment after ending the prayer. She was afraid to lift her gaze to Austin's. Had she gone on too long? Had she scared him off?

But when she made herself meet his eyes, the look he was giving her wasn't one of anger or fear.

If she wasn't mistaken, it was one of hope.

Chapter 27

The truck's heater purred, pouring warmth from the vents and thawing their toes and fingers. Despite the frigid temperatures, the sleigh ride back to the truck had been much too short for Austin's liking.

If he could have, he would have stayed in that gazebo with Leah all night. After they'd finished eating, they'd sat and talked for an hour, and he'd even convinced her to dance with him. In spite of his bad leg, he hadn't moved too badly, if he did say so himself.

The gazebo had felt like a separate world. Like none of the cares and concerns that weighed on them out here existed in there. Leah had been carefree and happy and even—dare he say it?—slightly flirtatious. And he hadn't thought once about his physical or Afghanistan or Chad.

But he'd felt it all stealing back over them as they'd ridden in the sleigh, as if it was borne on the cold wind that snaked down their blanket and slipped through to their core.

Leah had grown quieter, and even he had a hard time keeping up the light tone.

He sneaked a glance at her out of the corner of his eye now. She caught his look and dropped the piece of hair she'd been absently twirling around a finger.

"What are you thinking about?" Though it'd only take one guess for him to figure it out.

Her sigh was heavy. "Sorry. I was thinking about Jackson. I'm going to have a talk with him when we get back. Tell him—" She shook her head. "I don't know what I'll tell him."

She angled toward him. "What were you thinking about?"

Somehow, his sigh was even heavier than hers had been. "Chad."

"I've been praying for him." Her hand came to rest on his arm.

How could one tiny touch like that be so reassuring?

"Me too." He could barely get the words out, but Leah's face lit up.

He didn't know how to tell her that his prayers weren't anything like hers. When she'd prayed before dinner, he could hear the conviction in her voice. She really believed God would hear her. That he would answer.

His prayers were more like shots fired wildly into the dark at a target he wasn't sure was there.

"I'd feel better if I heard from him. I can't wait to get back over there. Then I can be the one to watch his back."

Her hand tensed against his arm, and he turned his head to find her staring at him, open mouthed.

"You're going back? I thought— With your leg—"

"I've been on the temporary disability retired list for the past year. But with any luck, I won't be for much longer. I had my physical today, and if they find me fit for duty, I could be redeployed."

"When?" Leah's voice sounded strangled, and he glanced at her again. Her left hand remained on his arm, but her right was balled in her lap.

"Soon. I thought you knew."

She shook her head, blinking rapidly, and he repositioned his arm so he could take her hand. This was not how he'd have chosen to tell her.

"This doesn't change anything, you know. Unless you want it to." His heart nearly crumbled at the thought, but he had to let her decide this. It wouldn't be fair to drag her into a long-distance relationship she hadn't been prepared for. "I'm not saying it wouldn't be hard. But lots of guys have girlfriends or wives back home while they're deployed. And I do get leave and—"

"Austin." Leah squeezed his hand. "It doesn't change anything. I mean, I'd be worried about you, but I know that God is bigger than I am, and he's always watching over you."

He let out a long breath. Whether that was true or not didn't matter. What mattered was that she'd said yes.

"But can I ask you something?" Leah's voice was gentle, and Austin nodded, though he felt like he should protest. But that was ridiculous. There was nothing she could say right now that would tamp down the joy building in his chest.

"You said *if*. What happens if you're not found fit for duty?"

Austin shook his head. "Not going to happen."

It couldn't. He had to get back over there.

"But *if*, Austin," Leah insisted.

He sighed. Fine. He'd tell her the process. But he was going back.

"They could find that my injuries haven't stabilized enough and keep me on the temporary disability list and order another physical in a few months. Or—" He pressed his lips together. He hated to consider the other possibility.

"Or?"

"Or they could move me to the permanent disability list. Retire me."

He could feel Leah's eyes on him as she considered his answer. "And could you be content with that?"

The gentle question ripped through him like shrapnel.

"No." His answer was flat and immediate.

Leah didn't say anything, and he risked a look at her. But she was staring out the window.

"We're home." And just in time too. If this conversation continued, they might end up destroying this relationship before it had gotten off the ground.

He pulled into her driveway and walked her to the door.

"Do you want to come in and have some cocoa?" Her voice was tiny, hesitant, and it sliced him to know he was responsible for that.

He stretched his neck, trying to force himself to relax. She hadn't been trying to crush his hopes.

"I actually have a little bit of a headache. I think I'll go home and go to bed." He touched a hand to hers, then took a step backward.

"Austin, don't—" Tears sprang to Leah's eyes, and he silently cursed himself.

Did he call this not hurting her?

He moved close enough to wrap his arms around her. "I'm not upset. I promise. I just need some sleep. I'll see you tomorrow, okay?"

At her slight nod, he slid his hands to the back of her head and leaned in for a kiss, telling himself it was only his imagination that she barely returned it.

Chapter 28

Leah swiped at a stray tear as she pulled off her coat.

Austin hadn't meant to hurt her. He just had a headache. One she'd probably caused.

She'd only been trying to help, trying to make sure he saw the situation realistically—that he was prepared in case things didn't work out the way he wanted.

She wanted him to know that God was with him no matter what.

But instead of reassuring him, she may have ruined everything.

She dragged herself down the hall, rubbing at her head.

"Jackson, I'm home." She knocked on his as-always closed bedroom door, running a hand over her face one more time. Jackson didn't need to know anything was wrong.

She'd go over to Austin's in the morning and they'd talk, and everything would be fine.

Wouldn't it?

She drew in a rough breath and knocked again.

Of course it would be fine.

"Jackson? Please open the door so I can say goodnight." Another, longer sigh slipped out.

A mutiny from Jackson was not what she needed right now.

Not when she just wanted to pull on a pair of fuzzy socks to warm her still tingling toes and curl into bed.

"You have ten seconds." She raised her voice to make sure Jackson could hear. "And then I'm coming in there whether you open the door or not."

She counted backward in her head. When she got to three, she switched to counting out loud. "Three. Two. One."

Weariness tugged at her shoulders. She'd rather go to bed and deal with Jackson in the morning. But she'd said she was coming in, so now she had to follow through.

She lifted her hand to the doorknob slowly, giving him one last chance.

When it didn't open, she turned it.

The lights were off inside, and she opened the door farther to let light from the hallway brighten the space. "Don't tell me you're sleeping . . ."

Her eyes fell on the empty bed, and she flipped on the light. The peanut butter and jelly she'd made him sat untouched on his dresser, and the room was vacant, aside from Ned, who gave an excited squeak and ran back and forth in his cage with his tail lifted over his back.

"Jackson?" She backed out of the room and retraced her steps toward the front door. Had he been in the living room or the kitchen and she'd missed him when she walked past? She *had* been rather distracted.

But the kitchen was empty, as was the living room.

She opened the door to the basement, quashing down the rush of panic that threatened to take over. There was no reason to overreact. He'd probably gotten bored and was exploring downstairs.

She pounded down the wooden steps, calling his name.

No answer.

She stood at the bottom of the staircase, her breaths coming heavier than they should. "Jackson, this isn't funny. If you're down here, come out."

The furnace kicked in, making her jump, and she pressed a hand to her heart.

After a quick search of the mostly empty basement, she sprinted up the stairs and straight out the back door. Maybe he was collecting nuts for Ned.

But the yard was dark and empty, no footprints marring the fresh snow.

She tore through the house to Jackson's room. Clues. She needed clues about where he could be.

Maybe there was something going on at school tonight that he hadn't told her about, and he'd gotten a ride with a friend. It was a long shot, one she already knew couldn't be true, but she clutched at it, searching the floor for his backpack. There might be a note in it.

But the backpack was gone, as was, she noticed now, the sweatshirt from Austin that always hung on the closet doorknob and the watch she'd given him for his birthday, which had remained in its box on top of the bookshelf since then. Nausea rose in her gut as she lunged for his dresser and yanked the top drawer open.

Empty.

So was the next.

And the next.

The room seemed to spin, but she staggered out of it, down the hallway, and to the front door.

She needed Austin's help.

Right now.

Chapter 29

Austin leaned into his crutches as he reached for a bottle of water from the refrigerator. He popped the aspirin into his mouth and took a swig out of the bottle. He hadn't been lying to Leah about the headache, though he'd also needed some space before he said something he'd regret.

He knew she was only doing what she thought was best when she'd asked what he'd do if he weren't redeployed.

But that possibility wasn't something he could think about.

He hooked the water bottle between his fingers and maneuvered his crutches to the couch, propping his good foot on the coffee table. His laptop taunted him, silent as ever.

When are you going to call, Chad?

The wallpaper on the screen—a picture of him and Chad in front of a spectacular sunset in the Afghan mountains—mocked him, and he dropped his face into his hands, the edges of his scar rough against his skin.

A second later, he jumped as footsteps pounded up his porch stairs, followed by someone beating on the door.

"Austin!" Even through the door, Leah's voice set his heart on fire. As much as he'd wanted space, he hadn't wanted to leave things the way he had tonight.

He glanced at his crutches.

She knew about his prosthetic. But she'd never seen him without it on.

"Austin!" The urgency in her voice made him forget the debate. He grabbed his crutches and hopped to the door, wearing his best apologetic smile. "I'm sorry, Leah. I shouldn't have—"

The look on her face stole whatever he'd been planning to say next. "What is it? What's wrong?"

Her eyes were too wide and wild, skipping past him to the living room, and her breath came in short gasps even though she lived fewer than fifty steps away.

"Is he here?" She barreled past him into the house. "Please tell me he's here." Her voice pitched up an octave.

"Is who here?"

But Leah was no longer in the living room. She'd sprinted down the hall and was popping her head into every bedroom.

"Leah." He followed her, his crutches thumping quietly against the wood floor. "Leah, stop." He grabbed her elbow, pulling her to face him. "What's going on?"

She shook her head, gasping harder than before. "I thought maybe he—" She choked on a short breath. "I thought he'd be here. I thought—"

"Jackson?" His own pulse spiked. Was she saying she couldn't find him?

"I was sure he must be here. But if he's not—" Face ashen, she clutched at her arms.

"Shh." He leaned one crutch against the wall so he could pull her close. "It's okay. We'll find him. You looked everywhere at your place? Outside?"

She nodded into his chest. "Everywhere." Her voice was muffled by his sweatshirt. "Austin, his backpack is gone."

"That doesn't mean—"

"So are his clothes."

Austin's heart dropped, but he schooled his face into a calm expression, gripping her shoulder and sliding her back until he could look into her eyes. "We're going to get through this. Together. Okay?"

He waited for her slow nod. "It's so cold out there." Her teeth chattered as if she were the one out in the cold. "It's so cold, and he's just a kid."

Austin shook his head. "No. It's going to be all right. We're going to find him. He's probably nice and warm somewhere. I'm going to call the police and file a report. Why don't you call everyone else and ask them to start driving around to look for him? Maybe someone can call his classmates."

Leah's hand shook as she pulled out her phone, but she started dialing.

Austin took out his own phone and dialed the police. He didn't mean for the prayer to come out as he waited for someone to pick up, but it did.

Please let us find him.

Chapter 30

Two hours. They had been searching for her son for two hours, and no one had seen a sign of him. Austin's breath puffed into the air between them as he leaned on his crutches and studied the map of Hope Springs on his phone.

They'd already searched the entire downtown, and Grace and Emma were calling all of Jackson's classmates. Not that she had much hope he'd gone to one of them, since he'd never referred to any as friends. The rest of her friends were going door to door through the town, asking if anyone had seen the boy, and Jade had offered to sit at Leah's house in case Jackson came home.

Because of the extreme cold, the police were organizing their own search of the fields and forests around the town as well. They'd already sent patrolmen to search the beach, and Leah's breath locked in her chest every time she thought about the cold Lake Michigan water washing up on shore.

Jackson wouldn't have gone into the water.

She was sure of it.

Wasn't she?

A strangled sob fought its way up from her core, and she lifted a hand to her mouth to stifle it, but she couldn't keep it in any longer.

Austin pulled her into his arms without a word, their embrace slightly awkward around the crutches. She leaned into him, letting his strength hold her up.

"It's going to be okay," he murmured into her hair. "We're going to find him."

But she knew he was just as uncertain—just as scared—as she was.

She pulled away, a completely unjustified anger straightening her back. "You don't know that. He's a kid, Austin. He has no food. No shelter. No money. Nothing. He's one hundred percent alone." She crossed her arms over her chest, so he couldn't take her hand and give her empty assurances that everything would be fine.

"He has you." Steam rose from Austin's mouth, floating on the cold night air.

"A lot of good that does." Leah snarled at her own helplessness. "I can't do anything for him now."

"Look, let's go check—"

But Leah shook her head, defeat engulfing her. "Let's split up. We'll cover more ground that way."

"I'm not going to leave you alone, Leah." Austin moved his crutches toward her, but she backed up, ignoring the hurt in his eyes. She knew it was unfair, knew this wasn't his fault. But if she had been home with Jackson instead of on a date with Austin, none of this would have happened.

"I want to be alone right now, okay?" She bit back the fresh sobs that tried to wriggle free of the tight hold she had on them. She could deal with her emotions later. Right now, the only thing she cared about was finding Jackson.

"Okay." Austin's whisper cut at her, but she turned away and started walking toward her storefront. Maybe Jackson had sneaked in there for the night.

"Leah," Austin called behind her. She stopped but couldn't bring herself to turn around. "I'll pray for him."

Leah's nod was stiff. She knew she should be grateful that Austin would consider it. And she should do the same—had been trying to do the same all night.

Up until now, she'd always rejoiced to know God was in control. It was why she'd always been fine when he answered her prayers with no.

But if she prayed for Jackson's safe return and God answered that prayer with a no, she wasn't sure her faith could survive.

So she walked away, keeping her mind carefully blank.

The toes of Austin's good foot had gone numb. If only there was a way to numb his heart too.

The punch of Leah's words—"I want to be alone"—hit him right in the solar plexus as he watched her walk away.

When she disappeared around the corner, he forced himself to go in the opposite direction, all his senses on full alert for the slightest sign of movement. It was so cold out here. How warmly was Jackson dressed? How long could he survive out here on his own? Would they find him in time, or would—

It was too much. First his brother.

And now Jackson.

He shook off the thought. He might not be able to do anything for Chad right now. But he could help find Jackson.

Come on, Austin. Think.

A thirteen-year-old who didn't have any money couldn't get farther than he could walk. Unless he had hitchhiked. Austin nearly choked at the thought, and he had to knock it aside so he wouldn't fall into the same despair as Leah.

His eyes fell on the dark bus station. It was the only form of mass transportation in the small tourist town, and it was only open during the day. But if Jackson had left Leah's house right after she and Austin had gone on their date, the boy could have gotten here before it closed.

And if he had . . . A sick feeling rose in the back of Austin's throat. If he had, he could be in another state by now.

Heaviness dragged at his limbs, but he forced himself to make his way to the station. Maybe there was a phone number on the door he could call to find out who'd been working. Ask them if they'd seen a young boy traveling alone.

But the glass door boasted only a closed sign and posted hours—the station wouldn't reopen until nine the next morning. That was nine hours from now. They couldn't wait that long.

He called the police station and filled them in on his hunch, and they promised to investigate who had been working and where the last buses of the day had been headed.

Then he circled the perimeter of the small building, checking in every nook and cranny he could find, even the dumpster. But there was no sign anyone had been there recently.

He didn't understand. This wasn't how it was supposed to be. Leah was a good person. She was only trying to help this kid. To give him the family he'd never had. She shouldn't have to go through something like this.

It just went to show that she was wrong when she said God was in control. When she said to trust him. She'd trusted this so-called God, and look where it'd gotten her.

There was no God.

When he returned to the front of the building, Austin tried to peer inside. In the faint glow of the security lights, he could see the building was empty.

But he didn't care.

He lifted a hand to pound on the door as hard as he could.

The shock of the impact reverberated through his body, and he hit the door again. And then again, putting all his fear and pent-up anger into each blow.

It didn't make sense. It shouldn't make him so angry to realize, once again, that there was no God.

But he'd been starting to hold onto a tiny tendril of hope that maybe Leah was right and there was a God and maybe he did answer prayers.

And now.

Now he knew he'd been wrong about that. Again.

He dropped his forehead to the glass, letting its cold pierce through him. He'd run out of ideas. There was nowhere else to look.

A knifing pain sliced through him at the thought of Leah's loss.

Of his loss.

He hadn't meant to get close to Jackson—he'd warned himself not to—and yet over the past few weeks, Jackson had become more than the neighbor kid to him. The boy felt more like a son.

He almost didn't register the clicking sounds over the harsh in and out of his own breaths. He kept his eyes closed and worked to slow his breathing so he could hear better. It sounded kind of like the bolt of a lock.

His eyes popped open just as the door next to him pushed out.

Jackson stood on the other side, mouth open, staring at the spot where Austin's foot should have been.

Austin swung forward on his crutches, then let them drop to the ground as he pulled the boy into him with one arm. With the other, he reached into his pocket for his phone.

Chapter 31

Leah had never understood happy crying.

Until tonight.

She hadn't been able to slow the tears flowing down her cheeks since the moment Austin had called to tell her he'd found Jackson.

As the three of them sat crammed into the front of Austin's truck now, she swiped at her eyes. If she didn't get herself under control soon, both guys were going to think she was crazy.

She'd insisted that Jackson sit up here with them instead of in the back so that he could warm up after spending half the night in the bus station.

From the little Jackson had told Austin—and Austin had relayed to her—by the time Jackson had gotten to the bus station, the last bus had already left for the day. So he'd hidden in a supply closet until the station was closed and locked up for the night. He'd been planning to use money he'd swiped from Leah's purse to buy a ticket in the morning.

Every time she thought of it, her heart skipped. If they hadn't found him—if Austin hadn't been there—Jackson might have disappeared from her life forever.

But God had put Austin in exactly the right place at exactly the right time.

Even after her faithless refusal to pray.

Leah's heart swelled at the reminder that in spite of her own frailties and sins, God loved her. He was still working in her life even when she failed to acknowledge him.

She turned toward Jackson and Austin. It was impossible not to notice how the boy's gaze kept tracking to Austin's missing limb.

Leah wanted to tell him that it was okay, that it didn't change who Austin was, but she needed to let Austin be the one to address that.

When they pulled into the driveway, Austin shut off the truck's engine, and the three of them sat, their breaths the only sound in the small space.

Finally, Austin opened his door and slid off his seat, then reached into the back to grab his crutches.

The movement unstuck Leah from her seat, and she opened her door as well. The moment she was on the ground, Jackson scooted out past her and trundled to the front door.

Austin came around the truck to stand at her side.

"Thank you." There was so much more she needed to say, but she couldn't. She wound her hands between Austin's crutches and his torso to crush him in the tightest hug she could manage.

His hands rested on her back, and he dropped the lightest touch of a kiss onto the top of her head. "I'll let you get some sleep."

She nodded, though she didn't see how that would be possible. What if Jackson ran away again the moment she closed her eyes?

Austin glanced toward her house. "Unless you want me to stay. I don't sleep much anyway. I could sit up in the living room . . ."

Leah shook her head, but even she could tell the gesture lacked conviction. "You don't have to do that."

But Austin was already working his crutches toward the house. "Whatever makes things easier for you, that's what I have to do."

Leah followed him inside, offering her eightieth prayer of the night to thank God for him.

"I'm going to go talk to Jackson. Or try to at least." She didn't hold out much hope that he'd respond, given the fact that he hadn't said a word to her since he'd been found.

Austin squeezed her arm as she walked past, and she tried to gather what strength she could from the gesture. It was well after one in the morning, and the need for sleep pulled at her eyelids, but she couldn't go to bed without talking to her son first.

She knocked on his door but didn't wait for his response before opening it. The relief of seeing him in here shouldn't slam into her like this—after all, they'd been home for all of three minutes—but still, she sagged against his door.

Her eyes fell on the PBJ on his dresser, and she reached for it, then passed it to him. "You have to be hungry. Why don't you eat this before you go to sleep?"

Jackson shrugged but snatched the plate from her and took a bite that devoured half the sandwich.

"I know things have been a little rocky between us lately." Well, not so much lately as from the moment Jackson had arrived at her house. "But I don't understand why you felt like you needed to run away. Are you that unhappy here?" She managed to hold off the tears that threatened but couldn't prevent the crack to her voice.

When Jackson didn't answer, she lowered herself to the edge of his bed. He watched her but kept eating.

"Look, Jackson. I love you."

The boy's eyes focused on his plate, but Leah wasn't going to let his lack of a reaction keep her from telling him how she felt. "I love you so much that no matter how many times you run away, I'll come find you. I'll search and search and search. Even if it's a hundred times."

"Like Jesus with the sheep," Jackson muttered.

Leah's heart just about burst. She knew Dan had preached about the parable of the lost sheep a couple weeks ago. But she could never be sure if the message was getting through to Jackson.

"Exactly like that." She swallowed. She wasn't sure she could make herself say the next part.

She gathered her hair at the nape of her neck and took a long, shaky breath. "If you really don't want to stay with me—" She sniffed and blinked to clear the moisture from behind her lids but forced herself to keep going. She had to do what was best for Jackson. No matter how much it hurt her. "If you think you'd be happier with someone else or in a group home, then I'll respect that. You're old enough to make that choice."

At last, Jackson looked at her, but she couldn't read his expression. Was he happy? Angry? Hurt?

His eyes were blank.

"I don't want to go to another family." Jackson's hands fisted in his comforter.

"Do you want to go to a group home?" Leah tried not to let the hope lifting her heart leak into her voice.

The boy shook his head, and any prayer she had of not getting her hopes up was shattered.

"Do you want to stay here? Maybe talk about adoption?" She bit her lip, trying to resist the smile that threatened to burst out. If that's what tonight had been about—showing Jackson that he belonged with her—then maybe it had been worth all the worry and fear.

"I don't want any family."

Leah's heart crashed to the floor of Jackson's bedroom. "Why not?" she managed to whisper past the glass shards blocking her windpipe.

Jackson got out of the bed and stomped to the other side of the room, leaning against the wall and crossing his arms in front of him.

"What's the point?" The combination of hurt and anger in his voice tore at her. "Families tell you they'll be there for you forever, but it's all lies. You know what my mom said the morning she—" His gaze collided with hers, and Leah longed to go to him and wrap him in her arms. No kid should have to know this kind of pain. But she forced herself to keep her seat and let him talk.

"She said, 'It's you and me forever, baby.' I'll never forget that, the way she called me 'baby.' And she made me a peanut butter and jelly, my favorite, and said that after lunch we could go to the park if I sat at the table and ate like a big boy."

"And I trusted her." Jackson shook his head as if he couldn't believe how stupid he'd been. "I ate my sandwich, and then I went to find her to ask if we could go to the park. But she—" He dropped his eyes to the floor, kicking at the crack between floorboards with his toe.

"She was dead," Leah filled in for him.

Jackson nodded, not blinking. "So forever lasted less than an hour with her. And then they put me with this family that I thought was nice. But they kept me for less than a year before they got rid of me. And then there was another family. And another one. Some of them promised to adopt me. But none of them did."

Leah stood, daring to take a few steps toward him. "Jackson, I'm so sorry you've had to go through all of that. I wish I could take it away. I really do. But I can't. The only thing I can do is tell you I'm not them. I *do* want to—"

"No." Jackson's yell startled her into stillness. "Don't say it. I don't want you to. You're dumber than me if you think I'll believe it this time. Why don't you save us some time and admit what all those other families found out? I'm a bad kid, and nothing's going to change that."

"You're not a bad kid."

Jackson pushed off the wall, striding past her to get to the other side of the room. "Yes, I am. I didn't know why until yesterday. But now I know there's nothing I can do about it."

"Until yesterday? You mean punching Trent? That doesn't mean you're—"

"It's not about punching Trent. He deserved it. He was making fun of Adam because he has one arm that's shorter than the other. He's a total—"

"Wait." Leah had never considered that Jackson might be standing up for someone weaker than himself when he punched Trent. Not that it made punching acceptable, but it did change her perception of the situation. "You were defending Adam?"

"He can't exactly defend himself."

Leah tried to sort out her thoughts. "We'll talk about why hitting isn't the way to do that later. But first, I want to know why you say you're a bad kid."

Jackson slouched against the wall. "I just am," he mumbled.

Leah waited. Maybe that was all she was going to get. Already, he'd said more in the past twenty minutes than in the entire month they'd been together.

"My mom was an addict." The boy's voice was low, and Leah moved closer so she wouldn't miss anything.

"I'm afraid she was, honey. But that doesn't mean—"

"Mr. Giles said in health class that addiction is hereditary." He lifted his gaze to hers as if challenging her to argue.

She paused, thinking. She didn't want to mislead him. But nor did she want him to go through life thinking he was destined to fall into addiction. "It's not quite as clear-cut as that. It's not like inheriting your blue eyes. Just because your mom was an addict doesn't mean you'll be one. God gives us all a free will, to make those choices about things like what we put into our bodies. And it's my job to help you make good choices. To resist those temptations. And, if you ever fall into them, to always love you and forgive you. And to remind you that Jesus loves and forgives you too."

Jackson didn't say anything, but the tension in his shoulders eased, and his head drooped.

"Why don't you get some sleep now, and we can talk more in the morning?"

Jackson moved to the bed. Leah waited until he was tucked under the covers, then flipped off the light. She stood in his doorway, watching him lying still in bed for a moment.

"Goodnight, Jackson. I love you."

He didn't respond, but that was okay. She hadn't expected him to.

She only hoped that he'd believed her when she said it this time.

Chapter 32

"Pancakes?" Leah's sleepy voice from the entryway to the kitchen lifted Austin's mouth into a smile.

"I thought you could use them after last night."

Leah had been too worn out after talking with Jackson to tell him much about their conversation, but from what he'd gathered it had made her, at least, feel somewhat better.

He, on the other hand, had sat up on the couch the entire night, unable to shut off the images of what could have happened.

It had been too close. Way too close.

Thinking about what he could have lost had almost brought him to his knees more than once during the night. He'd even gone so far as to say a quick prayer of thanks for Jackson's safe return.

"Is Jackson up yet?" Leah shuffled into the kitchen and started setting the table.

"He got up a while ago. We talked for a bit." Austin had used their time alone together to apologize to the boy for not telling him the truth about why he couldn't play hockey. Jackson hadn't had too many questions about Austin's leg—other than how it had happened and if it hurt—and afterward, he'd returned to his room.

Austin wasn't sure yet if that was a good sign or a bad sign.

"Thank you for staying." Leah touched a light hand to his arm as she reached past him for the butter, but her voice was semi-guarded.

Because of the way he'd left her last night after their date? Before everything with Jackson?

"Leah. About last night. I'm sorry."

She set the butter down and slipped her arms around him, crutches and all. "I am too. And I really am praying for you. That things will work out the way you want, and you'll be redeployed."

He nodded and let himself do what he'd been dying to do all morning.

Her lips were soft and yielding against his, and he let himself sink into the moment.

Until Leah pulled back abruptly, snatching at the butter and moving around the table.

Austin blinked. It took him a second to figure out why she'd pulled away.

But then he spotted Jackson, staring between them with a revolted expression.

"Good morning." The forced casualness in Leah's voice almost made Austin laugh, but he managed to hold it in.

"Want some pancakes, dude?" He only asked it out of habit, though he knew what the answer would be.

But Jackson wiped his hands on his shirt and said, "Sure."

Austin could feel his mouth open as he turned to Leah, but she grinned at him and raised her eyebrows. Apparently she had the same thought as he did—don't make a big deal about this, or Jackson might change his mind.

So, as if this was what he did every day, Austin loaded a plate with three pancakes and passed it to Jackson. Then he filled one for Leah and another for himself.

As they sat there eating together, Austin couldn't keep the thought from edging its way in: They made a nice family.

Chapter 33

"So, when will we be planning one of these for you?" Peyton nudged Leah as she dropped her cake decorating supplies onto the counter.

Leah continued garnishing the elegant cups of tomato soup with basil. The bride and groom had chosen the perfect meal for a December wedding, from the tomato soup appetizers to the beef tenderloin and roasted potatoes to the hot chocolate bar.

"You're getting a little ahead of yourself."

Sure, the week since her date with Austin had been perfect. She and Austin and Jackson had eaten dinner together every night, and they'd actually convinced Jackson to play a board game with them last night. And then there'd been the kisses she and Austin had shared, and the quiet conversations they'd enjoyed together.

But that didn't mean she was planning their wedding. It'd taken her this long to be ready to date anyone. She was nowhere near ready to get married.

Even if the flutter in her tummy every time she considered it said otherwise.

"Oh, come on, Leah. Anyone can see that's where this is going." Peyton bent to pipe a flower onto the three-tiered cake.

"*I* can't."

"Of course you can." Peyton added a last flourish to the flower and lifted the piping tip. "I can see it in the way you look at him. You're in love."

"I know, but—" Leah threw the basil to the counter and wiped her hands on her apron. She couldn't deny that she loved him, even if they hadn't said it out loud yet.

"You don't look very happy about it." Peyton laid a hand on Leah's shoulder.

To her chagrin, Leah burst into tears at the gesture. "I'm sorry. I—" She picked up the basil again, but Peyton pulled her into a hug.

"Did something happen?"

Leah shook her head and wiped her eyes, laughing at herself. "That's the thing. I don't want to get my hopes up. In case nothing does. Happen. Because what if I'm expecting it and then—nothing?"

Peyton patted her back, then pulled away to fill another piping bag. "I know this is hard for you because you like to be in control, but—"

"Are you calling me a control freak?" She sniffled through her half smile.

Peyton raised an eyebrow. "You've always had your whole life planned. You like to know how everything is going to go. You thought you were going to stay single. You *planned* for it. So now that things are changing, you're scared."

Leah searched for an argument. But she had nothing.

"But you've never been in control," Peyton continued. "You know that. That's God's job."

Leah nodded. She knew that.

And yet . . . did she?

What if remaining single wasn't God's will for her? What if she'd only told herself that so she wouldn't have to risk getting hurt?

"You need to submit it all to God, Leah." Peyton examined her handiwork on the cake. "Trust he's got this. He's got you."

Leah nodded.

But she had a feeling that was going to be harder than it sounded.

"You good?" Dan didn't break his stride, but Austin caught his glance.

"I'm good." Austin huffed the words out. He knew Dan was probably used to running at a faster pace than this, but he felt good about holding his own this morning.

After how cold November had been, the days this week had warmed into the thirties, and there were only a few patches of brownish snow left at the sides of the road.

Much as Austin hoped Leah would get her white Christmas, he was grateful that the sidewalks were clear and dry enough to run again.

They pushed it hard for the last mile, and by the time they slowed to a walk in the church parking lot, Austin's lungs burned.

But he felt good.

"So, Leah tells me you hope to redeploy." Dan lifted his hands behind his head as they walked it off.

He should have known this was coming when Dan had invited him on a run this morning. But he'd agreed to it because he had something he wanted to ask Dan too.

"Yeah." He tried to gauge Dan's level of overprotectiveness. "It won't affect my relationship with Leah, though, if that's what you're worried about."

Dan stopped at the sidewalk that led from the parking lot to his house and gave Austin a long look. "Of course it will. But she's strong. She can handle that. Can you?" Dan leveled a look at him, but Austin met it full on.

His love for Leah was one thing he had no doubts about. "I can. In fact, I wanted to talk to you about that."

Dan nodded, and Austin took it as an invitation to continue. "I'd like to ask Leah to marry me."

Another nod. Either the guy had the best poker face in the world, or Austin's declaration hadn't surprised him.

"I know your dad passed away last year," Austin continued. "So I was kind of hoping you'd be willing to give me your blessing."

Dan studied him, and Austin forced himself to stay still and not look away.

"You should know that Leah has a strong faith," Dan said finally. "It's important to her."

It was Austin's turn to nod. He did know, and it was one of the things he loved about her.

"She's not going to be content with someone who only goes to church to please her." Dan regarded him. "Who doesn't have a genuine faith."

Austin swallowed. He knew that too. And although he'd once sworn to himself that he'd never believe again, over the past few weeks, as he'd sat at her side in church, as he'd listened to God's Word, he'd almost wondered if he could believe again.

It was taking more and more work not to, especially after the way they'd found Jackson unharmed last week. It was hard to believe that was a coincidence.

Which meant God had answered that prayer.

Now if he'd just answer Austin's prayers for Chad's safety and his own redeployment, he might be convinced.

"So I don't have your blessing?" Somehow the words found their way out.

Dan clapped a hand to his shoulder. "You have my blessing. And my prayers. That you see how much God loves you, no matter how things turn out."

That wasn't exactly the vote of confidence he was looking for.

But at least Dan hadn't said no.

Chapter 34

As Leah gazed around the table at Austin and Jackson, one verse kept running through her head: My cup runs over.

It was the only way to describe how she felt right now.

Surely God had blessed her and made her heart run over with joy.

For the past week, she'd been unable to stop thinking about her conversation with Peyton. The one about giving over control of her life to God.

At first, she'd been annoyed and tried to force her thoughts to something else every time it came to mind. But over the past couple of days, she'd found herself softening to the idea.

And last night, as she'd lain in bed, she'd finally prayed the prayer she'd been putting off maybe her whole life. *Lord, you made me, and you know me better than anyone else in this world. You know I like to be in control. Because I feel like if I'm in control, I can't be hurt. But the truth is, Lord, I need you to be in control. Because you love me and know what's best for me. Help me to trust that. And help me, if it is your will, to be open to a future with Austin.*

Peace had enveloped her as she prayed. Not the peace of knowing she and Austin would marry—that she was still completely unsure of—but the peace of knowing that whatever happened with Austin was in God's control. And that no matter what, she would always have the agape love of her Heavenly Father.

"What's up with you?" Jackson asked around a bite of spaghetti. Leah couldn't help the surge of happiness she felt every time he talked to her voluntarily.

Dan had been counseling the boy for the past couple weeks, and it seemed to be making a huge difference. It was such a blessing that her brother could not only help Jackson deal with some of the trauma of his past but could also share God's Word with him in the process. The other day, Jackson had come home and told her that he thought he might want to be a pastor someday. Or a soldier.

"Nothing. Why?"

"You're smiling really weird."

"Am I?" But Leah already knew she was. And she couldn't stop.

"What about me? Am I smiling weird?" Austin stuck his tongue out the side of his mouth and crossed his eyes.

Jackson pushed away from the table, picking up his empty plate. "And adults think kids are weird."

"But you love us." The words rolled off Leah's tongue. Jackson hadn't yet gone so far as to say it, but Leah could tell his heart was changing—and if he didn't love her yet, he at least didn't seem to hate her anymore.

"Whatever." As Jackson fled the room, Leah could feel Austin's eyes on her.

He reached across the table and laced his fingers through hers. "Before we clean this up, there's something I want to tell you."

A shiver of anticipation went up her spine. They hadn't said "I love you" to each other yet. But Leah didn't need to hear the words to know that was what this was.

Which wasn't to say she'd mind hearing the words—or saying them.

"There's something I want to tell you too."

"Yeah?" His grin was slow and sweet, and she leaned closer to kiss him.

But as their lips met, his phone blared a sharp ringtone. He pulled back with a quick apology, then snatched the phone off the table and lifted it to his ear.

Leah worked not to be disappointed. He'd been jumping at every phone call lately, hoping it would bring news about his brother.

She couldn't imagine how agonizing this must be for him, not knowing if Chad was safe.

It was agonizing for her to watch him go through it.

She squeezed his arm, then got up to clear the dishes. She hummed a hymn under her breath as she worked, and it took her a second to realize that Austin had called her name.

"Hmm?" She looked over her shoulder with an easy smile, but the moment she saw his white face and shaking hands, she dropped her rag and rushed to him. "What is it?"

He pulled the phone away from his ear and hit the speaker icon.

"We're still looking, Austin. And I have no doubt he'll show up any day. But I wanted you to hear it from me first."

Austin stared at the phone, not blinking, not moving.

Leah reached to put her hand in his, and he gripped it as if afraid she'd disappear if he let go.

"I'm sorry." She directed her comment toward the phone, even as her eyes remained on Austin. "Is this about Chad?"

"Sorry, who is this?" The man on the other end of the line sounded confused. "Where's Austin?"

"I'm here." Austin's voice was rough, as if someone had scraped sandpaper over his vocal cords. "This is my—" He broke off, staring at their linked hands.

"I'm a friend." She couldn't worry about labels right now. And no matter what else they were—what else they might become—they were friends first.

"Did I understand you correctly? Are you saying Chad is missing in action?" Even though her voice was barely above a whisper, the words seemed to blare across the kitchen, and Austin's arm convulsed under hers. She gripped his hand tighter.

"No ma'am. Not officially. But he was on an intel assignment, and he's missed a couple of check-ins. I was just calling to prepare Austin. In case . . ."

Thankfully, he left the rest of the sentence off.

Austin asked a few more questions about people and places Leah had never heard of, then hung up the phone. As the room fell silent, Leah turned to wrap her arms around him. He returned the hug briefly, then slid back from the table.

"I have to make some calls."

"Of course." She told herself it was ridiculous to be upset by his abrupt tone. "You can use the living room. I'll stay out of your hair. Unless you want me to—"

"I think I'll go home. I've got some info on my computer." He'd already moved to the front door and was pulling on his sweatshirt and hat.

Leah followed him, a wave of helplessness washing over her. She grabbed his arm as he reached for the door.

He lifted his head but refused to meet her eyes.

Pushing past her own hurt, she offered him the same comfort he'd given her when Jackson ran away. "We're going to get through this. Together."

With a nearly imperceptible nod, Austin pulled his arm away and left.

$\mathcal{C}hapter$ 35

$\mathcal{A}$ ustin slammed his phone to the table.

Twenty-four hours of phone calls had gotten him no closer to answers.

What he really needed was to get his own boots on the ground. If he were there, at least he'd feel like he was actually doing something. Instead of being stuck here, useless.

He scrubbed his palms over his face. His eyes begged for sleep, but there was no way his mind would allow it.

His gaze went to the front window. The mail truck was just pulling up to his house.

Feeling as if he'd aged ten years in the past day, he forced himself to his feet. Maybe his reinstatement letter was in there today. Then he could get where he needed to be to help his brother.

Yeah, because your life always works out that way.

But he pushed the thought aside. God had taken enough from him. It was about time he cut Austin a break.

Outside, he couldn't keep his eyes from going to Leah's house. She'd stopped by three times already today, and each time he'd reassured her that he was fine and there was nothing she could do. He'd had to look away from the hurt in her eyes when he'd declined her offer to stay with him.

He had to be alone right now. He couldn't have any distractions as he tried to figure out how to find his brother from seven thousand miles away.

He reached into the mailbox, pulling out a stack of envelopes. An electric bill, a Christmas card, two credit card offers, and, at the bottom of the stack, an envelope marked *Department of the Army*.

His heart roared, and the world moved in slow motion as he ripped the letter open, slid the single sheet of paper out, and unfolded it. He gulped in a quick breath before letting his eyes skim the letter.

The shaking in his hands intensified as he scanned the page. He couldn't seem to focus. But four words stood out to him: *permanent disability retired list*.

He rubbed at his eyes and tried reading it again.

He had to be seeing it wrong.

But as he read the words more slowly this time, making himself absorb each one, his chest grew tighter and tighter, until he wasn't sure he was breathing anymore.

His eyes caught on more phrases now: *condition has stabilized, not fit for active duty, right to appeal the decision*.

Darn right he was going to appeal the decision.

He tilted his head up, squinting into the brilliant blue of the winter sky. "Guess you don't care after all."

Chapter 36

The scent of garlic and herbs made Leah's mouth water. She may have gone a little overboard, experimenting with four new recipes today. But she hadn't known what else to do, when Austin kept pushing her away.

She understood, she really did, that he wanted to be alone. But that didn't make her any less heartsick.

Heartsick not only for herself but for him and what he was going through and for his brother and whatever might have happened to him.

Please be with him, she prayed, trusting that God understood that by *him* she meant both Austin and his brother.

"Jackson, come help me carry some of this food over to Austin's."

It was too much to expect that Austin would come over for dinner. But the man still had to eat.

Jackson appeared in the kitchen. "Austin's not coming over?" Lines of worry puckered the boy's brow.

"I don't think he's up for it." She'd already explained to Jackson what she knew of the situation, and her heart had nearly burst when he'd volunteered to pray for Austin.

"Here, you take that plate and this container, and I'll take the pie." In truth, she probably could have carried it all herself. But she hoped seeing Jackson might help Austin. And it might make things less awkward between the two of them.

Not bothering to make the boy put on a coat, Leah followed him out the door and across the now snowless yards.

Austin's bloodshot eyes and haggard skin told her what she already knew—he hadn't slept since he'd gotten that call yesterday.

"Hope you don't mind being a guinea pig." She worked to keep her voice cheerful. "I tried a bunch of new recipes today and had way too much food, so here you go."

Austin gestured for them to come in. Jackson headed straight for the kitchen with his load, but Leah stopped to greet Austin with a kiss.

His lips were stiff on hers, and he pulled away after a quick peck. Leah stumbled slightly at his abrupt retreat but regained her footing and followed him to the kitchen.

"Any news?"

"No."

She set the pie she'd been carrying on the counter and reached for him. But he flinched away.

Blinking back the moisture that threatened, she busied herself dishing food onto a plate for him.

"I know what I forgot to tell you." She reached for the thin book she'd brought along with the food. "Dan did some digging, and he found out that your parents *did* go to Hope Church. There's even a picture of them." She paged through the book until she came to it. "This must be before you and your brother were born."

Austin's eyes flitted to the book, then jumped away. He pressed his lips together. "Thanks for dinner."

Leah blinked at the clear dismissal. Maybe he wanted to be alone. But too bad.

They were in this together.

"I know this is hard, Austin." She kept her voice low. "But we're just trying to help. To be here for you. I wish you'd talk to us."

"You want me to talk?" The words exploded out of Austin, and she had to stop herself from taking a step back. "Okay, what should I talk about? The fact that my brother is missing? And that there isn't a single thing I can do about it since the army has found me unfit to serve my country?" His chest heaved.

"What?" Leah dared to take a step closer, but Austin paced out of her grasp.

"Don't act all shocked. It's what you said would happen. What you wanted to happen."

"Austin, I never—" She reached for him again, but again he sidestepped her. "Can we talk?"

"Stop trying to fix me." Austin's voice lashed into her. "All your talk about going along with whatever God's will is. Well, God's will may have cost me my brother."

"Don't talk to her like that."

Leah's head lifted in surprise. Jackson had been so quiet on his perch at the breakfast bar that she'd almost forgotten he was there.

But now he jumped off his stool, facing Austin head-on.

"It's all right, Jackson." Leah moved toward the boy. "Why don't we give Austin some space? Come on."

Jackson stared down the larger man for another few seconds, then walked to the front door.

Leah followed more slowly, not quite sure how her heart was staying in one piece when it wanted to break for him.

And for herself.

"Leah. Jackson. Wait." Austin blinked back the moisture in his eyes as he reached for her. What was he doing? Was this who he'd become now? A man who yelled at the woman he loved? Who set this kind of example for the kid he'd come to think of as a son?

They both stopped. Jackson stared at the floor, but Leah was watching him with a look of mingled hurt and compassion.

He opened his mouth, but he couldn't force the words out past the missile-sized lump that had lodged there.

Finally, he managed to pull out two words. "I'm sorry."

Jackson threw him a disgusted look and marched out the door, but Leah's look was longer, more penetrating.

"I want to help." Her voice broke. "I really do. But you're right—I can't fix you. Only God can do that." She stepped outside but then turned back to him. "I pray you'll let him."

With a sad smile, she made her way down the porch steps and to her own house.

For a long time after she'd gone inside, Austin stood staring at her house, with the twinkling Christmas decorations they'd worked so hard to put up together.

They made the house look cozy and homey—the perfect place for a happy family.

Too bad he had finally realized the truth: He was too broken to have a family.

Chapter 37

Coffee.

She needed coffee.

Leah stumbled out of bed, banging her shin on the hope chest at the foot of it, and limped toward the kitchen. The sun was barely up, and only the dimmest light illuminated the hallway, but she didn't bother to flip on any light switches. She had never had such a horrendous night's sleep in her life, and she was pretty sure her eyes would seal themselves shut if she exposed them to light right now. It didn't help that she'd spent half the night on her knees, in tears. At first, she'd prayed that God would fix whatever it was that had broken between her and Austin. But after a while, her prayer had transformed into one for healing for Austin. She whispered it to herself again now as she turned on the stove to boil water.

"Please let Austin find what he needs, Lord. Help him find the one thing that can fix him. Help him find you. And if he has to lose me to find you, please give me peace with that."

When she'd told Austin yesterday that she couldn't fix him, it had been a revelation to her too. She'd been trying so hard to make everything better for him—and for Jackson. But she had to surrender all of that to God. Because he was the only one who could give them what they truly needed—the truth that they were forgiven in Jesus.

Leah blew out a long breath. She'd always thought she was good at surrendering to God. Hadn't she gladly sacrificed her desires for marriage years ago? But now she knew better. Peyton was right—she'd accepted being single because she'd wanted to be in control.

Now, though. Now she wasn't in control. And she was trying to be okay with that.

In spite of the tiredness that clung to her eyelids, a restless energy compelled her to the living room.

It had finally snowed again overnight, and the faintest light hit the tops of the trees across the street, setting their snow-covered limbs aglow. The image soothed her soul. If God could make such beauty with a little snow and light, imagine what he could do in her life. And in Austin's.

She let her eyes track to his house just in time to see him jump into his truck. Exhaust steamed the air behind the vehicle as he started the engine. Leah watched, a vague uneasiness creeping in as she wondered where he'd be going so early in the morning.

A second later, he hopped out of the truck and headed back into the house, emerging after a minute carrying a large duffel bag in one hand and his crutches in the other. He threw them into the back of the truck, then moved toward the house again.

Her stomach dropped. When she'd said she was willing to lose him so he could find God, she hadn't meant right now. Not this way.

Please give me peace with your will, Lord. The prayer had never hurt so much.

But if he *was* leaving, she couldn't let him go without giving him the Christmas gift she'd found for him. If nothing else, maybe it would remind him that there were people in the world who cared about him.

She ran to her room and grabbed the gift, which she'd wrapped in a silver and blue foil paper, then pulled on her coat and tucked the gift into her pocket.

She jogged across the yard, snow seeping into the slippers she'd forgotten to change. Oh well. She wasn't going to go back inside and risk missing him.

Austin looked up when she was halfway across the yard, and she couldn't tell if his expression held relief or regret.

He came around the truck to meet her as she reached the driveway.

"Going somewhere? Without saying goodbye?" She tried to keep the accusation out of her voice.

He didn't come closer but squinted at her through the morning light. "I didn't think you'd want to see me." His eyes slid to the road, and he tucked his hands into his sweatshirt pocket. "But I did want to say that I'm sorry about yesterday. I shouldn't have taken out my frustrations on you."

"I understand." Leah shuffled a few steps closer, and Austin's eyes traveled to her feet.

"What are you doing out here in slippers?"

She let herself smile a little. "It's what I do. Remember?" That first night they'd met, when she'd yelled at him for chopping wood at midnight, she never would have guessed that this was where they'd end up.

Although she could see him trying to fight it, a slight smile lifted Austin's lips, softening his face. She closed the rest of the space between them, though she was careful not to touch him.

"Where are you going?"

Austin sighed and leaned against the tailgate. "To see my old commander at Fort Benning. He has worked with other guys who wanted to appeal the decision to put them on the permanent disability list. If anyone can help me get where I need to be, it's him."

Leah pressed her lips tight but nodded. She wanted to argue, to tell him that was the worst thing he could do right now, that he belonged here in Hope Springs, where it was safe and there were people who loved him. But she held her tongue.

"I should make sure I have everything." He stepped away from the truck and started toward the house, but she reached for his arm.

"What will you do if you can't redeploy? Will you come back here?"

But she knew the answer before the dejected head shake. "I can't, Leah. You were right. I'm too broken. And you can't fix me." Red rimmed his eyes, and he sniffed and cleared his throat, opening his arms and pulling her in tight.

She wanted to argue, but there was nothing she could say. She would happily accept him as the broken man he was. But if she needed to let him go so he could find the One who could truly fix him, that was what she'd do.

"I really am sorry," he said into her hair. "For everything."

She inhaled his warmth, wondering how long she'd remember his comforting scent after he left.

Probably forever.

The realization gave her the courage to finally say the words she'd been holding back. "I love you, Austin."

He loosened his hold on her and slid his hands to her shoulders, nudging her back so that she could see his face. The torment in his eyes was clear, but so was how he felt about her. "I love you too." He swept a hand over her cheek, wiping away the moisture that had collected there, and she did the same for him.

"Would you—" Austin looked away, blinking hard. "Would you say goodbye to Jackson for me? Tell him I'm sorry and I'm proud of him."

She sniffled but managed to rasp, "I'll tell him."

Austin pulled away and took a few backward steps toward his house. "I have to check if I missed anything."

He walked backward nearly all the way to the door, his eyes not leaving hers until he disappeared inside. Leah took the gift out of her pocket as she reached numbly into the back of the truck for his duffel bag. She slid the gift into the bag, then zipped it and walked toward her house.

It'd be easier for both of them if she wasn't out here when he drove away.

Chapter 38

Austin slowed as the GPS told him to take the exit toward Omaha, his shoulders knotting and stomach churning now that he was close. He'd made it to Indianapolis yesterday, with the plan of driving the rest of the way to Georgia today. But last night, he'd felt compelled to open the emails from Tanner's wife—all fifty of them. As he'd read them, the love and forgiveness she'd poured into them had left him gasping for air until he'd had to give in to the sobs he'd been stuffing down for an entire year. He'd buried his face in a pillow to keep from alarming the people in the room next door, giving full vent to his grief for the first time. When he'd finally managed to calm himself, he'd picked up the phone and honored the request she signed each of her emails with. *Please call.*

And now he was on his way there. Omaha was nine hours out of the way, but it didn't matter. Somehow, he *knew* he had to go there. Today. Now.

Two more turns, and the GPS announced he was at his location. He parked on the street, rolling his shoulders and letting out a long, slow breath.

It took a few minutes to work up the courage to step out of the truck and make his way toward the front door.

The house was quaint, its Christmas lights not quite as elaborate as what they'd done to Leah's house but still festive. Two sleds lay in the middle of the yard, and boot prints crisscrossed the snow.

The home looked completely normal. Like a happy family lived here. Austin wasn't sure what he'd expected—curtains drawn, a black veil over the door, an empty yard?—but it wasn't this.

When he got to the door, he just stood there, staring at the doorbell. Could he really do this? Could he really stand here and talk to Tanner's wife? Could he ever justify why he was the one standing here, and not her husband?

Before he could retreat, he lifted his hand to the doorbell.

The action set off chaos in the house. A dog took up wild barking, and children's voices shrieked. Through the sidelight, Austin watched a boy of six or so walk toward the door, followed by his little sister. They were a little older than the last picture he'd seen of them, but Tanner had talked about them so much that Austin felt like he knew them already.

The sight of the kids set up an ache in his chest at the thought of his makeshift family in Hope Springs, but he stuffed it down.

The boy opened the door and sent a grin his way, and the air caught in Austin's lungs. Aside from the gaps where his front teeth should have been, the boy was nearly a mirror image of his father.

"Are you Mr. Austin?" The boy's voice was innocent and filled with admiration.

Austin nodded, but he couldn't speak.

The boy didn't seem to mind. "I'm Matthew. This is my sister Martha." He patted the little girl who had finally managed to catch up with him.

Austin swallowed. The kids were both so young, neither would remember their father. It was a blessing in some ways, he knew. He'd been young enough when his father was killed that he'd never experienced the sharp pain of missing someone who'd once been a regular part of his life. But he also knew they'd grow up with questions about their father—questions maybe he could help answer. Someday.

"Sorry. I was elbow-deep in dishwater." A slender, dark-haired woman hurried up behind the children. "I'm Natalie."

Austin shook the hand she held out. He recognized her from Tanner's photos too.

"I'm so glad you could make it." Natalie gestured for him to come in, then sent the kids to play in the playroom. "I've got some coffee and cookies in the kitchen."

Austin followed her and took the seat she indicated at the table, but he waved off the cookies and coffee. He couldn't have eaten right now if he'd gone weeks without food.

Natalie pulled out the chair next to him and poured herself a cup of coffee, picking up a cookie and dunking it. "I was surprised to get your call last night. I'd actually told myself that if I didn't hear from you by Christmas, I'd stop sending the emails. I figured either I had the address wrong or you didn't want to hear from me."

Austin slid his finger over a crack in the table. "I got them," he said quietly. "But I couldn't bring myself to open them until last night."

"And what changed last night?"

"I have no idea," he answered in all honesty. Maybe it was the anonymity of the hotel room. Maybe it was the emotional conversation with Leah that morning. Maybe it was loneliness. All he knew was that when he'd turned on his phone and noticed a new email from her, he'd clicked right to it and read it—and he hadn't stopped reading until he'd gotten through all of the messages.

"I'm glad you did." Natalie's smile was warm and kind. If he'd expected to find bitterness or anger toward him, he couldn't spot any.

He glanced around the cozy room. One wall was dedicated to pictures. Tanner stared at him out of nearly all of them. One holding each of his kids as newborns. Several family photos. One of him and Natalie on their wedding day.

Austin deliberately turned away from the photos. It was too painful to look at the face he'd only seen in his memory for the past year.

"How do you do it?" The question came out before he could consider whether it was insensitive. "How do you get through the days without him?"

Natalie paused with her coffee cup halfway to her mouth. Her eyes went to the wall of pictures behind him, but Austin didn't follow her gaze.

"Some days I miss him so much, I think there must be a hole clear through the middle of me." She pressed a hand to her stomach, and Austin was sorry he'd asked.

"I'm sorry. I shouldn't have—"

But she gave him a gentle smile. "But I know he's in his true home. In heaven. And I know I'll join him there one day. When it's time."

Austin grimaced. He hadn't come here to debate heaven. But as long as she brought it up. "How could it possibly have been Tanner's time? He was way too young."

Natalie shook her head. "There's no such thing as too young or too old. God calls us home when he knows the time is right. There's nothing that's outside of his control. Not even this."

Austin wanted to be angry at her answer. How could she believe in a God who would "call someone home," as she put it, on a whim?

"I get mad sometimes," she said, as if reading his thoughts. "But then I remind myself of the promise I made to Tanner every time I talked to him."

"What was that?" His throat burned around the question, but he needed to know.

"I promised him 'even if.'" She looked at Austin, as if waiting to see if he understood.

He didn't. "Even if?"

Her gentle smile held no judgment. "Have you ever heard the Bible account of Shadrach, Meshach, and Abednego?"

Austin shrugged. He'd probably learned about them in Sunday School. Long ago.

"It was Tanner's favorite Bible story."

A pang shot through Austin. Tanner had tried to talk to him about the Bible on so many occasions, but Austin had shut him down every time.

"Shadrach, Meshach, and Abednego worshiped the true God," Natalie continued. "And when they refused to bow down to a false god, the king of Babylon threatened to throw them into a fiery furnace. But these three men said, basically, 'Go ahead and throw us in there. Our God will save us. But even if he doesn't, we won't worship your false gods. We'll still worship the true God. Even if.'"

She leaned toward him, expression earnest. "That's the kind of faith Tanner wanted for us. Faith that even if something happened to him, we would continue to worship God. To trust in him and his will for our lives. I have to pray every day for that *even if* kind of faith. And God has been faithful in answering that prayer."

Austin blinked and looked away from her sincere eyes. He wasn't sure he could ever pray for that kind of faith.

"There's something Tanner wanted you to have." Natalie pushed her chair back and stepped toward the kitchen counter, grabbing a well-worn book and passing it to him. "This was his personal Bible."

But she didn't have to tell him that. He'd seen Tanner pull the beat-up book out of his pack more times than he could count. He'd offered to let Austin borrow it dozens of times. But Austin had always declined.

He half laughed as he took the book now. Apparently Tanner had gotten his way in the end.

"There's a letter for you in it," Natalie added. "It's from Tanner. Just so you're not freaked out when you open it and see your name in his handwriting."

Austin's throat threatened to close, but he managed to squeeze out a thank you.

"I'm glad you came." Natalie bent down to hug him, and Austin closed his eyes, wishing more than anything that she could be hugging her husband instead. "Tanner would be glad too."

Chapter 39

"*How* many of these are we going to make?" Jackson set down the candy cane-shaped cutout cookie he'd been frosting and picked up an angel-shaped one, dipping his knife into a bowl of blue frosting.

Leah couldn't help the laugh. They'd been working on the cookies for three hours already, and the boy hadn't shown any sign of tiring. Of course, it helped that for every ten cookies he frosted, he ate one.

But she couldn't bring herself to be upset about that. Not when she was having such a wonderful Christmas Eve with him.

The results of the house decorating contest had been announced earlier this morning. Their house had taken third place, earning them a fruit basket that sat in the middle of the counter now.

For the life of her, Leah couldn't remember why she'd thought it was so important to win the contest. She didn't need Hawaii to bond with Jackson. They were doing that right now, in the simple act of baking cookies.

With a thick layer of frosting covering the angel, Jackson set it down and sprinkled colored sugar over its wings. "Austin's not coming back, is he?"

Leah stopped frosting her own cookie and set it down, the heaviness of heart she'd managed to shake off for a short time returning. When she'd told Jackson two days ago that Austin had to go to Fort Benning, the boy hadn't said much. But Leah hadn't missed how many times he looked out the window toward Austin's driveway.

Wiping her hands on her apron, Leah stepped around the counter to stand next to Jackson. "I don't think so."

She wasn't sure she'd fully come to grips with it herself, but she was trying. Instead of being bitter about the time they wouldn't have together, she was focusing on being grateful for the time they had enjoyed together. And for the fact that he'd changed her outlook on life—on love.

Even though she was in no rush to meet someone and get married, she was no longer so certain that God had written that out of his plan for her life. Maybe someday . . . if the right man came along. Although at the moment, the only face she saw when she pictured the right man was Austin's.

Please be with him, Lord. She'd been repeating the same prayer constantly since Austin had left. She'd never stop praying for him, even if she never saw or heard from him again.

"Can't you call him?" Jackson looked at her as if it were the most obvious thing in the world. "Tell him to come back?"

Leah sighed. It wasn't like she hadn't contemplated doing that very thing. Every. Single. Moment.

But every time she pulled her phone out to dial, she put it away. If this was what Austin felt he had to do, she had no right to make it harder on him.

"It's not that simple." She piled the cooled cookies into a plastic container. She'd bring them to Christmas at Dan's tomorrow.

Jackson bit the head off a snowman. "Seems pretty easy to me. Call and tell him he's being an idiot."

Leah's heart twisted for the boy. Just when he'd thought he finally had a steady father figure in his life. "Austin loves you," she said quietly. "And so do I."

Jackson looked at her expectantly. "So . . ."

"It's complicated," she repeated.

"Mrs. Jenkins always says a problem is never as complicated as it seems if you break it down into its smallest parts."

Leah snapped the lid on one container and pulled out another. "Who's Mrs. Jenkins?"

"My math teacher. I think the smallest part is that you're scared to call him. Because you're afraid maybe he *might* come back."

"That's ridiculous." Leah pushed a piece of hair out of her eyes. "I'll clean this up. You go get ready for church."

Jackson popped the rest of the cookie into his mouth. "It's simple," he said as he trotted down the hallway toward his room.

Leah shook her head. She was so, so grateful for their wonderful day together. But this was not a conversation she wanted to have with him.

He was just a kid. What did he know about being scared to love people?

Probably a whole lot.

Wasn't that the reason he'd tried so hard to push her away? Because he'd been burned by people claiming to love him so many times?

But that was different. Leah wasn't afraid to love. She was just giving Austin the space he needed. She was completely willing to sacrifice herself for his sake.

That was all that was going on here.

Chapter 40

Austin threw his bags on the floor of the hotel room. After another whole day of driving, he'd made it back to Indianapolis. If it hadn't been for the detour to visit Tanner's family, he'd be in Georgia by now. But he couldn't regret making the trip to see them. Knowing that they were okay—that in spite of everything they could smile and laugh and pray—had eased his heart at least a little.

He dropped onto the edge of the bed and rummaged in his bag for Tanner's Bible. He hadn't been able to bring himself to look at it last night, but the promise of a letter from Tanner had been hovering in the back of his mind all day.

He ran his fingers over the Bible's soft leather cover. How many times had he seen Tanner do exactly the same thing, as if the book were an old friend?

Ignoring the tremor in his hands, he lifted the cover and inhaled as his eyes fell on the envelope. Despite Natalie's warning, the sight of Tanner's handwriting jarred him, and he had to look up quickly.

After a second, his heart rate slowing only slightly, he lifted the envelope out of the Bible and slid a sheet of paper out of it.

Hey Texas—

Austin couldn't help the soft laugh at the nickname. He was from nowhere near Texas, and Tanner knew it, but for whatever reason, he enjoyed the play on Austin's name. He let his eyes continue over the scrawled words.

So you're reading this, huh? I guess that means I'm chilling in heaven right now.

Austin blew out a breath. It was Tanner's voice, as sure as if he were sitting right here next to him.

I hope you know it's pretty awesome here, and I'm happy. And I also know that you did everything you could to keep this from happening. You might be wondering how I know this, since I'm dead and all. It's because I know you. And I also know that no matter how many people tell you my death isn't your fault, you'll insist it is.

Austin swiped at the tears blurring the words on the page.

Look, buddy, I'm sorry, but it wasn't your choice when I went home. That was all God. And another thing: I suppose you're using my death as one more excuse to harden your heart to him. Totally boneheaded move, man.

Austin shook his head. Even when he was writing his goodbye letters, Tanner couldn't be serious.

That's why I want you to have my personal Bible. I've been reading it and writing notes in it since I was thirteen. I hope you'll read it and that you'll let God open your heart through it. Because no matter how much you resist him, he loves you. He loves you so much that he sent his son to die for your sins so that you could come hang out with us here one day too. Looking forward to seeing you then.

Your brother,

Tanner

PS Check out Daniel chapter three.

For a long time after he read those last words, Austin sat holding the letter. How could one little sheet of paper covered with squiggles hold so much meaning? How had Tanner managed to capture the essence of himself in this letter? How had he known exactly what Austin needed to hear?

Finally, slowly, he opened the Bible and paged through it until he came to Daniel chapter three. He laughed as he read the heading—apparently Natalie knew her husband well. Tanner had directed him to the story of the fiery furnace.

With a sigh, Austin started to read it. He owed Tanner that much at least.

More than the story itself, Austin's attention hooked on the copious notes Tanner had written in the margin. But it was the final note that stuck with him the most. "Faith isn't faith if it only believes in God when he answers our prayers in the way we want him to. Faith is faith when we believe *even if*."

As Austin closed the Bible, his head spun.

He'd had faith once. And he'd thought it was an *even if* kind of faith. But after the things he'd seen, after he'd lost one too many buddies in battle, he'd let go of that faith, pretended it had never existed.

Could he find it again?

Not on his own. That much he was sure of. Bible still clutched in his hands, he closed his eyes.

"Lord, help me." He could only manage a whisper. "I need an *even if* kind of faith. I need faith to believe that you are with me even if things don't go the way I think they should. That you love me even if I can't be redeployed. That you are here even if something happens to Chad." Saying it nearly destroyed him, but somehow he knew this was what he needed to pray right now.

Eyes still closed, he focused on regaining control of his ragged breathing. He needed peace.

His mind slid to the first sermon he'd ever heard Dan preach. About asking God for peace with the things he was angry about. He hadn't wanted to be at peace then. He'd wanted to hold on to his anger.

But now he knew he couldn't live like this, always angry with God. "Please give me peace, Lord." His voice was stronger now. "Peace with Tanner's death and Isaad's. Peace with losing my leg. Peace with not knowing where Chad is. With all of it. Take my anger and give me your peace."

At last, his breathing slowed, and he opened his eyes.

Had the prayer done anything? He didn't feel different. Not really.

He reached for his duffel bag to put the Bible away and grab his sweats. He needed to at least attempt to get some sleep.

But as he reached into the bag, his hand fell on something sleek and thin. Another book?

He grabbed it out of the bag.

It was the church directory Leah had given him. He'd almost left it behind, but at the last minute, he'd thrown it in his bag. Even if he never looked at it, it was part of his family's history.

But something compelled him to open it now. As his eyes fell on his parents, young and obviously in love, smiling at the camera as if they had no fears about the future, he realized they hadn't known that their life wouldn't turn out as planned either. And yet, even after his dad was killed, his mom didn't turn away from God. She continued to bring Austin and his brother to church, continued to pray with them, continued to encourage them in their faith. She had been his living example of an *even if* kind of faith, and he hadn't even realized it.

Setting the book aside, Austin reached for his bag again. Now he really did have to get to bed.

But as he tugged his sweatshirt out of the bag, something hit the floor with a soft thump.

A present, wrapped in blue and silver paper, lay in the middle of the floor. He stared at it, uncomprehending. That hadn't been there when he'd packed.

And then he realized.

Leah.

As he reached for it, the ache he'd carried with him for the past three days of not being with her blazed into a need to hold her.

But that wasn't possible—would never be possible again.

Maybe if he opened the present and got it over with, he'd get some closure.

He snatched the gift up and tore the paper off in one quick movement.

His breath caught. It was a ceramic ornament in the shape of a gingerbread house that looked startlingly like Leah's house after they'd decorated it. But in place of the door was a picture—one they had taken during a walk on the beach last weekend. Austin stood with an arm around Leah, and Jackson stood in front of the two of them. There'd been no one else around, so Austin had extended his arm as far as he could to take the group selfie. The image was slightly out of focus, and he'd cut off the top of his own head—but the picture was perfect. All three of them were smiling as if there was nowhere else they'd rather be.

He ran his hand over the photo, regret slicing at him. If only things had turned out differently. If only he weren't so broken.

Austin flipped the ornament over. On the flat white ceramic of the back, in flowing handwriting, Leah had written, "'Though the mountains be shaken and the hills be removed, yet my unfailing love for you will not be shaken nor my covenant of peace be removed,' says the Lord, who has compassion on you. -Isaiah 54:10."

Austin laid on the bed, resting the ornament on top of his heart. God's covenant of peace, the verse said.

For the first time in a long time, he felt like maybe that covenant was for him too.

He reached for his phone to set the alarm. But as his finger hovered over the clock icon, a notification popped onto his screen—an email from Hope Church that the Christmas Eve service would begin live streaming in five minutes.

Austin hesitated. He was supposed to be leaving Hope Springs behind. But maybe one last night to remember wouldn't hurt.

Chapter 41

*I*n the glow of hundreds of candles, Leah joined the rest of the packed church in singing the final verse of "Silent Night." Listening to Jackson singing next to her, she knew she had gotten more than she ever could have hoped for Christmas.

The final chord of the song rang out, and Leah joined the others in blowing out her candle and sitting as the lights came up just enough to illuminate Dan at the front of the church.

A twinge of pride lifted her lips at the sight of her little brother up there, fulfilling the role their father had once filled. She missed Dad more than ever tonight, but it was a sweet sort of missing him. He was happier in heaven than any of them could ever imagine being here on earth—and someday, when it was her turn to go to her heavenly home, she'd see him again.

"Traditionally, I would preach from the account of Jesus' birth in Luke chapter two on Christmas Eve," Dan began his sermon. "But you all know I'm not a terribly traditional guy." There was a smattering of laughter among the congregation, and Leah couldn't help smiling along.

"Instead, I'd like to look at Isaiah 54:10."

Leah fought to keep from gasping out loud. Her brother couldn't have known that was the same verse she'd written on the gift to Austin. She hadn't shown it to anyone.

Dan read the verse she knew by heart: "'Though the mountains be shaken and the hills be removed, yet my unfailing love for you will not be shaken nor my covenant of peace be removed,' says the Lord, who has compassion on you."

Jackson gave her a strange look, and she realized she'd been mouthing the words along with her brother. She shrugged. This was too wonderful to ignore. She sat forward as her brother paused to take in the congregation.

"Here's a dumb question: Do bad things ever happen to you?" Dan paced from one side of the church to the other as all around people nodded. "Of course they do. It's part of living in this sin-fallen world, right? But you think you have it rough? Look at all those people in the Bible who went through bad things. There was Joseph—his brothers stole his coat, threw him in a pit, and sold him to slave traders. And what about David? He served King Saul loyally, and how did the king repay him? By chasing him down with the intention of killing him. Oh, and let's not forget Job. He probably had it the worst of all, right? God let Satan take everything from him—his land, his home, his health, and, most painfully, his children."

"Makes our problems seem pretty insignificant, doesn't it?" Dan paused.

In front of her, Leah could see a few heads nod, but she knew her brother well enough to know this was where he was going to flip everyone's expectations upside down.

"Actually—" Dan held up a hand. "Actually, I don't think it does. Because God doesn't see any of our problems as insignificant. He knows our hurts. He knows when we're sick. He knows when we worry that we won't be able to pay the bills. He knows when our hearts are broken because a relationship has ended."

Leah blinked back the moisture that pricked her eyes. It did hurt to know that her relationship with Austin had ended. And yet, it was comforting to know that Jesus understood. That he cared.

"And he knows what we're going through when we have to say goodbye to someone we love because they've gone before us to be with him."

Dan spread his arms wide, as if encompassing the whole room. "And how does he know all of this? Why can he relate to it?" After a heartbeat, he answered his own question. "Because he was one of us. He chose to set aside his glory and humble himself and come into this world to be born as a baby and live among us. He hurt the same ways we hurt—worse, because he knew what he had created us to be, the perfect life he had intended for us, and we had thrown it all away."

"But here's the thing to remember." Dan's smile took in the entire congregation. "These verses from Isaiah. God says that no matter what, his love for us will not fail. Even if the mountains are shaken. Even if the hills fall to the ground and are no more. Even if we are filthy, wretched sinners who fail him at every turn. Even then, his covenant with us will always stand. His promise to us. And what promise is that? It's the promise he was born on Christmas and died on Good Friday to fulfill. The promise he made at the beginning of the world, when Adam and Eve fell into the first sin. The promise that he forgives us for all of our sins. That we have the peace of knowing the promise of heaven."

Leah sighed, relaxing into her seat. No matter how many times she heard that promise, she'd never tire of the good news. Next to her, Jackson was leaning forward, taking in Dan's sermon. God's Word was working in his heart. Leah could tell.

But there was one more person's heart she prayed it worked in. *Please let Austin know this good news too, Lord. It's the only thing that will heal him.*

Chapter 42

Austin had sat up in the bed of his hotel room halfway through the sermon, and as Dan said "Amen" and the congregation began to sing a new song, he sprang to his feet.

That sermon. Those words. That *even if*. Again.

"Okay, Lord, you have my attention," he said out loud into the mirror over the room's small dresser. "Now what?"

But he already knew now what.

He shoved his phone in his pocket, grabbed his duffel bag, and cradled the ornament from Leah. With one last look around the room to make sure he hadn't forgotten anything, he jogged toward his truck. It was nearly nine o'clock, but if he drove through the night, he should reach Hope Springs by tomorrow morning—Christmas morning.

He set the ornament on the seat beside him, then started the engine and pointed the truck north. As he drove, he found himself falling into prayers he hadn't known he needed to pray.

Prayers for Tanner's wife and children.

Prayers for Isaad's family.

Prayers for himself, that he would find peace with the life God had given him instead of seeking the one he'd thought he'd have.

Dan had said once that he could be thankful for his blessings in disguise. That God knew what he was doing with his life even when Austin didn't. He hadn't seen it at the time—hadn't wanted to see it. But now he did.

These scars were exactly what had led him to where he was supposed to be—with Leah and Jackson. And more than that, walking with his Savior.

Thank you for your scars too, Lord. The scars that you willingly endured to save us when we were helpless to save ourselves.

Austin drove and prayed through the night, stopping only twice to stretch his legs. By the time the sun was peeking over Lake Michigan, he was pulling into Hope Springs. A fresh layer of snow had fallen overnight, giving the town the perfect Christmas atmosphere.

He wanted nothing more than to go straight to Leah's house and fold her into his arms. But there was something he had to do first.

He pulled into the church parking lot and stopped in one of the spots near Dan's house. Since it was Christmas morning, the preacher was likely already awake and preparing for services. But Austin didn't want to wake his family. So he sent a quick text.

Got any wrapping paper?

The immediate *yes* from Dan set off a grin he couldn't hold back.

Chapter 43

"It's not much, sorry." Christmas morning, Jackson passed her a card and a box it looked like he'd wrapped himself. She'd wanted to wait until after church to open gifts, but he seemed so eager to give her hers that she hadn't been able to say no.

She slid her finger under the flap of the envelope and pulled out a Christmas-tree shaped card. When she opened it, speakers inside started playing "O Christmas Tree," and she had to laugh.

But her laughter died as her eyes fell on the words Jackson had written:

Dear Mom,

Thank you for not giving up on me. I know I haven't made it easy.

Merry Christmas,

Jackson

She tried to blink back the tears but failed. "Thank you, Jackson."

The boy looked at the floor, a slight pink tinging his cheeks, and she couldn't resist pulling him into a hug.

He didn't exactly return the hug, but he didn't squirm away either.

After a few seconds, Leah released him and swiped at her eyes, then carefully unwrapped the box he'd given her.

"Austin helped me pick it out," Jackson mumbled as she opened the lid, and she nodded, trying not to let the name affect her.

A small laugh escaped as she lifted a pair of oven mitts out of the box. They were almost the same as her old ones—red and white checked—but had none of the worn patches.

"We thought you could hang up your dad's. So they wouldn't get more wrecked."

She hugged them to her. "I love them. Thank you."

Jackson's face grew pinker.

"How about you open one of your presents now?" Leah stood and moved to the tree, rummaging through the gifts she'd stacked there to find the perfect one to give him first.

"Uh, Le— Mom?" Jackson stumbled over the word, but it was still the most beautiful sound Leah had ever heard. She buried her head deeper under the tree. If he saw how emotional she got every time he called her that, he'd stop.

"Mom." Jackson's voice was more urgent now, and Leah stopped digging to look at him.

"What's up?"

But he was staring out the window. "Austin's here."

"What are you talking about?" Leah's mouth went dry, even as she knew he had to be mistaken. Austin was in Georgia by now.

She jumped as the doorbell rang, but Jackson was already running to answer it.

Leah's hands shook as she straightened, and she smoothed down her rumpled flannel pajamas.

The door blocked her view at first. All she saw was a hand reaching out to pull Jackson toward him.

But it was enough. She'd recognize that hand anywhere.

She wanted to take a step closer, but her feet refused to obey her brain. From the other side of the door came the sound of Austin's hand clapping Jackson's back.

She should tell him not to get the boy's hopes up. That if he wasn't here to stay, he shouldn't have come at all. Because it wasn't fair to Jackson. Or to her.

But like her legs, her mouth refused to follow her orders.

At last, Jackson took a backward step into the room, a massive grin filling his face. A second later, Austin followed, closing the door behind him.

"Hi." His eyes met hers, and all she could do was nod. He held a large wrapped box in one arm and, not taking his eyes off her, bent to set it on the coffee table. "I got your message."

"You called him?" It was the loudest she'd ever heard Jackson speak so loud she should probably reprimand him for yelling, but she still couldn't get her voice to work.

"Yes! I knew it." The boy clapped his hands.

Austin laughed, but Leah's heart dove. This was exactly why she hadn't wanted to call Austin. She'd left only a super short message right before she went to bed last night, wishing him a merry Christmas. But he'd obviously heard the sadness in her voice and let his guilt bring him back.

"You didn't have to come back."

"I know I didn't." His voice was too tender, and Leah had to look away as he stepped toward her. Still her legs wouldn't work.

"Leah, look at me. Please." His hands closed around hers, and her eyes were drawn to his.

"I didn't come back because of your call. I was already on my way. I came back because I realized you were right. Dan was right. Chad was right. Tanner was right. Everyone was right except me, apparently." He gave an ironic laugh. "I was so angry about everything that happened, so busy thinking that everything had to work out exactly how I wanted it to, that I missed the whole point. It's not about what I want. It's about what God wants for me. What he knows is best for me." He closed the last little bit of space between them. "And that's you." He lowered his face toward hers.

Leah's heart thrummed a thousand beats a minute as she lifted her chin.

"Eww." Jackson's voice behind them made them both pull back. But both were smiling.

"And that goes for you too," Austin said to Jackson. "You're one of the best things that has ever happened to me, and I'm not going to run away from that."

Jackson blinked and cleared his throat, staring at the floor, and Leah had to brush a tear from her own cheek at seeing his reaction to being so loved.

"I got you something." Austin lifted the present off the table, passing it to her.

Although it appeared easy for him to handle, she braced for the weight of the big box. But when he set it into her arms, she almost dropped it because it was so light.

"You got me air?" she teased.

"Guess you'll have to open it to see."

Leah lowered herself to the couch so she could set the box on her lap, then began carefully peeling the layers of wrapping paper.

"You might want to grab something to drink," Austin said over his shoulder to Jackson. "We might be here a while."

"This is how I open gifts," Leah shot back. "Take it or leave it."

"I'll definitely take it." Austin grinned at her, and she turned her attention to the box.

Once she had the paper all peeled off, she folded it and set it aside, then lifted the lid off the box, groaning at the sight of another wrapped box inside it.

"You're one of *those* present wrappers," she accused. But she started unwrapping the box immediately.

Three boxes later, she came to the smallest box she'd ever seen. This had to be the last one. There was no way another would fit inside it.

When the paper was finally off, she held a small velvet box in her hand—the kind jewelry came it. Her hands shook as she pried it open, and she nearly dropped it as her eyes fell on the ring inside.

She looked up, but Austin was no longer standing next to her. She'd been so busy unwrapping the boxes that she hadn't noticed him drop to one knee at her side. His left leg was propped at a slightly odd angle, but she still knew what the pose meant.

She could only blink at him, her heart leaping. Was this really happening? She hadn't been looking for it. And it was all so fast.

He cradled her hands in his. "Before I came to Hope Springs, I didn't realize anything was missing from my life." He laced his fingers through hers. "When I met you, I thought maybe that was it. Maybe you were what I had been missing." His smile went all the way to his eyes, which shone brighter than she'd ever seen them. "But you helped me see that what I was missing couldn't be found in a person. Or in redeploying. Or in anything else. What I was missing was God. And you helped me find him again."

Leah dropped the box into her lap and threw her arms around him. That was the best thing anyone had ever said to her.

After a second, Austin gently unwrapped her from his neck and slid her back so that he could see her face.

"The thing is, though, God had something to show me too." He lifted his palm to her cheek, caressing it with his thumb. "He showed me that even if my life didn't turn out the way I thought it would, he has been with me every step of the way. And he has led me to you. To both of you." He looked over his shoulder at Jackson, who was watching them with a half-disgusted, half-intrigued expression. "And I'd like to stay with the two of you for a very long time. Forever, in fact, if you'll let me." He dropped his hand from her face and reached for the ring still in her lap, pulling it out of the box and holding it out to her. "Leah, will you marry me?"

Her first instinct was to blurt the yes that had been hovering on her tongue the whole time he'd been speaking. But this was a big decision. It didn't affect only her. It affected Jackson too.

She swallowed. "Can I think about it?"

Chapter 44

"Merry Christmas, Austin." Sophie leaned in to hug him, juggling one of her twins on her hip, as Spencer carried the other, along with what looked like a year's worth of baby supplies.

"Merry Christmas." Austin reached to help Spencer with the extra highchair. Friends had been coming in and out of Dan and Jade's house all day, in between visits with their own families. Dan and Leah's mother had arrived just in time to go to church with them, and though Austin had nearly panicked at the prospect of meeting Leah's mother, he'd found her as easy to talk to as Leah was.

He hadn't mentioned this morning's proposal to anyone, though. He'd let Leah do that—after she made her decision.

Every time his eyes met hers, he felt it. This was *right*. This was where he was supposed to be. Who he was supposed to be with.

But he wasn't going to force it. For the past year, he'd been trying so hard to force his will that he'd lost sight of what mattered. But that stopped now. He was going to accept his permanent retirement and wait and see where God led him from here.

And right now, that meant giving Leah the time she needed to make a decision.

In his pocket, his phone vibrated, and he pulled it out, intending to decline the call. It was Christmas, after all.

But the moment his eyes fell on the name, his hands shook so hard, he nearly dropped the phone.

He swiped to answer the video call.

"Hey bro."

At the sight of Chad's pixelated face, Austin lost it.

Covering his mouth with his hand, he rushed down the hallway to the nearest empty room.

"Where have you— I thought—" He couldn't talk around his gasps. *Thank you, Lord.*

"It's okay." His brother's voice sounded so close and so far away at the same time. "I'm okay." He repeated it a few times, until Austin managed to pull himself together.

Finally, he scrubbed a hand over his face and cleared his throat. "Sorry. I—"

A knock on the door cut him off. "Austin?" Leah opened the door. "Is everything all right?"

"Is that your gorgeous neighbor?" Chad's voice was unnecessarily loud, likely intended to embarrass him, but Austin didn't care.

"Yes it is." He hurried to the door and grabbed Leah's hand, pulling her into the room.

"Leah, this is my brother Chad. Chad, Leah."

The tears that sprang to Leah's eyes touched him more than anything else could have, and he had to blink back his own emotion again.

"It's nice to meet you, Leah." Chad's voice was warm, and Austin still couldn't believe it was really him.

"You too." Leah wiped her eyes. "You had us all pretty worried. A lot of prayers were said here for your safe return."

"I appreciate that." Now it was Chad's turn to sound choked up.

"I'll let you two talk." Leah lifted onto her tiptoes to kiss Austin's cheek, and he reached an arm around her in a quick hug.

"Just neighbors, huh?" Chad's voice pulled his attention off Leah as she waved and closed the door.

"A lot has changed since the last time we talked." Austin chuckled, his heart buoyant.

Chad was alive and unharmed, he and Leah were together again, and he was in a home full of people he cared about—and who cared about him.

"So your girlfriend—"

"Possibly fiancée." Austin could not stop grinning.

Chad's eyes widened, and he leaned closer to the screen. "Seriously?"

Austin could only nod, still grinning. The only way this day could get better was if Leah answered his question with a yes.

But even if she didn't, it was shaping up to be a pretty amazing Christmas.

"Okay, then, your fiancée said that there have been a lot of prayers said there. Does that include you?"

Austin studied his brother. Despite the poor video quality, he could see the hope on Chad's face. His brother had been almost as persistent as Tanner in trying to talk to him about God.

Austin had never appreciated it before, but now he realized that each of those seeds Chad and Tanner—and later Leah and Dan—had planted had sprouted in his heart.

"I prayed for you, Chad. And I prayed for me, that I'd be redeployed so I could come watch your back." He blew out a breath. "God only answered one of those prayers with a yes."

On the screen, Chad blinked but didn't say anything, and Austin wasn't sure if it was because his words hadn't gone through or if his brother was waiting.

He gripped the phone tighter. "They moved me to the PRDL."

Still just a blink from his brother.

"Did you hear me?" Austin held the phone closer to his face, raising his voice in case the connection was bad. "They put me on the permanent disability retirement list."

"I heard." Chad's voice was quiet, but his expression didn't change. "How do you feel about that?"

"I'm—" Austin hesitated. Three days ago, he would have said he was furious, outraged, ready to tear down every obstacle to return to active duty.

But God had worked an amazing change in his heart since then.

"I went to see Natalie," he said quietly. "She gave me Tanner's Bible, and I read some of it."

Chad's laugh held admiration. "Gotta hand it to that guy. He never gave up."

"Yeah." Austin shook his head. There'd never be anyone quite like Tanner. "He wrote something in there about trusting in God *even if.*" He licked his lips. He could hardly believe the next part. "So I'm at peace with it. I trust God has something else planned for me. And that he's got your back better than I ever could."

"I'm happy for you, Austin." The sincerity in Chad's voice carried through the phone. "Looks like my prayers were answered today too."

Austin nodded, not trusting himself to say anything.

"I have to get to all kinds of debriefings, but I'll talk to you soon."

Austin expected the familiar panic to take over at the thought of not hearing from his brother for a while, but a new sense of peace cloaked him. Another answered prayer.

"Merry Christmas, bro."

After Chad hung up, Austin sat staring at the phone for a few minutes, pouring out his thanks to God for so many blessings, hidden and otherwise.

Then he pushed to his feet and hurried to the living room. He had to thank Leah and their friends for all the prayers they'd offered up for Chad—and for him.

"Today was a good day." Leah leaned into Austin as they walked up the steps to her porch. She couldn't remember ever feeling more content in her life.

"The best." Austin dropped a kiss onto the top of her head, then opened the door for her. When he hesitated on the porch, she grabbed his hand and pulled him inside.

"Can we talk?" She barely found the courage to say the words, and she could tell by the way his breath hitched that he knew what she wanted to talk about.

While Austin had been on the phone with Chad—praise the Lord for answered prayers—she'd had a chance to talk to Jackson about Austin's proposal and what it would mean for both of them, especially if he chose to let her adopt him.

"Austin—"

"Leah, wait." Austin took her hands and led her to the couch. "Before you give me your answer, can I say one more thing?"

She bit her lip but nodded. There was nothing he could say to change her mind, but she'd let him speak first.

"Whatever you answer, I want you to know that I will always be here for you and Jackson. As friends, if that's what you want. But I'm not going anywhere either way. And also, I want you to know that saying yes would mean being with a man who is broken but healing in his Savior, a man who makes mistakes but seeks forgiveness. Above all, a man who will love you and Jackson for the rest of his life." He sucked in a long breath. "I realize that was like four things. But I just wanted you to know. In case it makes a difference."

But Leah shook her head. At the flash of disappointment in his eyes, she rushed to clarify. "None of that makes a difference, Austin, because I already knew all of it." She lifted her hands to his cheeks.

"But before I give you an answer, there are a few things I need you to know. One is that you have totally upended my world. I had everything planned. I thought I knew where my life was going. I was happily single. And then you came along and—" She slid her hands along the light layer of scruff on his cheeks. "And I love you so much it literally steals my breath sometimes. And another is that I'm a mess too. I can't promise I'm not going to ever meddle or try to control things I need to leave to God. But I'm going to trust that you'll call me out when I do. And also, I want you to be a real father to Jackson—to teach him how to be a man of God. And finally—" She paused, and her eyes locked on his. "Finally, yes, I will marry you."

Austin's arms instantly engulfed her, and their lips came together, the long kiss solidifying everything they'd said—and all the things words could never express.

When they pulled apart, they both had tears on their cheeks, and both were laughing.

"Best Christmas ever," Austin whispered into her hair.

Epilogue

One Year Later

"Best Christmas ever." Leah could not stop smiling as she walked down the aisle on her new husband's arm. Technically, it was three days after Christmas because they hadn't wanted to take people away from family on Christmas day, but who was counting?

Austin had not stopped smiling once the entire day either.

The moment they exited the sanctuary into the lobby, he swept her up in his arms and brought his lips to hers.

"Eww. Are you guys going to keep doing that all day?" Jackson followed them, dapper in the tux he wore as Austin's best man and carrying a laptop under his arm. Chad hadn't been able to make it back for the ceremony, so they'd set up a video call with him so he could watch everything live.

"Not all day." Austin rumpled the boy's hair. "*Forever.*"

Jackson groaned but stepped into their outstretched arms for a family hug.

Leah had a fleeting wish that she could freeze time right at this moment and live it forever. But that wasn't how life worked. The three of them had a whole life to live together—so many more memories to create. She prayed that the majority of them would be happy, but even on this happiest day of her life, she knew they wouldn't all be.

But that was okay. Because they would weather them together—with God.

As the rest of the bridal party and then all the well-wishers at church gathered around them, Leah kept a careful watch on Austin. He'd been doing better in crowds lately, but she had promised herself that she'd do everything she could to make this day enjoyable for him. And if that meant escaping the crowds, that's what they'd do. Besides, that'd give them more opportunities to kiss.

As his eye caught hers, she leaned over for a quick kiss, whispering, "You okay?"

"Never better."

The rest of the afternoon and evening passed in a whirl of joy. After a delicious dinner prepared by her staff—she made a mental note to give Sam a raise—and a scrumptious cake made by Peyton, Jackson stepped up to the microphone that had been set up for toasts.

Leah gripped Austin's hand. "What's he doing?"

Austin grinned at her. "Best man toast."

Leah pushed down a flutter of nerves. When Austin had suggested Jackson as best man, she'd been so moved, she hadn't even considered this part of the job duties. He was only a fourteen-year-old kid. What was he supposed to say at a wedding?

But Jackson pulled an index card out of the inside pocket of his tux and cleared his throat, glancing at his wrist, which sported the watch Leah had given him for his birthday last year.

She stilled to listen.

"Uh, hi everyone. My name is Jackson Zelner. I'm Leah's son." His gaze flicked her way, and Leah gave an encouraging smile, telling herself that this was not the time to cry. "And, uh, I guess Austin's son too now—or at least I will be once the adoption paperwork goes through for that."

Well, it may not be the time to cry, but that didn't stop the tears that trickled down her cheeks. She was learning that there was definitely something to be said for happy crying.

"Uh, anyway," Jackson continued. "I just wanted to say that I don't think I ever really knew what love was growing up. I mean, people would tell me they loved me, but then they would leave me. Sometimes on purpose, sometimes not."

The wedding guests had stilled, and Leah didn't think a single person dared to lift a fork.

"Then this woman came along, and for some reason she decided she wanted to be my foster mom. I still have no idea why." A few people laughed gently. "I tried really hard—" He held out a hand. "I mean, really hard, to push her away. To get her to prove once again that there was no such thing as love. That it was just a word. But she wouldn't give up." He turned to Austin. "Just a warning that she's really stubborn."

The guests laughed harder this time.

"So anyway—"

Leah could tell Jackson was warming up to having everyone's attention. She never would have guessed that this was the same young man who'd barely said two words to her when she'd first brought him home last fall.

"Then there was this guy. Austin. Our neighbor. I thought he was pretty cool. But I don't think my mom liked him very much at first. Especially when he let me keep a squirrel."

Next to her, Austin laughed and wrapped an arm around her shoulders.

"But I could tell he liked her. And pretty soon she liked him too. And then they were in love. And I watched them. I was waiting again. Since Leah wouldn't give up on me, I needed different proof that love wasn't real. But the more I watched them, the more I wondered if maybe it *was* real after all." Jackson turned to face the two of them. "I don't think it was until last Christmas morning, though, that I really believed it. Austin came barging into our house and asked my mom to marry him. And I was sure she was going to say yes—it was pretty obvious she wanted to. And I figured that would leave me on my own again, since she'd found someone else to love. But she didn't say yes. She said she had to think about it. She wanted to talk with me about it. I think that was when I knew love was real, because she put aside what she wanted to make sure things were okay with me." Jackson blinked and looked down at his card, then raised a champagne goblet that had been filled with sparkling grape juice. "So what I guess I'm saying is that love is actually pretty great. And congratulations, Mom and Dad."

"Congratulations," the rest of the guests cried as both Austin and Leah flew out of their seats and trapped Jackson in a long hug.

When they finally pulled apart, Jackson looked from one to the other. "I can't believe I'm going to say this, but you two should kiss now."

He grabbed a spoon off the table and clinked it against his glass. The sound was echoed by people throughout the hall.

"What do you say Mrs. Hart, should we kiss?" Austin's hands were already around her waist, and he pulled her closer, his breath tickling her cheek and sending a warm shiver down her back.

She'd never thought she'd be Mrs. *Anyone*. And now here she was, married to a man God had created to be her perfect match.

She wrapped her arms around his neck. "Yes, Mr. Hart, I think we should."

As Leah's lips met her husband's, her heart welled with joy. She hadn't fixed Austin, and he hadn't fixed her. But God had taken the broken pieces of both of their lives and transformed them into something beautiful.

For Christmas and for always.

Thanks for reading! If you enjoyed NOT UNTIL CHRISTMAS MORNING, would you let others know by posting a short review? Your review is a blessing to me as it helps other readers find the book. And it lets me know what you love and want to see more of. Thanks so much!

And if you're not ready to leave Hope Springs, I have good news: you don't have to! You can read more sweet, emotional stories of faith and love in the rest of the Hope Springs series, which you can find on my website at www.valeriembodden.com/books.

A sneak preview of Not Until This Day (Hope Springs Book 6)

Red.

Why had she chosen red?

Isabel combed her fingers through her hair and leaned closer to the gas station restroom's grimy mirror as she waited for her daughter to finish up. Of course Gabby hadn't been able to wait the five minutes until they got to their new apartment.

But this was fine. It gave Isabel a chance to steady her nerves before they started their new life.

Again.

"How you doing in there, Bunny? Need any help?"

The sound of a toilet flushing answered, and her daughter emerged, swinging her long blond locks behind her. Locks that looked exactly like Isabel's own hair had once upon a time.

"I like your hair, Mama." Gabby flashed her signature toothless grin at Isabel as she walked to the sink.

"You don't think it's too red?"

Gabby shook her head as Isabel helped her reach the soap. "It's not red. It's burnt umbrella. That's what the box said, remember?"

Isabel laughed, ripped off a piece of paper towel, and passed it to her little goofball. "Burnt auburn. Not umbrella."

Gabby shrugged and wiped her hands on the paper towel, then threw it in the trash and slipped her still-damp fingers in between Isabel's.

Isabel squeezed. Her daughter couldn't possibly know what a lifeline she was. "Come on. We'd better get back out there before Chancy tears apart the car."

Outside, the sun had started to sink, and the air had cooled enough that Isabel shivered and hurried Gabby toward the car. She hadn't thought to pull their sweatshirts out of their bags this morning, since temperatures to the south had been hot and sticky for weeks already. She should have realized that early June would still be cool this far north.

Gabby giggled as she spotted Chancy in the driver's seat, poking his nose through the slight crack Isabel had left in the window. "I think Chancy wants to drive."

Isabel angled her ear toward her shoulder in a deep stretch. "He's welcome to." After driving for three days straight, she'd had enough. Thankfully, this was it. They'd finally reached their destination.

She settled Gabby into her booster seat in the back, then moved to her own door. Chancy licked her hand as she nudged him out of her seat and slid the temperature control from air conditioning to heat.

"Mama, I'm hungry."

"I know, Bunny. We'll get some supper as soon as we get settled in."

Settled in.

264

That had a nice ring to it. For half a second, Isabel let herself imagine what it would be like to settle in for good.

But they couldn't. Not here. Not yet.

Maybe not ever.

If they stopped moving, if they settled in for too long, Andrew would find them. And if he found them—

Isabel shivered and cranked the heat up another notch.

That wasn't going to happen. As long as she followed the rules she'd made for herself, they'd be safe: Keep moving. No friends. No men.

She let out a quick exhale and nodded to herself. Easy enough.

"What does that sign say?" Gabby piped up from the back seat.

"Hope Springs." The large wooden sign was painted in bright, welcoming colors, and the tightness in her shoulders eased as she said the words. In three years, this was the farthest they'd moved. She still wasn't sure what had made her choose this place. Not really. Except that when she'd Googled "where to find hope" a few days ago, an ad for this town had come up. The name had caught her eye. As had the fact that it was clear across the country from Andrew, small, out of the way, and picturesque. The last one she knew was frivolous, but if she was going to keep uprooting her daughter like this, she at least wanted her to have beautiful memories of the places they'd lived.

"Are we going to stay here this day?" Gabby asked around a yawn.

"*Today*. Not 'this day.'" Isabel shook her head. She corrected Gabby on that phrase nearly every day, but it was one of those things her daughter seemed to ignore. "And, yes, we're going to stay here for a while. What do you think of it?"

They crested a steep hill, and both of them gasped at the same time.

"Wow, Mama. I thought we were far away from the ocean."

Isabel blinked at the expanse of water, burnished with the red-gold of the sunset, a hint of peace filling her for the first time since she could remember. "That's not the ocean. It's Lake Michigan."

"Look at all those boats down there." Gabby rolled her window down, and Chancy pounced into the back seat to climb over her and stick his head out the window. "I hope we can go on one."

"Close your window." Isabel frowned into the mirror. The last thing they needed was for the dog to jump out of the car. "Those boats are too expensive. And too dangerous." Though she had to admit the bobbing masts made a pretty picture, glowing against the backdrop of the water.

She tore her eyes off the lake and examined the stores that lined either side of the street. A fudge shop, a bakery, an antique store. They probably couldn't afford anything in any of them, but at least they could have some fun window shopping. The tightness in her shoulders eased a little more.

This had been the right place to come, she could feel it.

Keep Reading NOT UNTIL THIS DAY
Visit www.valeriembodden.com/notuntilthisday

More Hope Springs Books

While the books in the Hope Springs series are linked, each is a complete romance featuring a different couple and can be read in any order.

Not Until Christmas

A fudge shop owner dumped a week before her Christmas wedding. The best friend who has sworn never to risk his heart. A Christmas tragedy that could tie them together or pull them apart.

Christmas isn't looking so merry and bright for fudge shop owner Ariana when her fiancé walks out of her life only a week before their Christmas wedding. As she turns to her lifelong best friend Ethan to help her pick up the pieces, she's careful not to let the feelings she once harbored for him surface. He's made it more than clear that he doesn't think about her that way.

Volunteer firefighter Ethan has kept his heart in a steel cage for the past ten years—ever since his entire family was killed in a car accident. But when Ariana needs him, he knows he has to be there for her. Even if the thought of risking his heart to her leaves him quaking in his fire boots. He knows what happens when you love someone: they can be snatched from you.

Just as he finally works up the courage to take the leap, the unthinkable happens. Now Ethan has to decide: Can he trust that all things—including his relationship with Ariana—are in God's hands? Or will he be spending another Christmas alone?

Not Until Forever

She chose her career over him. He put his family before her. When they get a second chance, will they choose to put each other first?

As she climbs the corporate ladder, Sophie doesn't let herself think about what she gave up when she declined Spencer's proposal five years ago. So when she's called home to say goodbye to her dying grandmother, she goes out of her way to avoid seeing him. Of course, that means he's the first person she runs into. Much as she fights against it, being near him stirs up old feelings and makes her question old decisions.

Leaving college to help on the family farm cost Spencer the woman he loved. But he couldn't turn his back on his family. Now that Sophie's back in town, Spencer's determined to protect his heart. Only he senses something new in Sophie—something that makes him think maybe they could have a second chance. But when his family needs him again, he feels like he's repeating the past.

Only this time, he's not sure what choice he should make. Is God giving them a second chance? Or are the heartaches of the past too much to overcome?

Not Until This Moment

She's looking for "the one." He knows it can never be him. Unless God has other plans for them . . .

Peyton has been looking for "the one" forever. She thought she'd finally met him when she started dating Jared. But when he told her he never planned to get married, she had to face the facts: maybe he wasn't the one God intended for her after all. Now, she's just trying to survive the annual ski trip with her bones—and her heart—intact.

Jared wishes he could give Peyton everything she desires. But marriage is the one thing he can never offer her. Not that it makes it easy to let her go. Especially when everywhere he turns on this ski trip, he sees her with another man—a man Jared knows can't be trusted.

Jared may not have any business worrying about Peyton anymore. But he promised himself long ago that he'd never again stand by and watch a woman get hurt. And he's not about to let anything happen to the woman he still loves. Even if that means losing her forever.

When a crisis rocks the trip, both have to reexamine what they want. But are their hopes for the future still too different, or can they trust that God has a plan for them?

Not Until You

She clings to the past like a treasured antique. He'd rather toss it in the trash. But if they can learn to trust in the God of second chances, they might just discover a future together.

The past is all she has... Since her husband's death three years ago, Violet has struggled to keep their antique store afloat and her grief at bay. She knows it's time to move on, but she's not sure she wants to. So when Nate moves in next door, she tries to ignore the feelings he stirs in her—feelings that were supposed to have died with her husband.

The past haunts him... Nate's star was rising in the world of Christian music. But all that was erased with a single, life-shattering mistake. One he doesn't deserve to be forgiven for. One that means he doesn't deserve a future—and definitely not with his beautiful new neighbor.

Can they have a future? As the two work together to save her store, neither can deny the feelings that are starting to develop. But when Nate's secret is exposed, they have to decide if they should walk away—or trust that the God of second chances has a plan for their future.

Not Until Us

Everyone knows former bad girl Jade and local pastor Dan don't belong together. But when what they know and what they feel are two different things, can they trust God to give them a second chance?

When Jade agrees to return to Hope Springs for the summer, it's with the hope that she might finally be able to escape her past. But small towns have long memories—and Jade knows she deserves every one of the judgmental looks the townspeople direct her way. What she doesn't understand is the handful of people who see past her reputation, including her ex-almost-boyfriend Dan, whom she left without so much as a word of explanation eight years ago.

Newly appointed as head pastor of Hope Church to replace his deceased father, Dan is under pressure to prove he's up to the task. He doesn't need any distractions. Not newcomer Grace, who on paper would make a perfect pastor's wife, and especially not Jade—who, well, wouldn't.

But as Dan and Jade get to know one another again, they can't deny that their relationship has grown from childhood crush to once-in-a-lifetime connection. When Jade learns a secret that could destroy both of their reputations, they have to decide: Trust God to see them through this, or walk away again?

Not Until Christmas Morning

She's a fixer... He's about as broken as they come... Can they learn to turn to God for healing and hope this Christmas?

Leah has always been a fixer. That's why she decided to foster a troubled teen. And it's why she's determined to give him the perfect Christmas. It might also be why she feels compelled to reach out to her grinchy, reclusive neighbor Austin. But she'll have to be careful that reaching out doesn't turn into something more—she's been hurt by crossing the line from friendship to romance once, and she's not willing to let it happen again.

After losing his leg, his friend, and his faith in Afghanistan, Austin figures he's about as broken as they come. For Austin, Hope Springs is simply a stopping point—a place to rehabilitate his leg, get over the burden of his PTSD, and get back into shape to redeploy. He has no desire to get to know anyone while he's here, least of all the meddlesome—if sweet—woman next door. But when she calls on him to help her make Christmas special for her foster son, something compels him to relent. Soon, his heart belongs to both of them.

But what if Austin is too broken for even Leah to fix? Can the two of them learn to turn to God for hope and healing—and maybe even a chance at love—this Christmas?

Not Until This Day

Three kids. Two broken hearts. One chance to become a family.

Isabel has three simple rules: Keep moving. No friends. No men. It's the only way to keep herself and her daughter safe. But when she arrives in the small town of Hope Springs, she finds that she suddenly wants to break all the rules. Especially when it comes to a certain sweet single dad.

Tyler has one goal: Keep his boys from ever getting hurt again. That's why he avoids dating, women, or anything having to do with love. So why does the mysterious single mother who works at his family's orchard have him rethinking everything?

As Isabel starts to think of Hope Springs as home, Tyler starts to think of her as more than a friend. But when Isabel's past comes to light, her fears and his doubts are tested in new ways. Will they give in to the fear and pain of the past—or can they turn it all over to God and trust him to give them a future?

Not Until Someday

She's waiting for her someday. He thinks his has already come and gone.

After spending the past five years caring for her ill grandfather, Grace Calvano is eager to honor his memory by turning his stately old house in Hope Springs into a bed-and-breakfast. All she has to do is fend off her mama, who keeps pressuring her to come home to Tennessee, marry the new youth pastor, and start raising a passel of children. Sure, Grace wants to settle down and marry someday. But only when God sees fit to send Mr. Right her way. Until then, she's content to wait.

After a career- and relationship-ending injury, former NFL quarterback Levi Donovan is sure his someday has already come and gone. Returning to Hope Springs for the summer to help out at his dad's construction company is not his idea of a bright future. But maybe it will be a chance to make up for lost time with his brother— and to make his dad proud at last.

The day Levi shows up to help renovate her bed-and-breakfast, Grace is sure of one thing—she and God must have gotten their wires crossed when she asked him to send Mr. Right to her doorstep. Because the motorcycle-riding, football-playing bad boy is the very definition of Mr. Wrong.

But as they get to know one another, Grace is challenged to rethink everything she thought she wanted. Can she and Levi move past their own plans to let God give them the someday neither has dared to hope for?

Want to know when my next book releases?

You can follow me on Amazon to be the first to know when my next book releases! Just visit amazon.com/author/valeriembodden and click the follow button.

Acknowledgements

I cannot even tell you how many times while writing this book I've had to sit and absorb its message for myself—the message that in all things God works for our good (even if things don't work out as we've planned), that God is in control in all things, that he loves us with an unfailing love. I am thankful for his daily reminders of that love and for the privilege of sharing that message with others. When I started writing the Hope Springs series, I had no idea how God would bless it—or how he would bless me through it. But the answer to both of those questions is *abundantly*! I thank God for that. And even more than that, I thank him for the promise of salvation through the perfect life and innocent death of his Son, Jesus. Without that promise, nothing else would matter.

God has also blessed me with a loving husband, who would totally take me to those gazebos in the woods, if such a place really existed. A husband who is my number one supporter. Who leads our family faithfully in all things. And who models Christ's love to me every day. Together, we have been blessed with four children: Hannah, Elijah, Titus, and Chloe. I thank God for each one of them. Being a mother has its challenges for sure (which is why I can relate to Leah!), but the reward of seeing my children grow in the Lord and share his love is more than I could ever ask for. I am grateful to our parents and extended family as well, for their continued love and support.

A big thank you also goes to Joe Davis, first, for his service to our country, and second for taking the time to talk with me and share his experiences with PTSD as I wrote Austin's character. Thank you also to everyone who serves or has served in our country's armed forces. Your courage and dedication astound me and bless our nation.

And to foster and adoptive parents everywhere, including my sister-in-law and her husband, thank you for opening your homes and your lives to give children their forever families. You are heroes.

And a super-sized thank you to my dedicated team of advance readers. Thank you especially to Marilyn Blackwell, Sheri, Lisa Lee, Donna Burfield, NJ, Ilona Stagg, Melanie A. Tate, Jennifer Ellenson, Sharon, Patty Bohuslav, Michelle Butler, Kathryn Rebernick, Judith Barillas, Pam Williams, Elle Ann Brown, Judith Seale, Sharika, Diana, Diane Markesbery, Evonne Hutton, Shavona Thompson, Jean S., Jenny Kilgallen, Annette Lawson, Jan Gilmour, Korkoi Boret, N. Fudge, Debra L. Payne, Ashley Lundquist, Deb Galloway, Rachel Kozinski, Seyi, Alina Bogateanu, Tandy Oschadleus, Sherry Johanson, Trudy Cordle, Vickie Escalante, Connie Gronholz, and Josie Bartelt, who have been such a support and encouragement to me, sending lovely notes to let me know how much this book meant to them. And thank you to Jess, my friend since before I can remember, who offered her wise insights into the title of this book and who never fails to share her enthusiasm for my books.

And finally, thank YOU. Yes, you! I am so grateful for every single reader who spends time with the characters who walk the pages of my books. Thank you for all you do to support and encourage authors. God's blessings to you!

About the Author

Valerie M. Bodden has three great loves: Jesus, her family, and books. And chocolate (okay, four great loves). She is living out her happily ever after with her high-school-sweetheart-turned-husband and their four children. Her life wouldn't make a terribly exciting book, as it has a happy beginning and middle, and someday when she goes to her heavenly home, it will have a happy end.

She was born and raised in Wisconsin, and aside from a short stint in Minnesota while her husband trained for the pastoral ministry, has lived there her entire life, in spite of an aversion to all things cold and snowy (except Christmas—a snowy Christmas is good). She periodically tries to coax her snow-loving husband and children to pack up and move to a warmer climate with her but so far has had no luck. So she tolerates the snow for them. That's some kind of love, if you ask her.

Valerie writes emotion-filled Christian fiction that weaves real-life problems, real-life people, and real-life faith. Her characters may (okay, will) experience some heartache along the way, but she will always give them a happy ending.

Feel free to stop by www.valeriembodden.com to say hi. She loves visitors! And while you're there, you can sign up for your free short story.

Made in the USA
Columbia, SC
07 October 2020